FORT WORTH LIBRARY

W9-CEK-455

Beaglemania

"Gutsy Lauren Vancouver easily wins over the hearts of animals in need—as well as readers . . . [Vancouver is] an ardent advocate for homeless pets."
—Rebecca M. Hale, *New York Times* bestselling author of *How to Moon a Cat*

"Animal lovers will delight in a new series filled with rescued dogs and cats needing loving homes. Lauren Vancouver is a determined heroine who will solve the intriguing mystery at her private shelter."
—Leann Sweeney

Praise for Linda O. Johnston's Kendra Ballantyne, Pet-Sitter Mysteries

"Humorous, cleverly constructed."
—*Midwest Book Review*

"A brilliantly entertaining new puppy caper, a doggie-filled whodunit . . . Johnston's novel is a real pedigree!"
—Dorothy Cannell

"A fabulous series."
—*The Best Reviews*

"Animal lovers will adore this series for the mystery as well as the animals."
—*CA Reviews*

continued . . .

"An incredible writer who creates believable, intelligent characters . . . [A] fun-filled, suspenseful story line that contains intrigue, mystery, murder, lots and lots of animals, and humor."
—*Fresh Fiction*

"Fast and fun."
—*New Mystery Reader Magazine*

"The author has done a great job of making the reader care about the animals. Plus their personalities really shine through."
—*Mystery Lovers Corner*

"Johnston's ability to blend pet love, mystery, and romance into one well-wrapped package makes this a summer treat for mystery and pet lovers alike."
—*Front Street Reviews*

"Exciting . . . Johnston is a creative storyteller who not only writes a fascinating mystery but also creates a deep character study."
—*Books 'n' Bytes*

The More
the Terrier

LINDA O. JOHNSTON

BERKLEY PRIME CRIME, NEW YORK

THE BERKLEY PUBLISHING GROUP
Published by the Penguin Group
Penguin Group (USA) Inc.
375 Hudson Street, New York, New York 10014, USA

Penguin Group (Canada), 90 Eglinton Avenue East, Suite 700, Toronto, Ontario M4P 2Y3, Canada
(a division of Pearson Penguin Canada Inc.)
Penguin Books Ltd., 80 Strand, London WC2R 0RL, England
Penguin Group Ireland, 25 St. Stephen's Green, Dublin 2, Ireland (a division of Penguin Books Ltd.)
Penguin Group (Australia), 250 Camberwell Road, Camberwell, Victoria 3124, Australia
(a division of Pearson Australia Group Pty. Ltd.)
Penguin Books India Pvt. Ltd., 11 Community Centre, Panchsheel Park, New Delhi—110 017, India
Penguin Group (NZ), 67 Apollo Drive, Rosedale, Auckland 0632, New Zealand
(a division of Pearson New Zealand Ltd.)
Penguin Books (South Africa) (Pty.) Ltd., 24 Sturdee Avenue, Rosebank, Johannesburg 2196,
South Africa

Penguin Books Ltd., Registered Offices: 80 Strand, London WC2R 0RL, England

This is a work of fiction. Names, characters, places, and incidents either are the product of the author's imagination or are used fictitiously, and any resemblance to actual persons, living or dead, business establishments, events, or locales is entirely coincidental. The publisher does not have any control over and does not assume any responsibility for author or third-party websites or their content.

THE MORE THE TERRIER

A Berkley Prime Crime Book / published by arrangement with the author

PRINTING HISTORY
Berkley Prime Crime mass-market edition / October 2011

Copyright © 2011 by Linda O. Johnston.
Cover illustration by Paper Dog Studio.
Cover design by Rita Frangie.
Interior text design by Laura K. Corless.

All rights reserved.
No part of this book may be reproduced, scanned, or distributed in any printed or electronic form without permission. Please do not participate in or encourage piracy of copyrighted materials in violation of the author's rights. Purchase only authorized editions.
For information, address: The Berkley Publishing Group,
a division of Penguin Group (USA) Inc.,
375 Hudson Street, New York, New York 10014.

ISBN: 978-0-425-24379-4

BERKLEY® PRIME CRIME
Berkley Prime Crime Books are published by The Berkley Publishing Group,
a division of Penguin Group (USA) Inc.,
375 Hudson Street, New York, New York 10014.
BERKLEY® PRIME CRIME and the PRIME CRIME logo are trademarks of Penguin Group
(USA) Inc.

PRINTED IN THE UNITED STATES OF AMERICA

10 9 8 7 6 5 4 3 2 1

If you purchased this book without a cover, you should be aware that this book is stolen property. It was reported as "unsold and destroyed" to the publisher, and neither the author nor the publisher has received any payment for this "stripped book."

Acknowledgments

Once again, I have had a wonderful time researching aspects of *The More the Terrier* and future Pet Rescue books.

Many of the same people who helped me when I wrote *Beaglemania* advised me again, and I thank them once more.

I want to particularly thank the members of the Small Animal Rescue Team (SmART) of Los Angeles Animal Services, and especially their team leader, Armando Navarette ("Nav"), who has invited me numerous times to observe training sessions and who has answered a lot of questions. I'd also like to thank Annette Ramirez, a member of both SmART and the Animal Cruelty Task Force, for her observations about how hoarders are handled within the Los Angeles system. I could single out the remaining members of SmART, too—since all have been friendly and helpful and patient with me when I've tagged along and asked questions. Thank you all.

I do want to point out, though, that although I have featured SmART in parts of *The More the Terrier*, I have used poetic license, as always. I made some stuff up, as well as the fictional team leader. All inaccuracies and exaggerations, again, are mine.

I've learned even more about pet rescues and the wonderful people who run shelters and other organizations. Thanks especially to the wonderful people at Pet Orphans of Southern California for teaching me even more about volunteering, and about how best to prepare pets for finding their forever homes.

This book is especially dedicated to my two adorable Cavalier King Charles Spaniels, Lexie and Mystie, and I thank the veterinarians who've worked with us to alleviate their different (and frustrating) health issues.

And no one who reads my books will be surprised that I once again dedicate this one to my dear husband, Fred.

Chapter 1

I love pet rescuers and all they stand for. That's why I became one—so I could do everything in my power to save and protect animals who are unable to take care of themselves.

But sometimes others who also rescue animals baffle me.

Like my former mentor, Mamie Spelling.

"I don't know what to do, Lauren." The hysteria in her voice, even over the phone, sounded way over the top. At least I thought so. I hadn't spoken with Mamie for years. This could be her normal tone these days. "Please, tell me what to do."

I was sitting in my office at HotRescues, the facility in L.A.'s northern San Fernando Valley that I run. My recently adopted dog, Zoey, mostly Border collie, probably part Australian shepherd, and all love, lay at my feet on a fairly new area rug—a woven oval in shades of brown—to protect her from the discomfort of the tile floor.

My assistant administrator, Nina Guzman, still stood at the door watching me. She had popped into my office a minute ago looking frazzled as she told me about the phone call that had just come in.

Nina was often frazzled. She'd been that way when I'd first hired her a couple of years ago—unsurprising, considering her personal problems then. That didn't make her any less of a helpful and energetic assistant.

I was amazed when Nina said the person waiting on the line was Mamie Spelling. After I'd answered the call, I'd felt my amazement turn into a whole gamut of emotions: bewilderment, to hear from Mamie after all this time; irritation, that she'd chosen me of all the people she must currently know.

And, yes, concern. I still didn't understand what was wrong in Mamie's life, and I was under no obligation to help her. But she had been there for me when I'd experienced some difficult times, advising me, helping me find a new direction in my life, and providing a shoulder to lean on.

So what if more than . . . what was it? Almost seven years had passed. I wouldn't turn my back on her—at least, not immediately. For now, I'd listen to her and see if I could help.

"Why don't we start at the beginning, Mamie?" I tried to use the most soothing tone I could dredge up. Not easy to do for someone like me, who's used to speaking her mind.

"But . . . I'm sorry I called you, Lauren. There isn't anything you can do. I just needed to talk to someone who understands people as well as animals and can deal with them. But even you can't stop her. I'd better go."

"Stop who, Mamie? Please, just tell me what's going

on." I leaned my elbows against my desk—a replica antique that I'd refinished when we first opened HotRescues, not long after I'd started losing touch with Mamie—and closed my eyes, trying to stay patient.

"She's threatened me. She's wrong, but if she does what she said . . . I can't live with what could happen. I really can't. So—"

"Wait, Mamie. Please tell me what you're talking about. And don't—You're not going to do anything foolish, are you?" My insides clenched in fear, even though I didn't really know this woman anymore. There was such desperation in her voice. Who had threatened her, and with what? And what did she mean, that she couldn't live with it? I had to keep her talking.

Something in my voice must have resonated with my concern, since Zoey sat up, looking at me questioningly with her brilliant amber eyes, her head cocked.

"No, nothing foolish. I'm fine. Really. Thanks for talking to me, Lauren." I heard a click, and she was gone.

I didn't believe she was fine. She'd sounded distraught. Suicidal? How could I know? I still didn't understand why she had called me out of the blue. A cry for help, yes . . . but for what?

"What's going on, Lauren?"

I'd forgotten that Nina had stayed in the doorway, watching one end of the HotRescues welcome area while also keeping an eye on me. I like Nina a lot—even though she's taller, curvier, and ten years younger than me. But we're usually on the same page when it comes to taking care of animals. Like me, she wore a blue HotRescues knit shirt over jeans, as all our personnel do.

"It was an old friend. We'd lost touch, but—well, something's wrong with her now."

I had an urge to run it all by Nina—how Mamie had been so integral to where I'd ended up—but there wasn't time. Even though I had too much to do, I had to go check on her. If I didn't at least try, and something happened to her . . .

I stood, and so did Zoey. "Do me a favor," I said to Nina. "Look online and find the address for Beach Pet Rescue. It's around Venice." Venice, California, was a part of Los Angeles between Santa Monica and Marina del Rey. I used to go there all the time to see Mamie at her shelter, but I seldom visit the area now. It had been long enough that I'd only guess at the address, and I didn't want to falter on my way.

"Sure, Lauren." She turned her back and hurried to the welcome area's staff table. She had a laptop there to work on. I had a computer beside me on my desk, but Nina was more adept at techie things than I. Besides, I wanted to talk to someone before I left.

Fortunately, Dr. Mona Harvey, our part-time adoption counselor and staff psychologist, was around. Her office was upstairs in the same building as mine. I hurried up the steps, passed the conference table in the middle of the second floor, and knocked on Mona's half-open door.

"Come in, Lauren." She was sitting behind her desk, and I quickly planted myself on her shrink's couch across the room. Mona was about Nina's age—mid-thirties. She smiled behind her glasses—but only for a moment. "What's wrong?"

I filled her in on the phone call. "I thought about calling 911, but I don't believe there's any immediate risk. I thought I'd visit her and check things out. You're a shrink. What do you think I should do?"

"You're not close to her any longer?" Mona's smile was replaced by a concerned frown. "Do you know any of her current friends? Relatives? They may be better able to deal with whatever is going on."

"I never really knew anyone close to her, not even when she was mentoring me. I don't even know if any of the people who used to work or volunteer at her shelter are still there, let alone how to contact them. Unless I just call the shelter . . . but if she answers, that defeats the purpose."

"Right. Well . . . From what you said, there's some kind of problem, but without talking to her I can't give you any guidance, other than to be gentle with her. You can tell me more later. Going to see her is probably a good thing—at least for your peace of mind. If you check on her and she's fine, you won't have to think about it anymore."

"And if she's not fine? If the threat she mentioned is real?"

"Then you'll figure out how to help, Lauren. That's what you do."

I thought about Mamie my entire drive down the 405 Freeway. I'd programmed the address Nina had found for me into my new GPS—a Mother's Day gift I'd received last month from my wonderful kids. Tracy and Kevin, both in college, were taking summer classes now. I missed them, especially when every direction that spewed from the electronic mouth of my gadget reminded me of them. At least I now had Zoey for company at home. I'd left her in Nina's care while I went on this mission.

Mamie had been in her late fifties, I'd guessed, when she had decided that veterinary techs—like I'd been at the time—needed better direction about how to really care for animals' welfare. I'd met her because she'd come to the clinic in Woodland Hills where I worked and asked the vets for occasional free care for animals she rescued.

I'd considered the vets there to be good doctors but not necessarily altruistic. Even so, Mamie had convinced them to donate a specified number of hours each month, as well as medicines needed to treat the animals she'd bring in. After her second time there, I'd walked out to her car with her.

We'd started our dialog about pet rescues then, and she'd convinced me. I had young teenagers at home and a jerk of a second husband who couldn't have cared less if those kids were okay. It therefore hadn't been easy for me to agree to find the time to occasionally volunteer at Beach Pet Rescue, but I'd done it, sometimes bringing Tracy and Kevin along on weekends.

I'd learned a lot, including how miserable people could be to the pets who loved them. How many animals were abandoned in an area as large as L.A. The large numbers, fortunately, of people who gave a damn, who helped out by donating time and money for pet rescue.

Mostly, I'd learned how important saving abandoned or abused pets could be to *me*. Largely thanks to Mamie.

But things changed between us when I divorced my miserable husband and interviewed for the job as administrator of HotRescues, the brand-new shelter that Dante DeFrancisco, the wealthy CEO of the huge HotPets pet store empire, was starting. Maybe Mamie, with all her experience, should have gotten the job—and the wonderful funding by Dante. But I'd put together one heck of a business plan, if I do say so myself. Dante had recognized it, and I became the new administrator.

And lost Mamie as a friend.

"Take the next exit to Venice Boulevard," intoned my GPS, and I eased my Toyota Venza into the exit lane. I continued to obey the instructions of the disembodied voice until I reached the address Nina had found for me. The drive seemed familiar, and I believed this was the same location where I'd visited Mamie seven or so years ago.

I parked along the street and looked at the fence around the property. A sign over the gate confirmed that this was Beach Pet Rescue. But that fence—I remembered it as gleaming white, not mottled, graying wood.

Maybe Mamie's problems had to do with insufficient donations to keep the place as nice as it once had been.

I got out of my car, grabbed my ubiquitous shoulder bag, and walked toward the gate. The whole neighborhood appeared to have gone downhill. I saw no people around, but the area seemed largely residential. A couple of houses appeared to be abandoned, and another had a car in the driveway with two flat tires.

From behind the fence, I heard a few barks. Some of the dogs in the shelter must have heard or scented this stranger's arrival. I assumed Mamie allowed visitors and walk-ins interested in adopting pets, so I didn't try to call from my BlackBerry or look for a bell to ring. I just opened the gate and entered.

And stopped, horrified—not just because of the repulsive smell that assailed my nose.

I couldn't believe it.

The person who'd first gotten me interested in pet rescues. Who'd taught me all I'd initially known about the process, how to find and nurture animals who required help and love and as much longevity as possible . . .

Mamie Spelling had turned into a hoarder.

Chapter 2

There must be a place in hell for animal hoarders. Or at least in purgatory. Hoarders deserve some kind of punishment, even though most of them start out with their hearts in the right place—wanting to save the lives of as many animals as possible.

I knew that was so with Mamie. But talk about hell . . . this had to be an alcove of it.

Behind the chain-link fenced-in areas of wall-to-wall pups, I saw the house I remembered: a small, now-dingy yellow cottage with white trim around the windows. There was a short set of stairs that led to the porch.

A woman had opened the front door as I walked in and the copious dogs raised even more of a bark-fest. "Lauren!" she shouted. Or at least I thought that's what I heard over the din. She ran toward me.

I'm not sure I'd have recognized Mamie if I hadn't

expected to see her here. The short lady who threw herself into my arms had bright, curly red hair; pale skin; and a myriad of wrinkles. My one-time mentor had been more or less the same height, but her hair had been straight and blond, and she'd looked young despite being twenty years or so older than me.

I didn't want to hug her. I didn't want to be anywhere near Mamie at that moment. What I wanted to do was to run to the nearest group of cramped, barking dogs—mostly mixed-breed terriers but also pugs, Dobies, and more—set them free from their confines, and hug every one of them. Assure them that things would improve, now that I was here.

Which, I hoped, was the truth. But embracing any of them right now wouldn't fix anything.

Embracing Mamie just might. No matter how much I wanted to shriek at her.

"I didn't really mean for you to come here, Lauren." Mamie pulled back and tried to smile at me, but tears flowed from her eyes as her frail body shook. "I'm so glad you did, though. I'm so . . ." A sob outmaneuvered her words, and she looked down. We just stood there for a minute.

I closed my eyes, willing myself to stay calm. I needed to remain cool and unemotional to help these poor, tortured animals . . . and, yes, the tortured woman before me.

The difference was that she had done it to herself, as well as to all the creatures around us.

When Mamie calmed a little, I said, "Let's go inside and talk, okay?" I was proud at how serene I sounded, as if I was soothing a child who'd been discovered committing some minor infraction and knew she'd be punished for it.

But taking away TV for a week wouldn't solve anything.

After I'd done what I needed to, Mamie would, in fact, be punished.

A short while later, we were in Mamie's kitchen—probably the only room in the house not stuffed with filled crates. That was what I'd gathered as we entered via the living room and walked down a short hall toward the back of the place. Some loose dogs and cats accompanied us, but most of those indoors were confined.

At least the home wasn't also filled with papers and trash and human detritus, as I'd seen in hoarding situations depicted in some reality horror TV shows. But even with only a few animals in here, the stench was overwhelming. How could she stand it? I wanted to scream the question but forced myself to pretend I was someone else—a heartless person who was blasé about animal mistreatment.

Fortunately, all the creatures I'd seen had appeared to be alive. Maybe I really could help them.

"I'll boil water for tea," Mamie said brightly, as if I was truly there as a friend invited for an enjoyable get-together.

"Fine." I smiled through gritted teeth. I doubted I'd be able to sip even a little without gagging.

Mamie fussed around for a little while, petted a couple of medium-sized dogs that jumped at her feet, then joined me at the gouged table in the middle of the room. Like everything else here, the kitchen needed an overhaul. "The water will be ready soon," she said.

"Fine," I repeated. When we were both seated, I struggled for a way to broach the subject in a way that might get us somewhere, the thousand-pound gorilla that hovered above us roaring and pounding its chest over what this woman had done. I finally just jumped in. "Mamie, I'll bet you can imagine what I'm thinking. What happened here?"

Rather than answering, she jumped up and grabbed some tea bags, put them into the cups on the table, then poured water from the kettle over them. I shuddered and avoided looking at those cups. Who knew what they might have been in contact with since their last arguably sanitizing wash?

"Please, sit down," I told her.

"Everything will be fine here." She turned her back toward me, facing the stove.

I rose. "You know better. You also know I can't leave things the way they are. These animals are suffering, Mamie." Even the ones now lying at our feet—a fuzzy tan-colored terrier mix and a black Lab—looked thin. "You can't like that any more than I do."

She shook her head back and forth, again like a child under chastisement. "Everything will be fine here," she repeated. "She can't do that to me."

She? In her confusion, Mamie apparently referred to me in third person.

"I need to do whatever I can to save the animals," I said.

"I know it, Lauren. But you won't threaten me like she does."

So *she* was someone else—maybe the person Mamie had alluded to when we spoke earlier. "Who threatened you?"

"Doesn't matter. Just do it. Take care of the animals, Lauren. That's really why I called you. I got scared and knew you're the best person to help my babies." She was facing me now, her jaw set belligerently despite the tears still flowing down her cheeks. "I only wanted to save them, you know? I kept finding more pets without homes, and

I couldn't find enough people to adopt them all. I didn't want to take them to city shelters. Some would die there."

"I understand," I said. "But, Mamie, in conditions like this . . ."

"I know, I know. I wanted to prove I was the best pet rescuer ever and help all of them. But it got too big for me to handle." She stepped toward me around the dogs and reached up, grabbing my shoulders and staring into my eyes with her wet, pale brown ones. "You'll save them all, won't you?"

I wanted to promise her I would. I wanted to promise *myself.* But all I could say was, "Why don't you show me around, and then we'll figure out what to do."

I'd been nearly correct. There were a few other rooms in the house not stacked with crates of cats and small dogs. Their inhabitants were larger dogs, roaming free in their own excrement. Uncaged cats occupied the two bathrooms.

Even Mamie's bedroom was overrun with animals.

All—canine and feline—appeared emaciated. Pets of all sizes, from Chihuahuas, to moderate-sized terriers, to big dogs like a Great Dane mix or two. Black cats, calico, some with young kittens. Pitiful. Filthy. In need of attention as well as food.

Fortunately, I still didn't see any dead animals, nor did I see any clearly suffering from anything but malnutrition— although a vet would need to make that call.

We went back through the kitchen and exited into the yard, where I saw a lot more of what I'd first viewed as I came through the gate: animals of many sizes. Most with large, sad, pleading eyes, even as the dogs barked again.

How many were there, total? I couldn't even guess.

When we returned to the kitchen, I said to Mamie, "You

know what I have to do, don't you? I need to get help for
these animals. They're suffering, Mamie."

"I want *you* to help them."

"That's what I'll be doing. But if you're asking whether
I can just pick them up and take them all to HotRescues,
I'm sure you know the answer."

She hung her head and nodded. "I want them all cared
for much better than I've been doing. And at least you're
not threatening me, Lauren. But that doesn't matter anymore."

I still wondered who'd threatened her, and why. If it had
to do with her hoarding, why hadn't that person done something to help the animals?

And what did she mean that it didn't matter? I looked at
her, trying to assess whether my initial fear when she'd
called was true. Could she be suicidal?

She seemed okay, but I'd keep an eye on her for now—
and I still had to take care of the animals.

I used my BlackBerry to call Captain Matt Kingston of
Los Angeles Animal Services. I had first met Matt a few
months ago when I'd shown up at a rescue of dogs from a
puppy mill. One of those who'd been guilty of that animal
abuse had later been murdered, and I'd been a suspect. So
had Matt. But neither of us had been guilty, and I'd helped
to discover who was.

Since then, Matt and I had become good friends. Maybe
more than good friends. For one thing, he'd brought my
dear pup, Zoey, into my life. Plus, we'd begun seeing a lot
of one another.

"Even if I wanted to," I murmured softly into the phone,
not wanting Mamie to hear everything—and knowing she
eavesdropped anyway—"I couldn't possibly take them all
back to HotRescues."

"From what you're describing," Matt said, "I think you know this has to be handled officially."

"Yeah," I said, "I do."

The HotRescues license to operate as a private animal rescue organization came with restrictions. Essentially, I was permitted to save healthy animals in danger of being euthanized because of overcrowding in public shelters, and I could accept owner relinquishments. But I doubted, even if Mamie agreed, whether I could genuinely call this a situation where the owner was surrendering her own pets into my hands.

"It's really awful, Matt. Please send help. Once all these poor creatures are out of here, I'll count on you to help me make sure all the healthy ones are saved somehow."

"I'll do all I can. You know that."

And I did.

While we waited, I told Mamie whom I'd called, and why. "I've gotten to know Captain Kingston and how much he cares about animals," I said. "Most people in Animal Services do, but they have their rules. By calling Matt I can be sure all these creatures will be handled as gently as possible within the system."

Mamie was crying again, and no wonder. But she sipped her tea and nodded. "I have to trust you, Lauren."

I hoped she hadn't misplaced that trust.

I wanted to visit all the pets who'd soon be rounded up and dealt with officially, give each one hugs and reassurances that might, in some cases, be empty. Instead, I made calls to a couple of other people I knew who ran private shelters that I found most acceptable: clean, caring, with staff eager to place animals into new forever homes. I gave them a heads-up that there would be a lot more dogs and

cats who might soon need to be rescued from the already
overflowing public system.

I also called my good friend Dr. Carlie Stellan, a veterinarian who owned a clinic in Northridge, not far from HotRescues' location in Granada Hills. She was the star of her own
cable TV animal health show, too, on the Longevity Vision
Channel called *Pet Fitness*. I told Carlie—fortunately in
town despite traveling a lot for her show—"The official
vets will look these guys over for now, but I'll want to bring
as many as I can to HotRescues once they're made available. I'll need you and your folks to check them out."

"Of course, Lauren. I just wish you'd told me you were
going there. I might have been able to film it for a show."

"I only knew I was coming a little while before I got on
my way," I told her, "and I'd no idea then that Mamie had
become a hoarder. Besides, I really wouldn't want you to
feature this on *Pet Fitness*. She was once a dear friend of
mine, and now she seems so unstable . . ."

The L.A. Animal Services vehicles and officers started
arriving a short while later. So did members of the
L.A. Animal Cruelty Task Force, mostly cops. Matt wasn't
with these officials, but he'd already warned he wouldn't
get there for a while, since I'd caught him in a meeting.

The officer in charge introduced herself and told Mamie
that the animals would be taken away for their health,
safety, and welfare. Mamie was also informed that someone would speak with her later.

When the officer went outside, Mamie and I followed.
The front gate had been propped open. Mamie stood beside
me, watching as the animals were gently packed up and
placed into vans.

"I can't stand this," she whispered hoarsely. "All my
little ones . . ."

I put an arm around her shoulder.

The excitement attracted public attention. Though I'd seen few neighbors around before, people started to line the streets.

A couple of media vans pulled up, too. I hated to see that, but I supposed the animals wouldn't care if their plights were screamed in the news. That might even be good for them.

Mamie cried out when one of the ACTF officers led a tan-colored terrier mix out the gate, possibly the one that had been in the kitchen with us. "That's Herman. Does he have to leave, too? He's my special baby."

"Yes, ma'am," said the officer.

"At least for now," I told her. "We'll see if we can do something to get him back for you later—no guarantees, of course." I suspected it would be a lost cause, but I hated to give Mamie no hope at all.

She knelt on the ground beside Herman and gave him a hug.

"It's about time!" said a voice from behind me. I turned to see a slender woman in a business-like suit, her hair a sleek, shoulder-length cap of gold, smiling down at Mamie.

Mamie rose, her complexion even paler than before. Her eyes were huge and furious. "This is all your fault, you miserable excuse for a—"

The woman laughed. "*I'm* a miserable excuse? What about *you*, and the way you treated those poor animals?" Her smile was vicious and looked out of place on a face that could have graced the cover of a fashion magazine—beautiful and perfectly made up, from eyes framed by long, dark lashes, to her becoming shade of lip gloss.

"But if it hadn't been for your threats," Mamie cried,

"I'd never have had to call for help. I would have fixed things myself."

So this was the person who'd been threatening Mamie. With what? Exposure?

"All you had to do was listen to me." Her tone was sweet despite the viciousness of her expression. "You know I run one of the most reputable shelters around. I'd have helped your animals if you'd linked your pathetic Beach Pet Rescue to my network of shelters. But, no, you had to be stubborn, and now it'll cost you, big time."

She was involved with shelters, had known about this situation, and hadn't dealt with it?

Just threatening Mamie, no matter what she'd said, hadn't helped the poor animals.

I held my temper in check, just barely, as I approached her. "Hi, I'm Lauren Vancouver. I run HotRescues, and I can't believe you—"

The woman approached me with one perfectly manicured hand extended. I noticed the pin she wore on her lapel: a circle of paw prints around the words "Pet Shelters Together." It was crusted with small, gleaming stones that looked like real diamonds.

"Of course I know who you are. Mamie has spoken highly of you. I'm Bethany Urber, and I save animals' lives, too. Aren't you glad I got Mamie to get in touch with you?"

Chapter 3

I had no answer to that. Not without yelling my own questions at her, like "Why didn't you do something to fix this as soon as you knew about it?" As much as I hated to pretend to be cordial, I shook her hand so briefly that it might as well have been the swipe of an angry cat.

"This way, Bethany," I heard from behind us. Bethany grabbed my hand again as she turned and posed us—for a couple of the news photographers who'd invaded the yard.

I yanked myself away and pretended that my attention had been grabbed by another wave of Animal Services folks exiting the house with filled crates—not much of a stretch. They, fortunately, also shooed the media vultures back outside.

I had in fact heard of Bethany Urber and her Pet Shelters Together organization. I belong to a different, unofficial network, one where pet rescue administrators trade data informally, and I visit its Web site frequently. It's called, not especially creatively, Southern California Rescuers. The shelter directors I'd already contacted also monitored the site.

Bethany and PST had been mentioned and dissected in its discussion group recently. Apparently some fellow rescuers considered Bethany's network a superb idea, where administrators shared not only ideas and information, but also banded together for fund-raisers and more.

Others considered it intrusive, with its requirement of ceding control . . . and I gathered that the majority of this group had met Bethany. Even so, no one said anything especially terrible about it.

Judging by this first experience with Bethany, though, I wondered if the organization was all about her, and not so much about saving animals. Otherwise, why would she have hesitated to call in official help right away? Had she been trying to create leverage to get Mamie to join? But why?

"I'm so glad that the Animal Cruelty Task Force and Animal Services are here," Bethany said from behind me, loud enough that a couple of those in uniform carrying the crates looked in our direction and smiled.

I chose not to respond. Instead, I turned toward Mamie, now standing beside me, also not looking at Bethany. She watched with tears once more streaming down her lined cheeks as Herman, too, was loaded into one of the official vans, among a bunch of other similar-looking terriers.

"Oh, Herman, I'm so sorry," she cried. She turned to me. "Don't you think I could get them to leave just one dog right now?" Her voice was so soft that I barely heard it over the shouts of the rescuers and the people who watched the show.

Not to mention barks from some of the frightened dogs, including Herman. Even cat cries and hisses. I wished I could explain to them what was going on.

Or not. I couldn't make promises to them, or even to Mamie. But I could to myself. I wouldn't stop until as many as possible—hopefully all of the animals—were healthy and well fed and placed in new, loving homes.

"I don't know," I began gently, only to be interrupted by Bethany.

"Why? So you could only mistreat just that poor animal instead of a hundred?" She spoke loudly enough that I glanced around but saw no reporters filming her.

"It's not like that." Mamie sounded as tormented as the pets she had crammed into such terrible quarters. "I loved them all. If I didn't take them in, who would?"

"Now, that's the question, isn't it?" Bethany taunted. "If you'd done as we'd discussed, worked with me and with Pet Shelters Together, we might have been able to fix things around here, and done it much faster."

"There were other ways of getting it done faster," I muttered, glowering at the woman. "Like as soon as you learned about the situation."

"Oh, but that wouldn't have taught Mamie anything. Anyway, I need to go talk to someone. See you later, Mamie, dear." Instead of walking off, though, Bethany took another step toward me. "We'll talk soon, okay, Lauren?"

I didn't have time to answer before she hurried out the gate. She stopped at a parked van—one from a TV station, not Animal Services.

"She did this," Mamie cried, gesturing toward the chaotic scene in front of us. "She ruined everything."

Maybe, to some extent, Bethany was right. Her timing and rationale might have stunk as badly as the interior of

Mamie's house, but her discussions with Mamie had in fact spurred my old mentor to call me, and thus, eventually, saved some animals' lives. I didn't want to throw that into the face of the distraught woman in front of me, though.

Which felt weird, upside down somehow. I was used to confronting people who abused animals, leveling threats and accusations of my own. I couldn't fault what was happening here, but I also wasn't going to rub Mamie's nose in it. Not now, at least. I don't like to see any creature suffering, not even someone who'd made such terrible mistakes, and that was definitely the case with Mamie.

"Oh!" Mamie cried again as a cart stacked with crates filled with cats was being maneuvered out to the street, to another Animal Services van. "My babies!"

I wanted to shake some sense into her but realized it would be futile. Plus, I didn't know how delicate her mental state really was. Maybe if I got her talking . . .

I turned and gestured for Mamie to follow me back in the direction of the house, a little farther from the chaos. She complied, though she looked reluctant.

"Do you want to tell me more about what happened?" I asked when we stopped. "I gathered that Bethany twisted your arm in an attempt to get you to join Pet Shelters Together, right?" Mamie nodded. "That's how she threatened you?" She nodded again. "What did she say?"

Mamie's smile was full of irony. "That she'd call in Animal Services if I didn't join and they'd arrest me."

Which still could happen. She might be hauled in for animal cruelty or some other charges, but I wasn't sure. I'd have to check with Matt about how this kind of situation was usually handled.

"So why didn't you just join?" I asked Mamie.

She shook her head, bouncing her red curls. "I considered

it. It sounded wonderful at first, but I needed to know more. I began to look into Pet Shelters Together, and Bethany. She had an amazing business background—did you know?" I shook my head. "Well, she did. I thought she knew what she was doing, running organizations and all, and that the animals would benefit. But when I started asking people who'd already joined some questions about what was good and bad about Pet Shelters Together, I wasn't so sure. Besides . . . I wasn't really ready to give up on my own shelter, you see?"

I did. Getting that kind of help would have meant ending her hoarding sooner. Bethany's threats or not, Mamie hadn't been ready to give up on her lifestyle.

"Have you considered joining Pet Shelters Together, Lauren? I mean, having HotRescues join it?"

I blinked at the unanticipated question. The answer was, of course, no. But my situation was unusual—ideal circumstances for a pet rescue administrator. I didn't need to band together or coordinate with anyone to get the funds HotRescues needed, thanks to its rich benefactor, Dante DeFrancisco.

Sure, we held fund-raisers now and then. But they were intended to publicize animal rescue in general, and HotRescues in particular—and not because we were hurting for money.

"No," I told her. "I haven't."

"Good. You'd only regret even considering it, like I do now. I told Bethany very politely that I appreciated her invitation but I'd decided to decline. That's when she started threatening to expose me. She said she'd save these animals anyway, and I'd be the one to suffer. She got so loud and mean that I started trying to avoid her, but she kept calling and coming here and making more threats—" And not saving the animals, damn her. "—and that's why . . ."

"That's why you decided to call me?"

She nodded.

I'd thought Mamie looked aging and frail before, but now, as she stared at me solemnly, then turned back to watch the loading process, I had the sense she was thinking about how her life had just ended, even though she was still alive.

Or maybe she was even considering how to terminate that part, too.

I felt so torn inside that I almost wished I could sever my own painful, ambivalent feelings from my heart. No matter how ill-treated the animals had been, abusing them hadn't been her intention.

Only the result.

I noticed another Animal Services car double-park along the street. It looked familiar, but many of the cars looked alike. The person who got out definitely looked familiar, though. It was Captain Matt Kingston.

He didn't seem to see me at first, or maybe he wasn't looking for me. He talked initially to a couple of the Animal Services folks while patting some dogs on the head, then conversed with a few uniformed cops who were apparently part of the Animal Cruelty Task Force. One of those cops turned and pointed toward me. The group headed in our direction.

What was going on?

"Hi, Lauren," Matt said when he reached where I stood with Mamie, at the side of the yard. "Is this Ms. Spelling?" He nodded toward Mamie.

He was wearing his official Animal Services uniform. He was also wearing his official Animal Services attitude. His expression, as he watched me for an answer, was remote, not at all the fond way he'd come to look at me when we visited each other at our respective rescue facilities or even got together for dinner or drinks or more.

I kept my own demeanor strictly professional, too. "Yes. Captain Matt Kingston, I'd like you to meet a long-time—" Well, former. "—friend of mine, Mamie Spelling. Mamie, this is Matt Kingston of Los Angeles Animal Services."

"And this is Officer Truax of the Los Angeles Police Department," Matt said. "He's a member of the Animal Cruelty Task Force."

A burly, uniformed man stepped from behind Matt. He didn't seem to pay much attention to the introduction. Instead, he neared Mamie—like a giant hawk approaching a mouse.

"Will you come with me, ma'am?" Though he phrased it as a question and his tone was soft, he clearly expected Mamie to comply.

I aimed a questioning glance of my own at Matt. He nodded. Softly, he said, "I'd asked that no one start talking to the owner of this property until I arrived, and everyone involved was kind enough to agree."

In other words, he'd done it for me. He didn't understand exactly what my relationship was, or wasn't, with Mamie, but even though he had encouraged the city's forces to come and rescue the abused animals, he'd been sweet enough to make sure he'd talked to me before anyone started dealing with her.

"That's very nice." My tone was a bit warmer than before. But I couldn't let go of my professionalism—or my concern about Mamie. "Matt, could I talk to you?"

"Sure." He looked at the others. "Officer Truax, why don't you hold off for a few minutes? Just keep Ms. Spelling company for now."

Fortunately, the guy didn't seem surprised by the request.

Or maybe it was a command, since Matt was a captain in Animal Services—although he wasn't a cop.

"Let's go over here," Matt said, and we went around the corner of the house. I noticed that the yard that had been so full of animals before was empty, except for the myriad of filthy enclosures.

"What's going to happen to Mamie now?" I asked as soon as I thought we were beyond her hearing.

"I understand your concern for your friend, Lauren." Matt reached out to clasp my hands in his. I hung on, but needed answers before I could feel reassured. "We treat hoarders different from most abusers, though. We consider hoarding largely a mental disease. The condition of Mamie's place wasn't the worst I've seen, but—What do you think? How does her mental state seem to you?"

"Awful!" I took a deep breath and stared into his brown eyes. They appeared full of sympathy. "I came here because I was afraid, from what she'd said on the phone, that she was suicidal. Now, I'm not sure . . . but I can't say that she isn't, either. She seems to be changing moment by moment, from flakiness to sadness to anger."

"That's helpful for us to know. Here's what's likely to happen." He described briefly how Mamie would be taken in for a psychological evaluation. "The hold is likely to be for a maximum of seventy-two hours, and then she'll probably be released. Most hoarders, at a minimum, suffer from obsessive-compulsive disorder, but there may be even more to Mamie's situation. Let's get that process started, and I'll explain to you later how the way she acts will affect how we deal with the animals. We'll keep them safe in any event, of course, and have them checked by a vet."

"Will Mamie be prosecuted for animal cruelty or something?" I asked.

"Yes, but she'll most likely wind up on probation. Incarcerating hoarders, with their mental conditions, is usually counterproductive—but we can monitor how well they comply with the terms of their probation."

"Most likely?"

"You know I can't give absolute assurances."

"I get it. And I will want to learn more later. But for now . . ." I squeezed Matt's hands, then let them go.

I returned to where we had left Mamie and the officer.

"I think things will be all right," I told her. She smiled and took a few steps away from the police officer. "The animals will be well cared for. But there are possible consequences for you. Mamie, do you happen to know any lawyers?"

She stared from the cop, to Matt, to me, looking confused. "My niece, but—"

"What's her phone number?" I withdrew my BlackBerry from my pocket, ignoring the glares from both men.

"I . . . I'm not sure."

I got her name, at least, from Mamie, did a search on my smartphone, and made the call—noticing, as I pushed in the number, that Bethany still stood near one of the media vans. She was pointing in our direction.

Obviously, she'd noticed the uniformed cop standing by Mamie, too.

Fortunately, I reached Janice Spelling immediately. I told her what was going on with her aunt. "Are you local— in L.A.?" I asked, since her law firm had a couple of offices.

"Yes, but I haven't seen my aunt in . . . Never mind. I'll be there in half an hour. Please tell her not to answer any questions."

"Okay," I assured her, then hung up. "Don't say anything till she's with you, okay, Mamie?"

"Okay, but—"

"Fine. Let's wait over here." I'd spotted a cement bench in what had once probably been Mamie's garden and led her over to it. We both sat.

I suspected what was coming. It was entirely appropriate. Psych evaluation and likely probation or not, Mamie might be questioned about whether this was her property, how long the animals had been under her care and control, and whatever else it might take to determine whether there was enough evidence to arrest her for animal cruelty.

I was certain what the answer would be.

Chapter 4

There wasn't much I could do after that, except to worry about the situation . . . and the animals. Would they all be okay?

And what about Mamie? What would happen to her now?

Did I care? Despite what she had become, yes, I did. I supposed it was because of our history.

A short while later, the woman I assumed was Mamie's niece arrived—a lady around my age in a business suit who hurried up to the gate, showed an ID, and was hustled inside by one of the cops guarding the entry.

I hurried over to her. "I'm Mamie's . . . friend, Lauren Vancouver. Are you her niece?"

"Yes, I'm Janice Spelling." She didn't meet my eyes as she spoke. "Look, I'll do what I can for her, but the thing is—well, the family has mostly lost contact with her." She gazed at the activity, watching animals being shuttled off the property.

"You knew of her hoarding?" I asked in as nonjudgmental a tone as I could manage.

"That's why we haven't talked to her for a while." Janice finally looked directly at me, and I saw the regret in her expression. "We saw what she was becoming, tried to get her help . . . but she got mad at us. Things continued to deteriorate between us, and— Well, I've read up on hoarders. What happened with our family isn't unusual. But maybe now I can do something . . . although I'm not a criminal attorney, and I think she'll need one. Can you tell me where she is?"

I pointed to the house, and Janice hurried in that direction.

In a bit, Mamie was ushered back through the gate. She shot me a frantic smile before being loaded into an official vehicle the way the animals had been—a cop car, not an Animal Services van. Her niece followed, a set of car keys in her hand. I figured she genuinely intended to do what she could for her aunt.

But what she'd said wasn't a surprise. I'd heard of families trying hard but eventually giving up on determined, psychologically unstable hoarders.

Matt again assured me that Mamie was being taken to a hospital for a mental evaluation. The animal evacuation was pretty much over by then. The crowd had begun to disperse, and so had the media vans.

I'd taken a place on the sidewalk near the gate where the animals were brought out, a good location for viewing as much as possible while staying out of the way. I stood there now with my arms folded, hugging myself in solace.

After Mamie was gone, Matt joined me again. "This really sucks." I didn't even try to keep the dejection from my tone. He'd know what I was feeling anyway.

Matt is around six feet tall. He looks good in his uniform—khaki shirt, green slacks, and jacket, with a nametag and all the patches and badges to show he was highly placed within Animal Services.

Right now, he appeared as grim as I felt. "I agree," he said. "At least none of the animals looked too ill or malnourished. With luck, they'll all be okay." At least he was confirming my initial impression and not making me feel like a foolish optimist.

"Isn't this great!" chirped a perky voice from behind me. I knew who it was even before I turned. Bethany was smiling, hands clasped in a gesture that suggested she might start applauding.

"What do you mean?" My voice must have sounded as menacing as I felt, since Matt put an arm around me and squeezed gently.

"All those animals have been saved and the person who hurt them will be punished. I'm just so glad I was able to do this."

I blinked at her. I'd never believed that attractive women were airheads, even those who used too much makeup. Plus, I'd gathered from the little I knew about her background that Bethany was probably a smart lady.

So what was she talking about?

"What did you do?" Matt's soft words echoed my thoughts.

"Didn't Lauren tell you? I'm a friend of Mamie's. I was so worried about her and the animals that I started trying to help her. She wouldn't let me, though, even when I pushed her a bit to join my network of rescuers." A slight pout creased her brow, but she didn't allow it to stay very long. Maybe it would stick and ruin her perfect looks. "But she did the next best thing and called Lauren. Lauren called Animal Services, I'll bet." She met my eyes.

My eyes are green, set in a mid-forties face that has weathered fairly well, but isn't especially glamorous—and certainly not slathered with a lot of makeup.

Hers, on the other hand, could have been ready for a Hollywood camera operator to start filming the second she began to speak her lines. Her words definitely sounded enhanced with fiction.

"Since you obviously knew about this situation before," I said between gritted teeth, "I'd still like to understand why you didn't get help sooner for both Mamie and these poor animals."

"I was just so hoping that Mamie would come to her senses herself."

Liar! I wanted to shout. But I could only guess at her real agenda, and I was sure it had to do with garnering her lots of favorable publicity.

"Right." I no longer wanted to try to be civil to this woman. "Would you walk me to my car, Matt?"

"Sure."

As we started down the sidewalk, I heard Bethany call, "Nice to have met you, Lauren. You, too, Captain Kingston."

I hadn't parked far away. As we stood at the door of my car, I said to Matt, "Can you tell me now—I mean, what's likely to occur with Mamie and the animals?"

"Well, basically, the animals are considered to be her property. The best-case scenario for them and for her would be if she decided to surrender them, but most hoarders don't do that. If she wants, she can contest the legality of the seizure. She's not likely to win. A seizure is considered legal if the officers conducting it believed that immediate action was necessary to protect the animals. After the hearing, assuming it's decided against Mamie, she'll start being assessed fees for the care of the animals, and if she doesn't pay, she'll be deemed to have abandoned them. With that number of animals, the cost will get pretty steep, so eventually she'll probably have to stop paying and lose legal ownership of them anyway."

"I see." I wondered if I could convince Mamie to surrender the animals right away. She seemed lucid at least part of the time.

But as much as I found myself worrying about what would happen to Mamie, I was even more concerned about her supposed property.

"You'll keep me informed, won't you?" I asked Matt. "About how all the animals are doing? And you'll make sure that someone—"

"Calls to let you know if any is in danger of being euthanized. Of course. That's my main assignment from you these days, isn't it?" Though his words were sarcastic, he sounded amused.

"Sure is," I agreed with a smile. The truth was that I enjoyed Matt's company. Enjoyed our relationship, whatever it was. Just friends with benefits? A prelude to something more? Not as far as I was concerned.

"I figured." He glanced around, as if assuring himself that no other Animal Services folks were around, then bent and planted a quick kiss on my mouth. "I'll be in touch."

I drove back to HotRescues as quickly as I could, trying not to think too much about what I'd just experienced.

By then, it was late afternoon. I pulled into my designated spot in the parking lot and got out of my car—my dark gray Toyota Venza crossover. I loved this car, partly because I'd gotten it with a variety of pet-friendly accessories, which worked well for the director of a pet rescue facility.

The air, unsurprisingly, was filled not only with the usual sounds of a few barking dogs, but also by mechanical and hammering noises.

I smiled to myself as I got my purse from the car floor and used my key fob to lock the door. Those had been the usual sounds for a couple of months now. I was thrilled about the new building Dante was having constructed at HotRescues after buying the property next door.

After the terrible things that had gone on at HotRescues a while ago—including a murder—I'd been certain that, despite having a security company on call, we had to have someone here at night. Having better sleeping quarters would be wonderful.

The main buildings on the original HotRescues site consisted of our office at the front, a middle building containing other offices and some of the rescued animals, and a storage structure at the back that also contained our laundry facilities. There was no good place for someone to hang out overnight.

Hence, the new building. The existing center building's second floor, where the overnight security people slept on a couch in an empty office, would be converted into an apartment. All the offices currently located there would move into the new structure when it was completed, and there would be room for more small animals downstairs. The new property next door would also be fixed up with more kennels for larger dogs.

HotRescues was growing.

I walked through the side door into the welcome area. Nina was there at the table behind our attractive leopard-print reception desk, working on the computer. She turned just as Zoey, from somewhere near her feet, dashed toward me. I knelt and gave my dog a hug, hanging on as she wriggled in my arms and licked my cheek. Under other circumstances, her enthusiasm at our reunion would have made me laugh. Not today.

"What happened?" Nina demanded. "Or shouldn't I ask?"

With a final pat on Zoey's head, I rose. My face must have reflected my angst. No matter what that egotistical brat Bethany was claiming, she hadn't done anything to save those poor animals. She certainly hadn't acted fast enough, once she suspected what was going on.

I'd been the one to call in the authorities. Not that I gave a damn about who received any public kudos. I knew I'd done the right thing. But I couldn't help wondering about how all this would really affect Mamie.

"Do me a favor, will you?" I asked Nina.

"What's that?"

"Check on the Internet to see all you can find about why people who care about animals become hoarders. And what usually happens to them after they've been found out. I know what's likely to happen with Mamie officially, since Matt told me, but I want to know any unofficial scoop. Do they hoard again? Do they hurt themselves . . . ?"

"You found a hoarding situation there?"

I nodded and sighed. Putting my bag on the floor, I lowered myself into a chair beneath the window, at the small table where we asked people interested in pet adoption to fill out initial forms. Zoey lay down at my feet.

I glanced around at photos we had hung on the bright

yellow walls—lots of happy pets with their new adoptive humans. That made me smile. It always did.

Nina joined me. "Tell me about it, then I'll go online."

I gave her a thumbnail version of who Mamie had been to me and what had happened that morning.

"I think you need a hug, Lauren," Nina said when I was done, and I let her make good on the offer.

"Any visitors today?" I asked. "Potential rehomings?"

"A couple of real possibilities." She described a young lady who had just gotten her first job and post-school apartment and had fallen for one of our kittens, and a couple whose dog had recently passed away and were looking for a new companion.

"Great," I said, cheering a little. "I'll talk to you more about them later." I crossed the welcome room to the hallway with Zoey at my side, then turned back toward Nina. "No hurry about finding statistics on hoarders. Even if there's something that can be done to help them, Mamie's in the system now, at least, undergoing psychological evaluation."

"I hope they hospitalize her forever," Nina spat. "Or throw her in jail. Sorry, Lauren. I know she was your friend, but—"

"You're absolutely right," I told her, then headed toward my office. *But maybe you're a little wrong, too,* I couldn't help thinking.

I sat down at my desk. To help understand my own hypocrisy, I decided to call Dr. Mona but only got our semi-resident shrink's voice mail.

I still wanted to discuss this with someone official. The HotRescues vet tech, Angie Shayde, was sweet and young and would have an opinion, but I decided instead to call Carlie. As a veterinarian, she's a wellness aficionado. Besides, her TV show is on the Longevity Vision Channel, a cable network that focuses even more on human life than animals.

I explained to her what I'd seen today, as well as my strange ambivalence.

"You poor thing." Her immediate sympathy made me feel a little better. "I'm nearly done here for the day. Want to get together for dinner?"

"As long as it includes a bottle of wine."

Chapter 5

Before I left the office, I made some phone calls. Matt had
said that Mamie was likely to be released in a few days,
although he had assured me that if she appeared suicidal to
the doctors, they would continue to monitor her. He had
checked in about their initial assessment, though, and
extending the seventy-two-hour detention seemed unlikely.

Assuming they didn't keep her, where would she go?
Home, no doubt.

She'd be lonely, but as sad as that was, she'd have to deal
with it. In fact, I'd tell her outright that she had better not
start collecting animals again. She'd be watched—not only
officially, but by me, too. I'd suggest that she get some kind
of counseling, and would at least pop in on her now and
then to be sure all was well.

One thing I could do for her now was to make sure the
home she returned to was livable. So, I called a cleaning
service I'd used and got their price and availability. Then I

called Dante to see if our benefactor would be willing to help in this kind of situation, too.

"It may help keep animals safe if we can make things as nice as possible for Mamie—and trash all the reminders that might make her start collecting again."

"Interesting image," he said. "I'm picturing your having to make over her whole house to get rid of any reminders. Maybe everything else in her life, too. But go for it."

I contacted Matt to find out when the cleaning could start without stepping on any official toes and ruining any evidence that needed to be collected. He promised to get back to me on the timing but believed that tomorrow would work out fine. Plus, he indicated he'd be able to get someone to let the cleaning crew onto the property, since the authorities retained access to it as a crime scene for now. He agreed with my opinion, though, that even though she wasn't reachable yet, it would be best to get consent from Mamie.

Instead, I contacted her niece, who was thrilled by the idea and granted permission from the family. Did she have the right? As far as I was concerned, she did. Mamie might have another opinion, but by the time she could assert it, her place would be clean.

Finally, I set up the day and time with the cleaning company and agreed to pay for rush service, since I didn't know when Mamie might be released. I was sure Dante would be okay with that.

Then, at long last, I went to meet my friend. I needed the distraction.

Not to mention the wine.

I wasn't very hungry, so I let Carlie choose our meeting place. She usually picked restaurants closest to her veterinary clinic, The Fittest Pet, in Northridge. Since Granada Hills wasn't far from there, that was okay with me.

But this time she chose a location nearer to HotRescues— an Italian restaurant I hadn't tried before.

"One of my patients recommended it," she'd told me as she gave me the address.

"Really?"

"Actually, the owner of one of my patients. But I equate them, you know?"

I did know. Pets were family members.

The restaurant looked appealing from the street, with a few tables located on the sidewalk outside. Some were occupied on this warm June evening. I wished I'd brought Zoey, but, not knowing this place's amenities, I'd left her with the early evening crew at HotRescues.

The place was crowded. Carlie was already there and, bless her, a glass of red wine sat on the table in front of the vacant seat she'd designated as mine.

"Merlot." She held up the bottle.

"Perfect." I sat and took a sip, and she did the same from the glass in front of her.

I'd met Carlie six years ago, when she was the first person to adopt a pet from HotRescues just after we opened. She often mentioned her beloved Max, an adorable cocker spaniel mix, on her TV show.

I could have started disliking Carlie because, though she was my age, she was a lot better preserved—and not artificially, unless you counted her highlighted, shoulder-length blond hair. She had lovely violet eyes, and softly chiseled features overlaid with smooth skin.

Not that I looked antique. My dark hair has almost no gray in it—naturally. I keep it cut short, since it stays out of my way as I care for animals, and I don't have to look glamorous in front of TV cameras the way Carlie does. I've kept my weight low, I exercise some—mostly by walking dogs—and I have high cheekbones that would look good if I ever guest-starred on one of Carlie's *Pet Fitness* shows . . . which I didn't intend to do.

We studied the menus briefly, then ordered. I chose a small salad followed by mushroom ravioli. I'd get a doggy box for my predestined leftovers—for me, not Zoey. She'd get her own food, but maybe extra treats, since I'd been away from her so long that day.

When the server walked away, Carlie said, "Okay, tell me about your hoarder."

I hadn't said much when I'd phoned for commiseration, but I did mention that the hoarder was the friend who'd gotten me interested in pet rescues in the first place. Now, I briefly related how Mamie had helped me when my life had been so awful—when I'd needed a new career direction and impetus to divorce my second husband, whom I'd mistakenly married to give my kids a new dad after my beloved first husband, Kerry, had died.

"I didn't think I could make a living at pet rescuing, though it had a lot of appeal. Then I heard Dante DeFrancisco was opening a new animal shelter and funding it, so I put together a business plan and applied, and—"

"And the rest is history. So tell me, did your friend Mamie think she should have been the one to open HotRescues?"

I blinked at Carlie. I shouldn't have been surprised, though. She was nothing if not perceptive—and maybe a little psychic at times. "Yes. She pretended not to care, but she snapped at me a lot when we talked. Then she stopped returning my calls. So we lost touch . . . and sometime after that she became a hoarder." I fidgeted with my wineglass's stem before I took a swig of the pungent, fruity drink.

"I want to hate her now for what she did to those poor animals. I certainly hate how she treated them. And I'm really angry with her." I shook my head. "But I don't hate her."

"That's because you're a kind person." Carlie poured us both more wine. "You have to be, or you wouldn't be an animal rescuer."

"But I have no qualms about hating people I know are animal abusers, like the people who ran that puppy mill I watched being shut down. This is just another form of abuse."

Carlie nodded. "True, but it's also a psychological defect. Mamie is probably an obsessive-compulsive person." I'd heard that from Matt, too. "From the way you described her, she at least started out as an animal lover. Probably still is, in her warped way."

"I suppose."

Our meals were served, and I decided to change the subject—at least a little. "Have you ever heard of Pet Shelters Together?"

Carlie laughed. "Have I ever. Its CEO keeps contacting me. She wants me to feature her organization on one of my shows. I'm going to do something on your hoarder—" She raised her hand as I started to object. "We'll talk about it first, and I'll be more or less kind. But to do a show on what seems to me to be a Pac-Man kind of association that gobbles up animal shelters in its path . . . Well, let's just say that Bethany Urber wouldn't like my take on it, so she ought to just back off."

"I have the sense she doesn't back off on much of anything."

"You've met her? Has she tried to drag HotRescues into her web?"

My laugh was both bitter and wry. I explained how Bethany's apparent threats and attempts at coercion had been the impetus for Mamie's awkward attempt to seek help. "Bethany knows who I am, but she didn't overtly attempt to recruit HotRescues. Not yet, at least."

"Watch out for her. Do you know her background?"

"Just generally," I said, recalling Mamie's description. Carlie told me that she'd been the founder of Better Than Any Cosmetics. "Hey, I use their stuff sometimes."

"Who doesn't?" Carlie described how the well-known manufacturer had recently been bought out by a huge conglomerate. While she was the owner of the company, Bethany had participated in fund-raisers for animal rescue groups and apparently had gotten hooked on the idea—or at least that was what she had said in a lot of TV interviews that I had fortunately missed. After selling her cosmetics company, she'd decided to devote her life to pet rescues. "She got the idea of combining smaller shelters, using economies of scale to help get better funding and other benefits. It's gotten mixed reviews."

"I know. And if she's the media hound she appears to be, I won't want to be bad-mouthed in public—any more than I already am."

Because of the connection with Dante, HotRescues was occasionally mentioned in the news—and therefore I was, too. The recent events at the shelter, including a murder, had also been considered newsworthy. I'd even gotten to know a paparazzi-type reporter for the *National NewsShakers* tabloid TV show, Corina Carey. I shuddered at the thought.

"I'll definitely watch myself around Bethany," I finished, "especially if she tries to go after HotRescues."

I picked up Zoey at HotRescues on the way home. That gave me the opportunity to say hi to Brooke Pernall, too.

Brooke, a former P.I., was now the security director of HotRescues, having been hired for that position by Dante—after he had also paid her expenses to deal with a life-threatening heart condition. I had first met her when she came to HotRescues to relinquish her beloved dog, Cheyenne. She had lost her job and her home, and had thought her life in danger, too. But she was a lot better now. She had even added herself to the stable of security people she hired to stay at HotRescues overnight.

She also supervised EverySecurity, the company hired by Dante to watch over his entire business empire. They'd done a less-than-stellar job at HotRescues before. Now, under Brooke's watchful eye, they handled whatever she needed just fine.

"Hey, Lauren, tell me about that hoarder situation," Brooke said when I walked into the welcome area. Her color was good, her formerly mousy hair in a nice, becoming style, and she had even put on a little weight beneath her black security staff T-shirt and jeans.

"Word gets around." I petted Zoey and Cheyenne, a golden retriever mix, as I gave Brooke a synopsis.

"Glad you got involved," she commented when I'd finished. "At least those poor animals have a chance now, thanks to you. I know that woman was your friend, but . . . well, enough said."

Zoey and I soon left for our home in a gated community in Porter Ranch. In the car, Zoey sat in the backseat, as always, in a special safety harness. Also as always, she seemed to navigate, most often watching over my shoulder between the seats. Now and then, she would put her paw on my shoulder, as if telling me it was time to turn. Did I mention what a smart dog she is? We also did training sessions in public parks and at the HotRescues visitors' park now and then, teaching each other essentials like shaking hands, dancing, and speaking on command.

As soon as I'd fed Zoey, I headed for the living room, where I sat on my comfy, blue-upholstered sofa. I booted up my laptop and used the remote to turn on the TV. I checked for news reports on Mamie and the hoarding situation.

Both my kids—twenty-year-old Tracy, a junior at Stanford, and eighteen-year-old Kevin, a freshman at Claremont McKenna College—had called me right after the puppy mill rescue I'd attended, because I'd ended up on YouTube. Fortunately, I'd been ignored this time, thank heavens—maybe because I hadn't gotten to hug any of the poor creatures today. In the last incident, I'd embraced rescued puppies including adorable beagles, which was why my picture had been online. I was so pleased that all those puppies had found new homes via the public shelters and some private ones, too. Most had been adopted quickly, and I'd kept in touch to be sure about the rest. Plus, we had recently placed Missy, the overworked mama beagle we'd taken in, into a wonderful new home.

Now, I called both of my kids and told them about the hoarding situation in case they heard about it, withholding some details. And then I called Matt.

"I'm not sure whether our vets have checked them all yet," he warned. "But I haven't heard of any casualties. I'll make arrangements for you to come to the West Los Angeles Animal Care Center soon and take a peek. They're still there, although they'll be moved to the Northeast Valley center, since it has more available space and we have to hang on to them for now. They're still owned by Mamie, and they're also evidence."

The Northeast Valley center was also where the dogs

saved at the puppy mill rescue had been taken. "Please get the okay for me to see them as soon as you can."

There was one more call I needed to make. Fortunately, it wasn't too late. I pushed the button for my direct line to Dante.

"I was wondering when I'd hear from you again, Lauren," he said. "After we talked about getting your friend Mamie's place cleaned, I got a strange call from a woman named Bethany Urber. She said you'd suggested that she call me—something about getting HotRescues to join a network she started with a lot of pet rescue organization members. Interesting that you didn't tell me about that."

"I didn't tell her to call you, Dante. In fact—"

"In fact, she sounds like some kind of shark. I figured you'd heard of her, might even have met her at that hoarding rescue, as she said. But if you'd have been interested in her network, you'd have let me know. Is she as much of an egocentric twit as she sounds?"

I laughed. "I don't know her well, but I think you've got her pegged."

"How's Mamie?" Dante asked. "Are you going to do more for her besides cleaning her home?"

I hesitated. My opinion of Mamie had so many angles that it might as well have been one of those sparkling mirror balls hung above dance floors. But as much as I reviled her actions, I'd already realized that I couldn't hate her. And the woman obviously needed help.

"I'm not sure," I told Dante.

His laugh annoyed me, but I didn't tell him so. "Knowing you, Lauren, I'll wait to hear the next episode."

Chapter 6

The next morning, I took my time getting to HotRescues. For one thing, I was still exhausted from the previous day, though I hadn't done much but watch animals being rescued.

For another, I needed a break. Not much of one—just an hour, after my quick breakfast of toast and coffee. I sat and read the *Los Angeles Times* online edition on my laptop computer, with Zoey lying at my feet. I put one of the morning news shows on the TV but kept it on mute.

It became even less of a break than I'd hoped for, not that I was surprised. The *Times* featured an article about the hoarding situation with links to stories on other sites. I read them all as eagerly as if they were a riveting novel I couldn't put down. But this wasn't fiction.

I finally had enough. Even so, I hadn't yet visited the Southern California Rescuers Web site. I intended to add a post on the group link alerting my fellow shelter administrators, rescuers, and fostering organizations about the hoarding situation, in case they hadn't heard—since I had only informed a few of them. I also wanted to start a list of those who'd step up and take in some of the rescued animals as soon as the city facilities were ready to give them up. That wouldn't be until the legal issues with Mamie were resolved, since she technically still owned all of them.

When I got onto the site, I wasn't entirely surprised to see it already overflowing with information about hoarders, this hoarding in particular, and what could be done to attempt to prevent such situations. Of course no participant in Southern California Rescuers would ever do such a thing. Or so everyone said. But Mamie had once been a reputable pet rescuer, too. And knowing what I knew about my profession, I was certain there were others.

I, for one, know how hard it is to realize that so many sweet, loving potential pets are lost in the official system simply because they have to make room for the next bunch that get there. Rescuers who run private facilities, like me, would love to save them all.

I always refer to HotRescues as a no-kill shelter, even though there are varying definitions. We don't keep suffering animals alive, so we're not strictly no-kill, but we've never euthanized an animal for behavior issues—and certainly not for lack of space.

Mamie obviously would have loved to save every animal, too. The difference was that I, and others like me, have to be strong and responsible and only take on as many as we can adequately care for in our facilities.

Which was one reason I was so delighted that HotRescues was currently in expansion mode.

But staring at this Web site, reading the posts both critical of Mamie and supportive of the rescue, I realized something.

Bethany Urber read this site. I'd never seen her post before, so she must have been lurking. But now she was all over it, bragging as if she had saved those abused dogs and cats all by herself.

She had even scheduled an emergency meeting for all animal rescuers who could attend, to discuss hoarding and what could be done about it. She was holding it at her own facility, the chief location in the Pet Shelters Together network.

Okay. I know I like to be in charge, too. Even to micro-manage. I also tend to want to protect my friends.

Mamie had once been a friend.

And I was damned curious now. Who was this Bethany Urber, really? As awful as the first impression she'd made? I'd have bet one of my favorite thick dog towels from Hot-Pets on it.

What was her network of rescue sites actually like?

Could I get her to shut up about Mamie by pointing out some of *her* shortfalls?

And exactly what would she say at her meeting?

First thing, I called Matt. Fortunately, he was able to confirm that Mamie's psychological assessment was still progressing well and that she'd probably be released on schedule. He also promised to talk to the people at the West L.A. Care Center again soon to check on the rescued pets—but swore that they'd promised to let him know if any of the animals was in danger of being euthanized.

"What I've heard so far is that they were all in surprisingly good shape. Some were malnourished, a few had festering sores because of the poor hygienic conditions, but there were none in danger of needing to be put down . . . although don't hold me to that. I'll ask for confirmation again."

"Thanks, Matt." I inhaled deeply. I'd been so worried about bad news that I'd been holding my breath.

"So when are we getting together for dinner?" he asked.

"Soon," I promised, feeling good about seeing him again.

I called Dante to give him that news. Then I posted the information on the Southern California Rescuers site—with the same kind of caution that Matt had given. No guarantees, but it appeared that the animals just might all survive.

Then I said to Zoey, "Time to go, girl." My beautiful pup rose immediately and started wagging her tail in anticipation. "We'll go to HotRescues first. This afternoon, I'll leave you with our friends. I have a meeting to attend."

I hadn't gotten the impression that Bethany had a grain of modesty anywhere in her professionally beautiful body, so I wasn't surprised at the name on the sign outside the facility whose address she had posted on the Internet: "Better Than Any Pet Rescues."

I knew immediately where it had come from. It was a play on the name of the company she had owned: Better Than Any Cosmetics.

The name wasn't the only thing that gave the impression of superiority, though. A lot of people were apparently coming to her meeting, and I'd had to park a block away— no easy feat in this commercial and highly developed part of the Westchester area of Los Angeles. Following the crowd—none of whom I recognized—I stopped and stared at the main gate that led into the shelter. It looked like the entrance to a movie studio, white and ornate with a tiara-like symbol at the top. The only thing that identified it as a pet rescue facility—besides the name—was that the tiara had profiles of a dog and cat, nose to nose, at the top.

Someone at the forefront of our ad hoc group must have pushed an intercom button; within moments, the gate rolled open in two massive sections, revealing grounds that were equally ostentatious. The vast, plantation-style office building—did Bethany live there, too?—sat behind an attractive, well-nurtured garden. Not a bark could be heard.

On the porch stood Bethany. She again wore a business-like suit, although for a moment I pictured her in a Southern-belle gown. "How wonderful to see you all," she cried. "Please, come in." She gestured for everyone to follow.

She'd set things up as if this were a convention and we were all attendees. A woman sat behind a table where rows of nametags were laid out. I saw some names I recognized from the Southern California Rescuers Web site. The efficient-looking nametag distributer wore an ID herself: Cricket Borley, Assistant Manager, Better Than Any Pet Rescues. Below her tag, she wore a pretty pin that read PET SHELTERS TOGETHER, with a circular logo decorated with paw prints, similar to the one I'd noticed Bethany wearing but not as ornate. Cricket had short curly hair, a harried smile, and busy hands as she handed out the tags.

"Hi," I said when I reached the front of the line. "I'm Lauren Vancouver, of—"

"I know who you are, Lauren." Cricket smiled. "I don't think we have a nametag for you, though. Was Bethany aware that you were coming?"

"No." I hadn't known for very long myself.

Speaking of Bethany, she had been standing in the middle of a crowd of the attendees but broke away to hurry in my direction. Lucky me. I immediately quashed the seething anger that was a residue of what I'd felt toward her yesterday. After all, I was her guest here today.

"Oh, Lauren, it's so good to have you here!" she exclaimed. "Would you like a tour of our shelter before we begin?"

I didn't know whether the media was expected for this gathering, but I didn't doubt it—especially considering how perfect Bethany's dark suit and gold blouse looked. Her makeup was perfect, too, which I guessed was usual for her. The diamonds on her PST pin seemed to glow like her personality.

"I'd love one." I was curious about whether the over-the-top theme was also carried out where the animals were housed.

"Cricket, why don't you take Lauren and any others who'd like to come for a quick tour? Our program will start in . . ." She looked at the gold watch on her slender wrist. "Fifteen minutes. This is Cricket Borley, my assistant, by the way."

Cricket nodded and smiled almost shyly, as if having her presence acknowledged was a treat.

Bethany looked around, then called out, "Darya, could you help us here?"

A tall, reedy woman, also in a suit, looked up from where she conversed with a group of people. I wondered how she had heard Bethany in the din of conversation, but she excused herself and came our way.

"Lauren, this is Darya Price," Bethany said, "the head of the Happy Saved Animals organization. She recently signed on as a member of Pet Shelters Together." Bethany reached over and squeezed Darya's hand. "Darya, this is Lauren Vancouver, the administrator of HotRescues." They shared a look, and I felt sure Bethany was attempting to communicate something to her flock's newest member.

"Welcome, Lauren," Darya said as Bethany smiled beatif-ically. I supposed that Darya had gotten her message.

Darya's pretty oval face was framed by light hair pulled back in a bow, and her long body was so thin that I won-dered how she could handle some of the larger dogs that might show up at her facility. Like the others, she wore a PST pin on the collar of her shirt.

"Thanks." But that was all I had time to say before Cricket swept her followers out the door for our tour.

The shelter was, in fact, as over the top as the entrance. Each rescued dog and cat—maybe thirty canines and twenty felines—had a small yet nearly palatial enclosure, and I wondered how they kept the intricately tiled floors as clean as the matching walls. Bethany must have poured a lot of money into her shelter, but I didn't find it nearly as efficient as what we had at HotRescues.

I wasn't about to ask Dante for a major remodel to dupli-cate this. I did, however, feel as if the place was admirable, which irked me to no end. I didn't want to like anything about Bethany.

As always, I wanted to play with all the residents, but there was no time. When we got back to the main building, everyone had poured into a conference room that was larger than any I had at HotRescues. A man joined Darya, and since I wound up sitting near her, she introduced me to her husband, Lan—also on the skinny side for a guy, and even taller than she.

I recognized a few of the group now, other rescuers I'd met including Kathy Georgio, who communicated with me on the Southern California Rescuers Web site. She was one of the people I'd first contacted about the hoarding situa-tion, and we greeted each other warmly. The other rescuer I'd contacted, Ilona Graye, wasn't there.

Chairs had been set in rows, all but a few occupied. Bethany took her place at the front of the room and began to talk.

"We're here today to discuss something that we all need to watch out for in our own shelters, and in others'—hoarders." She actually did a good job describing what animal hoarding was, and how shelters that started out perfectly well could end up in disrepair. She had facts and figures, and I found myself listening with interest. Yes, I admit it: The meeting was quite worthwhile in its education about hoarding and how easy it is to let things get out of hand. Not that I ever would, of course.

Bethany put in a plug for Pet Shelters Together when she described what to do about hoarding. "As a group, we can band together to prevent such things, especially among our members. People like that shouldn't exist and need to be punished once they're discovered. They deserve to rot for what they do to those poor animals."

She didn't always stick to her topic. "It's particularly important that all of our members do things right, like running our individual organizations ethically. Our donated funds are for caring for the poor animals we've rescued, and for no other use. Remember that, everyone. I certainly will."

That sounded odd—as if she was conveying some kind of message. No one in the audience seemed to react to it, though.

When Bethany returned to the topic of hoarding and began describing the situation with Mamie—not unjustifiably, I suppose—the anger inside me started to spark again. She not only blamed my former mentor, but claimed that she, Bethany, had recognized what a terrible person Mamie was and had tried to get her to see the light by joining Pet Shelters Together.

Bethany's tirade continued, growing more vituperative by the second. Of course, she didn't mention that she had done nothing to stop the animal abuse when she'd first observed it.

My muscles tensed, as if I was a feral cat about to spring. I wanted to leap up there and expose her hypocrisy. Why hadn't she done something to help those poor, suffering creatures as soon as she learned of their plight?

But taking a few deep breaths, I calmed myself. Shrieking about it now would do no good, and she had told this group to immediately turn in hoarders they learned of.

Too bad she hadn't heeded her own advice.

Escape seemed like my better course of action for now. I glanced at the door.

Which was when I saw who was standing there.

Mamie.

"You bitch!" Mamie screamed. "Liar! It wasn't like that at all. You never said you'd help like that. You're the one who deserves to rot . . . in hell!"

I stood and ran to her, grabbing her arm and steering her out of the room.

I'd accomplished my escape. I also agreed with Mamie—even more so after seeing the triumph on Bethany's face, and the confusion reigning in her audience. Bethany had known full well Mamie was there when she castigated her.

And now Mamie had wilted so much that I practically had to drag her out, down the plantation's steps and through those huge front gates.

When we were finally out of there, I said, "When did you get out of the hospital? And what are you doing here?"

"They released me," she said softly. "At last. They told me things like I should get counseling because of my . . . something disorder."

"Obsessive-compulsive?" I suggested.

"Or Humpty Dumpty. It made as much sense."

"Counseling's a good idea," I told her, then added, "You should listen to what they told you. You'll feel better in the long run."

"I'm fine now, you know. That's why I took a taxi and came right here. A friend called on my cell to tell me about the meeting of shelter operators, and I wanted to hear. I want my shelter back." She stopped talking, blinked, and looked at me with eyes as hopeful as starved puppies we'd taken in at HotRescues who had smelled newly opened cans of moist food for the first time. "When can I get my shelter back, Lauren?"

Her red curly hair was plastered damply around her face. Her wrinkles seemed to have multiplied and deepened. She looked so aged and pitiful that I wanted to cry.

"I don't think you ever can," I said sadly and truthfully.

"It's all your fault," she yelled, startling me. "If I'd gotten the job at HotRescues like I should have—" She stopped as quickly as if she'd bitten her tongue—which she may have done figuratively, if not literally. "I'm sorry, Lauren. I know it's not your fault. I'm just tired. Can I go home now?"

"Of course," I said. I'd received confirmation from the cleaning outfit I'd hired that the top-to-bottom overhaul of Mamie's place had been accomplished as fast as I'd requested.

I drove Mamie home, silently pondering her tirade. She probably had been serious, lashing out at me because she didn't want to accept any blame herself. She'd mentioned before that she had wanted to prove she was the best pet rescuer ever. She hadn't had that mind-set when I'd known her but had only wanted to help as many animals as she logically could.

Had her change in attitude been the result of my being hired by Dante and not her?

I refused to let myself feel guilty even about logical things, and that kind of possible cause and effect was irrational. But if I'd insisted that we stay in touch back then, would things have been different now?

There was no use second-guessing. Dante had made the right decision. I couldn't fix what Mamie had done. But if I stepped in, tried to help her through this, maybe I'd feel a little better about the situation.

We stopped for groceries, and then I saw her into her house.

"This place is . . . different," she said, wonder in her tone as soon as we entered the front door. "Janice told me it would be cleaned while I was gone." I couldn't tell from her tone whether she was glad or sorry that the place no longer reeked like a sewer.

But as we walked farther inside, Mamie said, "I miss my babies," so sadly that I knew without looking that she was crying again.

"I know. But you understand that things will get better for them now, don't you?" I hoped.

"Yes," she whispered, nodding like a child.

"And do you understand that you're not allowed to bring in any animals at all, at least for now?"

She opened her mouth as if ready to protest, but at my unwavering glare she stared back and repeated, "Yes."

"Would you like to come home with me tonight?" I asked impulsively when we reached the front door again, knowing I'd probably regret it if she said yes. But she didn't.

"No, Lauren. Thank you, but I need to be alone right now."

"You'll be okay?"

"Yes," she said firmly. "I'll be fine."

Hoping that was true, I started home.

I didn't expect to sleep well that night, and I just dozed now and then. My mind was racing.

My landline rang around six in the morning. I grabbed it in anticipation. Of what? I didn't know, but I'd felt something was coming.

A call for help from Mamie?

It was her on the other end. But the help she asked for was not at all what I had anticipated.

"Lauren? Please, help me! I'm at Better Than Any Pet Rescues. I'm with Bethany . . . and she's dead!"

Chapter 7

Mamie sounded panicked. Not surprising.

I took a deep breath while I thought about what to do. My mind overflowed with questions—like, are you sure she's dead? If so, did she die of natural causes . . . or did you kill her?

I didn't ask, though. My first inquiry was calm and logical. "Have you called 911?"

"No! I can't. I didn't. I—"

"That's okay," I lied. "I'll take care of it." Still holding my landline receiver to my ear, I hurried to pick up my smartphone and made the call, all the while soothing Mamie as best I could while I simultaneously answered the emergency operator's questions—also as well as I could, when I didn't honestly know what was going on.

And then?

Well, it wasn't really my business. It shouldn't have

been my concern. Even so, I felt that someone needed to be there for Mamie.

Her niece? Maybe, but I wasn't sure how much Mamie's family would get involved now. I didn't want to be involved, either.

But I knew I already was.

The street was crowded again this time when I looked for a parking space near Better Than Any Pet Rescues. Mamie had confirmed she was in the plantation house, where the shelter's office was—and which had also been Bethany's home.

I was already thinking of Bethany in the past tense. I didn't know if Mamie was rational enough to determine whether Bethany was alive or not, but my mind had been circling around the possibility of death and had landed on it.

This time, the parked vehicles were unlikely to belong to any pet rescuers, as many had been last night when I was here. Instead, there were a lot of official vehicles, including an ambulance and several cop cars with rotating lights. Also, there were the inevitable media vans. Word had gotten out. I still wasn't sure what had happened to Bethany, but the situation had already grown legs and antennae. Maybe that happened with all 911 calls.

I finally located a spot where my Venza could be shoe-horned in. I sat for a moment before opening the door.

Maybe it was because I'd been a suspect in a murder investigation not long ago, or maybe it was Mamie's near hysteria, but I felt certain that something bad—not natural causes—had happened to Bethany. If she really was dead, Mamie might have caused it.

I hadn't kindled any ill will between them. I had, however, known that Mamie was emotionally unstable, and I'd nevertheless left her home, alone and possibly angry. Not that I'd much choice. If Mamie had gone off the deep end, I'd done nothing to cause it.

Or to stop it.

A couple of police officers in LAPD uniforms stood guard at the massive white gate, which was now ajar. The symbolic dog and cat in the tiara at its upper edge had been separated, thanks to the opening, and now stared in different directions.

Could I get inside to help Mamie? Should I, even if I could? I wasn't sure.

Even so, I strode up to the nearest officer. "Sir, I'm the person who contacted 911. Someone inside there, Mamie Spelling, called me. May I go inside and see her?"

"Wait here, please, ma'am." The request sounded like a no-nonsense command. He moved away and talked into a radio. I couldn't hear what he said.

In a couple of minutes, a woman in a pantsuit exited the gate. After seeing Bethany, her assistant, and others yesterday dressed similarly, I wondered if wearing business clothes was de rigueur for hanging around this place. Me? I'd put on what I usually wore for a day on the job: jeans, a blue HotRescues knit shirt, and athletic shoes. I guessed I didn't belong here—a good thing.

"Are you Ms. Vancouver?" the woman asked. I'd given my name to the 911 operator, so I wasn't surprised this lady—probably a detective—knew it.

"Yes," I said.

She pulled a shield from her pocket. "I'm Detective Greshlam, LAPD," she said, confirming my speculation. "I'd like to ask you a few questions."

"Of course. But would it be possible for me to see Mamie

Spelling? She's a . . . an old friend." I stumbled over that as my thoughts again hashed over my feelings toward Mamie. For now, what I'd said was accurate enough.

"Maybe later." Which I translated to be something like, "When all the rescued animals here tell us exactly what they saw."

We went onto the porch, where I'd last seen Bethany reign. There weren't any chairs there now, so we stood off to one side. I saw a lot of people traipsing around the shelter grounds, and heard dogs barking almost mournfully. They'd been relatively quiet yesterday. I've always felt that pets have emotional connections with people they care about that far exceed relying on them for food and shelter. If someone is hurt—or worse—they sense it.

Whatever I might have thought about Bethany and her treatment of people, from what I'd seen here I knew she took good care of the animals she rescued . . . and they undoubtedly appreciated it, especially since most had probably come from sectors of hell.

"I understand that you were the person who called 911 about this situation," the detective said. She was a large woman, tall and wide, and there was an incisiveness about her eyes that made it clear she was smart—and out to get the facts. "Is that correct?"

"Yes."

"But you just arrived here?"

As she made notes in a small spiral notebook, I explained what she must already have known, since I'd told the 911 operator. "Someone who was present called me."

"And that would be?"

"Mamie Spelling."

Answering the detective's questions, I gave sketchy details about who Mamie and I were, how we knew Bethany Urber, why I'd been here yesterday, and what had occurred when Mamie showed up.

"I drove Mamie home afterward," I said.

"And you didn't know she was coming back?"

"No."

A few more questions, and then we seemed to be done.

My turn to ask what I'd been dying to know. Figuratively, of course. "How is Bethany, Detective?"

"She is the apparent victim of a homicide, Ms. Vancouver."

"Oh." I paused. "How did she die?"

"That's still under investigation." In other words, the detective wasn't about to tell me. Someone came running through the gate and up the porch steps.

Cricket Borley did not resemble the shy but efficient assistant she had when she had smilingly passed out nametags at the meeting the day before. Her face was ashen and tear streaked, her gray shirt only partly tucked into black slacks, and only one of her tennis shoes was tied.

"What are you doing here, ma'am?" asked Detective Greshlam.

"I need to see Bethany. Help her. I'm her assistant. I always help her. Please—"

She must have known how impossible that was, since she sank to her knees on the porch and cried. I had an urge to comfort her, but I didn't move, since the front door opened and the person I was most eager to see spilled out of it.

Mamie wasn't alone, though. Another suit—a detective, too?—followed her. Her face was pale, but she managed a brief, sad smile. "Oh, Lauren, you came. That's so nice. But I have to leave. These detectives want me to help them figure out what happened to Bethany. I'm going with them to the police station."

Chapter 8

I couldn't get a minute alone with Mamie, but I did manage to move close enough to ask if she ever watched cop shows on TV.

She nodded, her expression puzzled and wary.

"Remember how they tell people they're questioning that they have the right not to answer, and to have an attorney present? Just to make sure someone's there to answer *your* questions, why don't you call your niece Janice—the lawyer—and have her meet you there?" That was partly for the cop's benefit, so he'd know Mamie was represented—perhaps. Mamie's niece had said she wasn't a criminal lawyer but surely she'd get involved enough to at least refer Mamie to one.

"Oh, yes, Janice is such a good girl. Pretty, too. It runs in the family." Mamie touched her red curls.

"Call her," I said, not even attempting to comprehend Mamie's state of mind. Only then did I look up to catch the baleful look in the eye of the detective accompanying Mamie. They soon headed out the front gate. I could only hope that Mamie understood enough not to say anything that would incriminate her—any more than her presence at a murder scene, and anything she'd previously said, had already done so.

I remained fully cooperative after they were gone, answering a few more questions for Detective Greshlam—not that I knew anything likely to be useful. Plus, I wasn't about to give any opinions about the relationship between Mamie and Bethany. Quite a few people had been at Bethany's presentation on hoarders and could draw conclusions they'd likely be thrilled to tell the police. Like Cricket. I watched as she was approached by a guy in a suit, probably another detective, and I'd little doubt that she'd give all the details she could about Mamie's appearance yesterday at the meeting.

Could Mamie have killed Bethany? Honestly, I suspected it was possible, but I hated to think it could be true.

When Detective Greshlam was done questioning me, she and the guy with Cricket walked off together for a few minutes. I used the opportunity to learn what Cricket had been asked.

"They wanted to know about poor Bethany," she replied softly. "And about Better Than Any Pet Rescues. Now that Bethany's gone, I guess I'm in charge." She started to cry.

Quietly, I gave her a falsely cheerful pep talk. The one thing accurate about it was that I told Bethany's former assistant that pet rescuers were all in it together, and that if she needed any help running the facility or taking care of any animals, she should give me a call.

"But I have everyone in Pet Shelters Together to call

on," she responded in a soggy but nevertheless condescending voice. She must have learned well from Bethany.

In a few minutes, Detective Greshlam returned and told me I was free to go.

I hurried out before she could change her mind.

The media was a lot more forthcoming than the detectives. I'm not sure how they got their information, but I heard on the radio that Bethany had apparently been shot with her own gun.

I'd left Zoey at home that morning, since I'd come straight to the Westchester area to check on Mamie. Now, I headed there to pick her up. I didn't want her to be alone that day.

I didn't want to be alone, either. Not that it was possible to be alone during time spent at HotRescues—even if no other humans were present. And since this was Saturday, we'd have not only our usual staff, but more volunteers present—high school and college kids who helped out on weekends. A few of them and their parents even acted as foster families. We sometimes believed it to be in an animal's best interests not to stay in our facility while we tried to find them new homes—often very young kittens and puppies who needed special TLC.

With luck, we'd also have more possible adopters drop in, as frequently happened on weekends, too.

I felt relieved, as if I had finally come home, when I pulled into my spot in the HotRescues parking lot. I leashed Zoey and gave her a short walk before we went through the side door into the welcome area.

Nina stood immediately, and when I released Zoey from her leash, she dashed to my assistant for a pat. Nina had apparently been working on paperwork behind the counter. "What happened, Lauren?"

I'd called earlier to let her know I'd be late, told her an overview without details.

I like Nina. She is bright and efficient, and I'm proud of her attitude. We're both divorcees, but the marriage she had ended had been even worse than mine. She'd been the victim of abuse.

Right now, Nina's narrow face looked drawn. She cringed a little, obviously awaiting bad news.

But all she knew about Mamie was the little I'd described about the prior relationship between me and my mentor. No sense for Nina to worry about the situation. One person in this room worrying about something she couldn't fix—a rare occurrence, one I abhorred—was enough.

"I don't have all the facts." I motioned for her to join me at the table under the window. Zoey followed and lay down by my feet. "Bethany Urber is apparently dead, and Mamie found her. The police took her in for more questioning. I wouldn't be surprised if she's their main suspect."

"But—"

"I'll go talk to her soon and try to learn more," I said. "Assuming they don't keep her in custody. Meantime, there's nothing any of us can do. So . . . anything interesting going on around here?"

Her face brightened. "Actually, yes. Remember the Andersons?"

"The cat lovers who were here the other day?"

She nodded. "They're in the cat rooms with Ricki right now, picking out two of our residents to adopt." Ricki was one of our youthful volunteers. "As long as you approve of them. They'd love to take them home today, but I told them we don't usually allow that."

"They filled out the paperwork last time they were here, right?"

"Yes, and I was just going over it with them before you came."

We both stood in unison and went behind the leopard-print counter, Zoey in close pursuit. Nina handed me the Andersons' application, including a signed contract of how they would care for any felines they were permitted to adopt. They owned their home in Santa Clarita, north of Granada Hills. Mr. Anderson—Frank—was a car salesman, and his wife, Jen, had an eBay business buying and selling high-end cookware. Interesting backgrounds. Plus, someone would be home a lot of the time. It sounded like a good adoption environment.

As Nina and I discussed the application, Ricki walked in with her temporary charges. "Hi, Lauren," she called. "The Andersons have picked out two kittens in the Flip litter." That was shorthand for the fact that one of our residents, a small, buff-colored female we'd named Flip for her flippant attitude, had been pregnant when we rescued her. She'd been here long enough to give birth and for her four offspring to reach an age where they were ready for new homes. They'd been fostered for a while, then housed here most recently with the other youngest cats. To prevent spreading unwanted germs, we didn't allow cats from one area to fraternize with those from another. Plus, we required that people going into the cat areas use a lot of disinfectant on hands and shoes before moving from one to another.

Now, Ricki absolutely beamed. She was a college-age African American who'd been volunteering here for quite a while. Like all our volunteers, she wore a yellow HotRescues knit shirt. She was about to start school to become a veterinary technician.

The two people with her were also African Americans, older than her, and they seemed to mirror her pleasure.

Still, despite the seemingly perfect application, I needed to be as sure as possible that this couple was a good match for the kittens.

"Wonderful, Ricki," I said. "Hi, Mr. and Mrs. Anderson."

"Frank and Jen," the woman contradicted with a smile.

"Frank and Jen, would you mind coming into my office for a few minutes so we can talk?"

"Sure thing," said Frank.

I left Zoey with Nina. The Andersons and I sat in my upbeat and well-decorated conversation area. The adoption counseling discussion went swimmingly. They'd owned cats before, but had recently lost a beloved pet to old age. No kids at home, so I wouldn't need to meet the rest of the family. "We want to get two so they'll have each other as company," Jen said. They would remain indoor kitties.

I believed they were serious about taking the cats into their hearts. Plus, they had been here before and come back. Therefore, a little while later, after making it clear I could drop in anytime to make sure the kittens had a good home, I made the rare decision to allow them to leave right then with two of our youngsters—plus a supply of food and other supplies from Dante's HotPets shops. The kittens had already had preliminary shots and been microchipped but would need to be neutered when they were a little older—a vow the Andersons made.

Life was good.

Except that, when I was alone once more in my office, organizing the paperwork for filing, my mind again wandered to Mamie and her desperate situation. Too soon for me to visit her.

But maybe . . .

On impulse, I used my BlackBerry to call Matt Kingston.

"Sure, Lauren. It'll be fine for you to visit at least some of our unhoarded rescuees this afternoon—but there's a price."

"Dinner?" I guessed, since it had been a price before, one I didn't mind paying.

"That's it," he confirmed.

"I'll look forward to it." I grinned.

The West Los Angeles Care Center was located on West Pico Boulevard. It was a relatively new building, with curb appeal from the outside and, much more important, efficient and well-maintained facilities for caring for animals on the inside.

Matt met me in the animal receiving area, and he took me to visit some of the pets that had been rescued from Mamie's.

I vowed not to think too much about Mamie just then—how she was, whether she was under arrest . . .

Matt looked a lot more relaxed than I'd seen him yesterday. I felt a lot more relaxed than I had then, too.

Matt was a good-looking guy, tall and muscular from his training with his special Animal Services groups, with brown eyes and an angular, masculine face. I couldn't help smiling back when he looked around, then bent down to kiss my cheek. For the moment, there were no other Animal Services folks in the area to observe the act, which could be regarded as unprofessional. Even so, the brief, friendly kiss whetted my appetite for something hotter. Did I mention that I found this guy pretty sexy?

"C'mon," Matt said. "A few of the dogs and cats are still at the vet's, but they're all doing okay. The rest are here. A lot of them. They're in quarantine for now."

He led me to a crowded area where there were multiple enclosures, and I saw some doggy faces that looked familiar—some Chihuahuas, some terriers, Great Dane mixes, and more. The haunted, hungry looks I'd seen in their big, brown eyes previously now appeared a little less intense, or so I thought. They looked better fed, curious, and perhaps a little lonesome. In need of new forever homes where they would get a lot of personal attention.

I'd do all I could to ensure that their dreams came true.

We went into a different area where I got to see some of the cats, again looking much healthier than when I'd last viewed them.

Yes, I felt sorry for Mamie and what she was going through—especially since I didn't see her as the kind of person who might shoot someone else, even someone she hated. But I was thrilled that these animals had survived despite her actions. That they had a future.

I'm sure I was beaming as Matt and I walked back through the shelter area toward the entrance. Of course there were a lot of other animals there as well. As always, I wished I could save them all. But I was nothing if not realistic.

We left my car in the care center's parking lot, and Matt drove us to a fun pizza place we'd eaten at before, not far from the shelter.

We sat in a booth in the crowded joint, and I ordered a beer along with our everything-goes pizza. When we'd been here before, we'd sometimes sat outside and I brought Zoey along. Occasionally Matt also had his dog, Rex, a black Lab mix. But Rex wasn't with us, and I'd left Zoey at HotRescues.

"Do you want to talk about the Bethany Urber situation?" he asked once the server had brought our drinks.

"Not especially," I said. "You can get the tabloid version on TV and online, if you're interested."

"I'm only interested because of its effect on you. I did hear that Mamie Spelling was found at the crime scene. Do you think she did it?"

"Honestly? I don't know. I can't believe it of her, but she's so different from the kind mentor I used to know." I took a sip of beer.

"Are you going to do anything more about the situation?"

He and I both had gone through the angst of being potential murder suspects. Did I want to get involved again?

But if I didn't look into what had happened, would anyone pay attention to the fact that Mamie just might be innocent?

"I don't know," I said. "Let's change the subject."

I expected him to get into something personal, but was surprised—and maybe a little relieved—when he said, "Have you found anyone to bring in to HotRescues as a new animal trainer?"

To make our residents, especially dogs, as adoptable as possible, it was important to have a part-time trainer on staff to help modify their behaviors. Our last trainer had gone a different direction with his life, and I'd been looking for a replacement.

"No, I haven't hired anyone yet."

"I've got a recommendation." He proceeded to give me information about a trainer whom he'd come in contact with in some recent meetings, a guy named Gavin Mamo. "He's Hawaiian by background, I think. I saw him in action with a couple of pit bulls that had been brought in from a dog fighting rescue. He calmed them pretty quickly."

"I'll check him out," I said. "Thanks."

Our pizza was served, and we talked about a rescue Matt had attended that the Small Animal Rescue Team, known as SmART—one of the Animal Services teams reporting to him—had undertaken that day. "Some kittens were born in a tiny area between buildings in a schoolyard. It wasn't easy, but our team rescued them all."

I smiled. "Please congratulate them for me. They're an amazing crew." Ever since I'd seen them save those baby beagles from the storm drain at the puppy mill site, I'd watched SmART's accomplishments on their Facebook page and YouTube. They did everything from climbing trees to rappelling down mountainsides.

When we were done eating, Matt took the bill from the server. "My turn," he said.

"This time," I agreed.

We went back to the West L.A. Care Center, and he parked his official Animal Services car beside my Venza. Sadly, he had to go back to his office in the Valley and complete some paperwork, so spending time together that night wasn't going to happen.

"Like I said, I'll keep you informed about the status of the animals rescued from the hoarding situation," he told me. "It would help if your friend Mamie gave up any supposed legal rights to them, but that never happens. And . . . well, will you do something for me?"

"What's that?"

"Stay away from Mamie and all that's going on with her."

With my hand on the car door handle, I glared. "Why?"

"Because I think there's a lot of potential for you to be hurt, Lauren. The lady may be your friend, but she's also, possibly, a nutcase. She may really have killed Bethany Urber."

But what if she didn't? my mind niggled.

There must have been something resistant in my look, since Matt sighed and reached for me. He held me tight, which was okay here. We were alone in the parking lot, since visiting hours for the shelter were over. I reveled in the feel of him against me, despite the controversy in our discussion.

"Okay, let me amend what I said." Matt spoke into my hair. "You know I worry about you, Lauren." When I moved away, ready to state, as I often did, that I wasn't ready for anything serious between us, he said, "I know. I'll back off. But if you decide to get more involved in the murder investigation, will you at least let me know?"

"Okay." I nodded. That sounded fair.

Matt's concern filled me with warmth. I really had started caring for him—much more than I was comfortable with. I wasn't sure where things might go from here but appreciated that he seemed to understand and never pushed me.

We gave each other some pretty sexy goodnight kisses, and I got in my car to head back to HotRescues to pick up Zoey.

Chapter 9

The time was nearly nine o'clock. I felt exhausted, ready to go home. Almost. I could never leave HotRescues without a final walk-through of the shelter.

Zoey greeted me inside the welcome area, leaping around as if I'd been gone for weeks, not just a couple of hours. Smart and obedient pup that she is, she immediately settled down when I said "Sit." Her butt wriggled on the tile floor, though, and her beautiful amber eyes never left mine. She wanted my approval, which she got. A hug, too.

I went to put my purse in my office. When Zoey and I came back down the hall, we were greeted by Brooke Pernall and Cheyenne.

"Hey, Lauren," Brooke said as I gave Cheyenne a pat in greeting. Unlike how I felt, Brooke appeared wide awake and alert, and I marveled again at how much she had improved since she had first come here ill and ready to relinquish Cheyenne for the pup's own good. "You're just getting here?

Are you taking on a security job? This is like the hours my guys and I keep."

"Just picking up Zoey and taking my last walk-through of the day. Care to come along and do your security thing?"

"Wouldn't miss it."

Inevitably, Brooke asked me about the Mamie situation. Word had gotten out. I told her what I knew, which wasn't a lot.

"They were still questioning her? Do you think she did it?"

"Honestly, I don't know." But the same thoughts kept reverberating in my mind—along with the germ of a crazy idea.

By then, we were in the outdoor shelter area. Our chain-link kennels on both sides of the walkway were nearly all full, particularly here, near the front. I stopped at the first on the left to pet Hannibal, a Great Dane mix, and Babydoll, a shepherd, in the one beyond. With both, as always, I waited until they were calm, then slipped inside their enclosures, rewarding them for behavior that might ultimately help them get adopted. Then I went to the cages on the right side and did the same with Dodi, a sheltie mix. Junior, a Doberman, woofed at us from the left as we started walking past the center building. I didn't acknowledge him till he'd quieted down, and then I greeted him, too. Despite his breed, he wasn't aggressive. We always tried to avoid taking in aggressive dogs, since they were less adoptable.

The area was crowded with dogs that needed loving homes. I've always believed that letting visitors see as many residents as possible right from the get-go was more likely to trigger compassion than allowing them to feel they weren't needed because we couldn't fill our habitats.

The enclosures were well built and maintained, partly

due to Dante's generous support of HotRescues—and lots of bedding and toys, and, of course, food from his stores. In addition, I always prided myself on making each enclosure as welcoming as possible. Naturally, each animal had plenty of water—in bowls from HotPets.

For ease of keeping things clean, the kennels resembled cages, each with dual parts: a roomy outside run that led to a door into a narrow temperature-controlled building. Toy dogs were all housed in our center building, beyond the first row of enclosures on our right, but in separate rooms from our kitty locales. Most cats hung out together in areas filled with climbing toys and litter boxes, with a kitchen in between. We also had rooms for other kinds of small pets like rabbits and hamsters, but all we'd sheltered recently had been adopted.

Dogs were kenneled together, or allowed to mingle in our visitors' park, only after observation to make sure they got along well. That minimized the possibility of fights.

The four of us—Brooke and I and the dogs—continued down the path toward the back shed, turning the corner so we could visit the enclosures at the other side of the uneven U formation.

"There'll be a lot more room here soon," Brooke observed. "More potential security issues, too."

"Will you need more people here overnight when the two properties are joined?" I asked.

"Nah. I think we've got that EverySecurity bunch under control now. They report to me first, and they're already planning to add cameras and all to the new building and animal enclosure areas."

"I hope so." My prior experience with EverySecurity also hadn't been great. In fact, there had been a murder here at HotRescues as well as other security breaches, and the company hadn't helped much in resolving them.

That's one reason Dante had hired Brooke, a former P.I.

Her background was now feeding the idea that had taken root in my mind.

We looked through the gate toward the construction on the property next door. "The building's nearly done," I commented. "At least the outside."

"Couldn't be finished fast enough for me," Brooke said. "I'm a little tired already of using that office upstairs in the center building as makeshift sleeping quarters. I'll be glad when the other offices are finished in the new building and the whole upstairs is remodeled into a real apartment."

That was because someone always slept here at HotRescues—now. We'd survived six years with only a security company on board till the problems that had occurred a few months ago, though I'd always been concerned about whether more watchfulness was needed.

Brooke had a few part-time security employees who took turns with her in being our overnight contingent, although she now most often stayed here herself.

Finishing our visits to the canines outside, we entered the back door to the center building, where we looked in on the smaller dogs, as well as the cat rooms. All the animals seemed fine, if, perhaps, a bit lonely. But Brooke would walk through again at least twice more to check on them.

I was heading home.

First, though, as we strolled back toward the entrance, I asked Brooke, "How's Antonio?" Detective Antonio Bautrel was her new boyfriend. He happened to be with the LAPD, in the Gang and Narcotics Division.

"He's fine." Her voice went soft and mushy, unusual for

our security specialist, but only for a moment. "Why, do you need me to ask him something on that situation with your old friend?"

She was nothing if not perceptive. "I don't need it, but I'd appreciate it. I'd really like to know what the cops think happened to Bethany Urber."

I explained briefly what I knew about Bethany, a little about her Better Than Any Pet Rescues, and her network of Pet Shelters Together.

"The cops might have zeroed in on Mamie as the killer, and it may be true . . . or not. I'd like to know something about any evidence they have against her besides just her presence, although I know a lot of that is kept confidential. Also, the media are saying that Bethany was allegedly killed with her own gun. Is that true?" I'd been wondering whether she'd taken it out herself and her killer had gotten it away and used it in self-defense . . . or whether the killer had been around Bethany's place enough to know where the gun was hidden.

"I'll see if Antonio can tell me anything." Brooke's grin was suggestive. "Of course, I can be pretty convincing."

I laughed. "I'll just bet you can."

She sat down behind the counter in the welcome area, and the dogs stayed with her.

I retrieved my purse from my office and checked my cell phone. I'd received a call from an unknown number. The person had left a voice mail message, and I listened to it. It was from Gavin Mamo, the dog trainer Matt had told me about. He'd said he was available until eleven that night, so I pushed the button to return the call. We arranged for me to visit him at his training facility on Monday afternoon.

Then Zoey and I left HotRescues for home.

The usual lights, on timers, were turned on in our small

but comfortable house in its gated Porter Ranch community. I missed my kids, as always, but was glad they both liked their colleges enough to take summer courses. They'd found jobs, too. Tracy was working in a Wal-Mart, and Kevin at a car repair shop. Both were responsible kids. Both were wonderful.

I also kept in close touch with my parents, and with my brother Alex and his family. They all lived in Phoenix. I hadn't talked with them for about a week and would call them soon.

"Let's go to bed," I told Zoey as we entered the house from the garage.

My cell phone rang then. It was past ten o'clock at night, and I didn't recognize the number.

I answered. "Hello?"

"Oh, Lauren, it's so good to hear your voice!"

"Mamie?" Was she still at the police station? Had they arrested her, or—

She answered my questions right away. "I'm home at last. I did like you said and called Janice, and she got that very nice Mr. Caramon to come and help me. He's a lawyer, too. He stayed with me, and then drove me home. I'd really like to talk to you, Lauren. Could you come see me tomorrow? In the afternoon would be best, 'cause I'm really tired now. Will you come? Please?"

Chapter 10

First thing, when I got up the next morning, I took Zoey for a walk around our pleasant residential neighborhood. We ran into others walking their dogs along our quiet streets, past similar-appearing houses of stucco and wood, and I proudly but subtly let Zoey show up every one of them. She was smart and obedient, and she recognized not only hand and voice signals, but also body language. If I stopped, she stopped. If I started going again, she heeled, whether or not I told her to.

She had been owned by a senior citizen who'd passed away without making arrangements for her. When she was brought into one of the city shelters, Matt, who knew my partiality for Border collies and Australian shepherds, had given me a first right of refusal to adopt her.

I hadn't been able to resist.

I admitted to myself, though, that my mind wasn't fully centered on my pup, or on the bright and warm June day in the San Fernando Valley.

I couldn't help thinking about my impending visit to Mamie. What did she want to talk about? Would she confess to me that she had murdered Bethany?

Zoey and I took one of our longer routes around several blocks, then went home. There, since it was late enough for me not to feel bad if I woke my kids, I called first Tracy, then Kevin, just to see how they were doing. Both were already awake and even sounded pleased to hear from their worrywart mom.

I had intended not to mention to either of them that I knew another murder victim—or a probable suspect. They'd been through enough when I'd been a suspect myself.

Even so, Tracy said, "I heard that someone involved with that pet hoarding situation was murdered, Mom. Did you know that?"

"Yes," I said with no elaboration, "I did."

Same went for Kevin, who'd spoken with his sister and knew about the murder. He sounded even more concerned. "You aren't connected with that, are you?" he asked.

"Not really," I said, "although I'd met both the person accused of hoarding and the lady who was killed." No need to worry him. My involvement in this case was definitely a lot less than when I was accused of murder.

After I'd hung up with Kevin, Zoey and I drove to HotRescues. Brooke was still there, but since our regular Sunday staff had begun to arrive, she and Cheyenne were preparing to leave. Zoey and I caught up with them as they made their final walk through the shelter area.

"Everything okay here last night?" I asked, stopping as always to slip inside and pat our nearest well-behaved canine residents before going on to the next enclosures.

Brooke, who also chucked one quiet dog then the next under the chin, looked a little tired—her eyes dull, and her attractive features drawn. That concerned me. Was her health situation acting up again? She'd looked great last night, though.

"Fine." She gave Junior a final pat and moved on. "No noises at all. I did my couple of rounds and all our animals were just fine."

"Then it's time for you to go home and get some real rest," I said firmly, then added, "Please let me know, though, if you get a chance to do any checking on the Bethany Urber situation."

"Already have." Her expression perked up. "Lost a little sleep over it—nice long talk with Antonio—but it was worth it." The smug smile that told me volumes about her relationship with the cop was back. It also partly explained how tired she looked. "Here's what I've learned so far."

As we continued to walk, she filled me in. "The investigation is ongoing, but the detectives on the case feel pretty sure that they're zeroing in on the right suspect. The autopsy's not complete, but the cause of death appeared obvious: two gunshot wounds to the chest. The weapon was likely the one Mamie was holding and handed over to the first patrol officer on the scene. No threat there—she wasn't in danger of being shot. Of course her fingerprints were on the gun but there were others, too, which were smeared and could be Bethany's—or not. Mamie has been very cooperative, including telling the investigating detectives how she had despised Bethany."

"What!" I exclaimed. "Even with her lawyer present?"

"I don't know when she said it, and that's all I've got so far. More to come, I hope. This seems like an interesting case, especially if your friend Mamie is innocent. The physical evidence includes the gun, and it belonged to

Bethany. I've gathered that, per the interviews conducted so far, she let her nearest and dearest friends know she had one, though not where she kept it. Apparently, she knew she rubbed people the wrong way at times and figured she'd scare them off from retaliating."

"Didn't work this time," I observed.

"Right. One more thing: Bethany apparently insisted that all Pet Shelters Together members wear a little pin she designed. One of them was found in her blood—not her pin, though, since she'd gotten one with diamonds in it."

"Whose is it?"

"The cops are still checking into that. Mamie didn't own a pin, since she didn't join the group, so that's something that's keeping her from being arrested."

"Good," I said. "At least there's one indicator that she could be innocent."

We'd stopped near the back entrance to the center building, and Brooke regarded me shrewdly. "You really think she is innocent, don't you?"

I shrugged. "I don't know her well now. But . . . well, though she obviously still loves animals, she was abusing them, intentionally or not. As far as killing a person? I hate to think so, but I really don't know." Mamie had considered Bethany a threat, but I'd, in fact, been the one to do what Bethany had threatened her with: tell the authorities about her hoarding. If she was going to murder anyone, wouldn't I have been a better subject?

I didn't tell Brooke that, though.

"Well, if you're going to visit her—" She looked at me inquisitively, and I nodded. "Be sure to see if you can get anything out of her about who she thinks could have killed Bethany."

"If it wasn't her," I said.

"If it wasn't her," Brooke agreed.

As I had the last time I'd been here, I parked on the street outside Beach Pet Rescue and walked through the dilapidated gate. Fortunately, the outdoor odor from pet excrement had dissipated, although I didn't believe that the housecleaners would have done anything out there. Collapsed fencing and crates were piled in the yard. I supposed that, to prosecute Mamie for animal abuse, the authorities didn't have to confiscate all the equipment. Some examples and photos would probably be enough to show a judge or whoever needed to be convinced about what had happened.

Assuming Mamie even faced legal action now for what she had done to the pets in her care. Maybe she would only be prosecuted for murder.

At least she apparently hadn't started collecting animals again. I'd warned her against it, but that was a frequent occurrence with hoarders anyway. I'd double-check inside her house, though. I'd already planned to visit her now and then to make sure—but I hadn't anticipated there'd be an additional reason, like a murder, to bring me here.

She must have been watching for me, since, once again, she appeared right away, hurrying out the front door to her shabby house. "Lauren! You came!" She dashed toward me and threw herself into my arms.

She seemed even smaller, frailer, than the last time I'd seen her, which was only yesterday.

"Please, come in." She stepped back. "I've boiled more water for tea. Is that okay?"

"Sounds wonderful," I lied politely. I followed her into

the gleaming kitchen. The place smelled of disinfectant instead of poop. Heaven! And no animals begged for attention. In fact, I'd seen none . . . so far.

Mamie had again set two places at the gouged table in the middle of the kitchen, both with chipped tea cups in a floral pattern and mismatched stainless spoons. Everything appeared clean this time. Mamie waved toward the half-full box of tea bags that sat in between. "Please, help yourself." A kettle steamed on the battered gas stove, and she picked it up. I put a tea bag into my cup, and she poured water over it, then into her own, which already contained a tea bag. After returning the kettle to the stove, she sat across from me. Her smile was brittle, and her eyes looked both terrified and exhausted.

She said nothing, though, so I decided to prompt her. There were two topics I wanted to cover, and I started with the one most important to me.

"Mamie, has anyone talked to you about what happens to your animals now?" They were, in fact, hers—and that was part of the problem, as Matt had explained it to me.

She nodded solemnly. "The lawyer Janice found for me —Mr. Caramon—he's really nice. He said we could protest how they'd stolen my friends from me, but . . . well, he didn't think we'd win. He also said they could start charging me a lot of money for taking care of my babies, or I could give them up." Her eyes welled, and I reached over to squeeze her hand.

"I understand how hard that is, but they'll have better lives if you surrender them, Mamie. I'll make sure that they're either rehomed by Animal Services right away, or, if there's any danger to them, I've contacted other rescuers who'll take in any that I can't—and I should be able to handle a bunch." I paused until she looked up, and I met her gaze solemnly. "Please promise you'll surrender them, Mamie."

Tears rolled down her papery cheeks, but she nodded slowly. "If you really think that's best for them . . ."

"I do."

"But—"

"It really is," I insisted firmly. "They'll find families who'll love them. You know that's the right thing to do."

She drew in her breath. Her nod was sad but resolute. "Okay, Lauren. I'll do it. I'll let Mr. Caramon know."

"You're the greatest!" I went around and gave her a big hug. I'd let Matt know, too, so he could follow up on it.

Mamie still looked dubious as I sat back down. It was time for the next subject. "Tell me how things went at the police station. You said your attorney was with you there, right?"

She nodded, and her red curls wafted around her lined face. "Mr. Caramon is a very nice man. He told me to tell the truth, since he knows I didn't kill Bethany."

"I don't want to interfere in any way with whatever Mr. Caramon told you," I said, "but can you tell me why you were at Bethany's so early in the morning?"

Her eyes welled up, and she took a sip of tea. "I couldn't sleep. I missed my animals so much . . . I knew that Bethany lives—lived—at her own shelter, so I doubted she'd be sleeping too late and I decided to go talk to her. See, your place, HotRescues, is so far away, or I'd have asked you. I don't drive the freeways much these days. Too much traffic. My car is still at Bethany's, I think. Or maybe the police took it."

"You'd have asked me what?" I felt utterly confused.

"I went to see Bethany to apologize for yelling at her during her meeting. I meant it, of course, but I wanted to work there, even volunteer, to be near animals again. I know she thought me a hoarder, and so did you." She dipped her head, and I had to strain to hear her. "It wasn't . . . Well, maybe you were right, but I never meant to hurt . . . Anyway, as hard as it would be, I was even willing to let Bethany supervise me, tell me what to do, as long as I could help rescue pets again."

"I see." My voice was subdued. I *did* see. Mamie wouldn't quite admit to herself that she was a hoarder. Even so, she was willing even to beg the person who'd threatened her with disclosure in the first place, if only she could be around animals.

Unless she was a really good liar, and claiming she'd gone there to beg was part of her act.

"What was Bethany's response?" I asked.

"That's the point. When I got there, no one answered the buzzer, but the gate wasn't locked. The animals heard me come in—some dogs barked, and they sounded very upset. I didn't want to go see them without talking to Bethany first, observing whatever rules she wanted. I thought that would show how sincere I was. But she didn't answer the doorbell, and the house was open, too. I just went inside and called out to her. She didn't answer, but I thought I heard something, so I kept calling her name. I went upstairs, found her bedroom . . . and found her." Mamie inhaled sharply. "It was so awful. Blood everywhere. A gun on the floor. I didn't know what to do. That's when I called you."

She sounded sincere. Her story even appeared logical. Maybe that was another reason she hadn't been arrested, at least not yet. The cops might need more evidence than her presence to get her convicted of murdering Bethany.

Even though she had all the elements I heard of in crime-scene TV shows: motive, means, and opportunity. I'd even discussed them with the detective who had been investigating me as a potential murderer. This time, though, the means . . .

"The gun, Mamie—where was it?"

"On the floor, near Bethany."

"Had you ever seen it before?"

"Well, yes. Bethany waved it at me when we were arguing before. I heard that she did that a lot."

Interesting. So there could be others who knew about it. "Did you touch the gun when you saw it near Bethany?"

"Yes, to look at it, and to hand it to the police." Was she really that naïve? She must have realized how dumb that sounded, since she added, "I wouldn't know how to shoot a gun even if I wanted to, Lauren. If I'd decided to kill Bethany, I'd have figured something else out."

Maybe. But it was time to move on.

"So . . . do you have any ideas who might have wanted to kill Bethany?" I asked.

"Who else, you mean?" I felt my eyes widen. "I know you still think it could be me, Lauren. But it wasn't, damn it. And, yes, I do have some other ideas. I told the detective that, too. But—" The anger in her voice suddenly tapered off. "But I'm afraid it's no use."

"What do you mean?" I asked gently. Despite all my doubts, I realized that I had started to believe her.

"He pretended to listen to my ideas, and Mr. Caramon encouraged me to make suggestions. But I think the cops have already decided they know who did it, no matter what I say, and they're just taking their time so they can get whatever evidence they can make up to prove it."

"They think it's—"

"Me, Lauren. They seem sure that it was me."

Chapter 11

On my drive back to HotRescues, I pondered the meager list of additional suspects that Mamie had strained to tell me about. She claimed not to have known Bethany well. Even so, she had met her weeks ago, had had a lot of interaction with her while they discussed the possibility of Mamie's Beach Pet Rescue joining the Pet Shelters Together network.

But that didn't mean she knew Bethany personally. Mamie probably didn't know her well enough to figure out everyone—else—who might have wanted Bethany out of their lives.

That left it up to me . . . somewhat.

I wasn't an investigator. I'd no reason to believe that the cops were mishandling anything. They were treating Mamie like a suspect . . . which she was. But they hadn't arrested her. That indicated they weren't necessarily jumping to conclusions.

Yet I also couldn't say with any certainty that they were

doing anything besides getting all their detective mojo lined up so they could prosecute Mamie with no hitches when they were ready to pull her in.

A little thing like her not being guilty might not stand in their path once they decided to prosecute.

But *was* she guilty?

And why was I putting myself through this?

I knew the answer, of course. I always helped friends. Mamie had once been a friend—a really good one. The fact that I'd won the position at HotRescues, and not her, might have angered her, but I now believed I should have made a greater effort to stay in touch.

I'd unintentionally turned my back on her then when she might have needed my help. I wouldn't do it again.

Besides, if she had decided to kill anybody, I'd already figured it was more likely to have been me. She apparently still resented that Dante had chosen me to run HotRescues, and I'd been the one to call Animal Services on her.

Not that I felt bad about either. Both had been the right choice.

They also made me feel a little sorrier for Mamie.

I used my hands-free device to call ahead to HotRescues. Brooke, having finished her overnight security duties, had already left. Everything there was fine, Bev, our senior volunteer, assured me. Since it was Sunday, Nina wasn't around. Most likely she was volunteering today at one of the L.A. city shelters. Pete wasn't around, either, and the place was largely staffed by our volunteers. I also heard noise in the background as I talked to Bev that suggested . . . A. she was outside, and B. the construction guys were there, next door, working on the new building.

Since everything sounded in order, I pulled over once I got off the freeway and asked Bev to look something up for me. "I need some information to do a home visit on my way to HotRescues," I told her.

After about five minutes, she called me back with information about one of our recent adoptions—a cat placement in Northridge, not far off my route to HotRescues.

I called the number of the very nice lady who had adopted the calico kitty we'd called Queen J a few weeks ago. I'd done one follow-up visit nearly immediately, since Q.J. had been sent to her new home at the end of an adoption event in a park, and I was always concerned about how those quick placements would work out—so much so that I almost never permitted them. The people had appeared to be great prospective adopters, but, micromanager that I tend to be, I always did at least one extra visit to assure myself that all was well.

"Carmen?" I said when a woman answered the phone. "I'm Lauren Vancouver, the administrator at HotRescues."

"Oh, yes, Lauren. Good to hear from you. Queen is doing just fine, if that's what you're calling about."

"It is. Would you mind if I stopped by for another visit?"

"Not at all." She was home, and I headed my car in her direction.

Her house was a modest one, on a street off Nordhoff. The area was familiar. I'd visited another house just a block or two away last week, to check on a dog placement.

When I reached the front door, I assumed that Carmen Herrera had been watching for me. She opened it, and the sweet calico we'd rehomed here was in her arms.

"She's still a house cat?" I confirmed as I followed Carmen into her living room.

"Absolutely. I'd be so worried if she roamed around outside."

This was one of those situations where a person resembled her pet, or vice versa. I couldn't be sure whether Carmen had selected Queen J based on the fact that her hair was fluffy and multicolored, too, but intentional or not, that was how it was.

I only stayed a few minutes. All looked well. Queen J was still the cat's name, and she appeared pampered and happy.

All in all, a good rehoming. I'd mark the visit in our online files once I got back to HotRescues. I didn't think we'd need to come back again, unless we got word that conditions had changed.

"Thanks so much for letting me visit, Carmen," I said as I walked out the door. "You, too, Queen J."

"Anytime," Carmen said. "And thank you, Lauren, and all of HotRescues. It's so wonderful to have a kitty like Queenie in my life. You know, I've told everyone about you, and my neighbors around the corner adopted a new dog from HotRescues just a couple of weeks ago. They're the ones who told me about you."

"I know," I said. "And I appreciate the referral. The more pets we can adopt out to good homes, the happier we all are."

Just for the heck of it, I drove around the corner and passed the house where that dog we'd recently adopted out now lived. He'd been sweet and shaggy, a reddish Briard mix we'd called Beardsley, and the house had a fenced yard much larger than Carmen's. He was, in fact, the second dog we had placed with this family, as well as a cat who'd come here first. The humans consisted of a single parent, Margie Tarbet, and her teenage son, Davie. I'd interviewed both of them before the first placement and liked them a lot. Davie, in particular, seemed fascinated by the whole idea of pet rescue.

The cat, Nemo, and the first dog, Moe, had both been adopted more than a year ago and had seemed a good fit, even getting along together. We'd made sure that Beardsley was okay with cats by bringing him into one of our cat areas, and then had Margie bring Moe to HotRescues to confirm that Beardsley and he got along. No problems there, either. I'd spoken with Margie after she brought Beardsley home, and she had assured me that he and the others were all adapting fine to one another. I still wanted to check it out, though—as well as how the human family was relating to them.

I didn't see either pup or the kitty outside, a good thing. I impulsively parked and went up the front walk of the cottage-like house, then rang the doorbell.

Dogs barked, but no person answered the door. That was fine. I'd no belief that there were any issues here. Beardsley was guarding his new home along with Moe, as he should. Nemo was probably observing the foolish, excited dogs, bored as he washed his paws.

I could only grin as I returned to my car. Even so, I'd do a follow-up visit here soon.

Back at HotRescues, I left a message on Brooke's cell phone and gave Zoey a hug. My pup had been hanging out in my office, sleeping under my desk. I invited her to come along while I did my next shelter walk-through, and she eagerly agreed.

Bev was still staffing the welcome area. When Zoey and I passed through on our way outside, she was conversing with a young couple. Shamelessly eavesdropping, I learned that the pair was newly moving in together and couldn't decide on the size of the dog they wanted to adopt.

Bev, a senior citizen, was short and thin, slightly bent over as if she perhaps had osteoporosis. But she was more animated than volunteers a fraction of her age.

"Since you're renting half a house and have a yard, you don't have to stick with a toy dog unless you want to. Plus, kids your age will probably love going on long walks or even runs with your new pet. Now, we have several mid-sized dogs I'd like to introduce you to. Unless—" She looked at me. "Care to do the honors, Lauren?" She looked back at the couple. "This is the really nice lady who runs this place, and she knows a lot about all our animals."

What the heck? Zoey and I took them through the shelter area, listening as they discussed each dog we passed. The guy seemed to like the big, husky-like canines best. The girl was into terriers and small spaniels.

Until . . . "Isn't he sweet?" the girl said, stopping outside the enclosure housing a mid-sized furry mix whose breeds I couldn't even guess. The pup had an elongated muzzle, pointy ears, and a wistful expression in deep brown eyes. We called him Big Boy.

The young man also knelt down and reached inside the enclosure. All three smiled and stared at one another, and I believed we had a match.

Assuming, of course, that I approved their application. Which, a short while later, after reviewing it with them and seeing the couple interact with Big Boy in our outdoor visitors area, I did, but they would have to come back later to talk with Dr. Mona before adopting their new pet. Moving in together was a big change in their lives, so I wanted to be sure our staff psychologist thought them a good fit, too.

Brooke returned my call a short while later. Sitting behind my desk once more, I gave her a rundown of what I'd learned from Mamie, which wasn't a lot.

"So she's not under arrest but expects it momentarily?"

"That's what I gather."

"And you still don't think she's guilty?"

"I still don't know. But in case she's not . . . could you ask Antonio if the detectives are seriously considering other suspects, or if they're just putting together their case against Mamie?"

"Will do. If they've got others in mind, will you still want to pursue this?"

"I don't really want to pursue it even if they have fully open minds and don't think Mamie's their only candidate."

"But—"

"But if that's not the case, I'll at least want to look at some other possibilities. Just for the sake of fairness."

And nosiness. And taking charge of anything in which I'm involved, whenever possible. And watching out for friends, even those with whom I was no longer close. But I didn't say any of that.

"Got it. But, Lauren . . ." Brooke paused, which made me lean forward a little in my desk chair, anticipating she was about to say something profound. "Okay, let me be honest here. From the little I've seen about this case, I think your friend Mamie could be guilty."

"I know it's possible," I said with a sigh. "One problem, though, is that I'm concerned no one is trying to find another answer just in case she's innocent."

"Except you?"

I nodded. "Except me."

"Then we'll stay on it," Brooke said. "I'll let you know what I find."

Chapter 12

I slept well that night, at least after I finally dropped off.

I never second-guess myself. Once I make a decision, I stick with it. Even so, I kept asking myself, over and over, if I was just wasting time by trying to help Mamie. What if she really was guilty?

Ah, but what if she was innocent?

At least the animals she'd been hoarding were still doing amazingly well. The one call I'd made after I got home was to Matt. I told him that Mamie had agreed to surrender them, and he sounded as jazzed as I felt. Plus, he'd mentioned their continued improvement. They would soon be out of quarantine. Some might be available for possible adoption as soon as Mamie's surrender became effective.

The next morning, Zoey and I headed to HotRescues early. When we arrived and I parked, I opened the back door to unhook Zoey from her harness and attach her to a leash. Usually, she trots proudly to the door into the welcome area, as if she runs the place. As my new best friend and companion, in some ways, she does.

Today, though, she sat down and made a small growling sound in her throat, putting her nose in the air for a sniff. Then she dashed off toward the far end of the parking lot.

Fortunately, I had a good grip on her leash. I could have ordered her to stop. Being the excellent dog she is, she would probably have obeyed. Though we hadn't been together long, I knew enough about her to realize she had something important in mind. Keeping a rat off the property? Maybe, and, if so, that was a worthwhile endeavor. I suspected something even more significant, though.

Zoey pulled me past where the large shelter van was parked, toward the back of the lot, which was shielded from the alley behind HotRescues by a wooden fence. It was more for a semblance of privacy from the commercial buildings on the far side than for security, since the parking lot wasn't enclosed. Zoey tugged until we went around the fence. I had to slow her down as a vehicle turned into the alley— Pete Engersol's minivan. Our handyman, who also helped to pick up supplies, had a designated parking space outside the rear storage building, which was part of the enclosed and secure area within HotRescues.

But Pete didn't pull into his spot. Instead, he stopped behind the storage building and exited his van. The thin senior citizen, in jeans and a blue HotRescues knit shirt, was a lot stronger than he looked, thanks to all the large bags of kibble he maneuvered onto carts for piling inside the building. Or, he was just naturally fit enough to heft the kibble.

"Not again!" he exclaimed as Zoey and I hurried toward him. I turned in the direction he was looking.

Right in the middle of his parking spot was a Doberman. Its leash was tied to the knob of the door into the storage building. The dog sat there, cringing as it looked at us with apparent fear. I wanted to hug him—or her. I couldn't tell the sex yet.

"Another one?" I all but echoed Pete. Around the dog's neck was a collar. No ID tag dangled from it, but a note was fastened to it.

"If people want to relinquish their dogs at a shelter, why don't they have the guts to meet with you first?" Pete muttered.

"I agree." I knew what the note would say—a sob story about how the owner couldn't keep this dog anymore. There would be no identification, so we couldn't check it out.

The thing was, in Los Angeles, private shelters like HotRescues could take in owner relinquishments, but not strays—not unless they'd been through the official system first and Animal Services or another public shelter had ceded them into our care.

Someone apparently knew that. I was afraid that the dogs who had been left here over the last several weeks were strays, and the person who'd found them was trying to circumvent the official system, possibly to ensure their lives would be spared.

But I worried about whether I could keep HotRescues' license valid and take these animals in.

I told Pete to do the obvious and bring the poor dog inside HotRescues. I didn't let Zoey perform a nose-to-nose sniff, not until our newcomer was checked by a vet to make sure he carried no communicable disease.

Yes, he was a he; I could tell when he stood up after Pete took his leash. I directed Pete to take our new friend to the quarantine area, in a special place inside the center building. It would be located in the new building next door when the construction was finished, but not yet.

Before they left, I gave the new guy a reassuring hug using just my hands around his face. I'd wash my hands before touching Zoey or any of our inhabitants here, but I couldn't resist that sad, scared look.

"Does the note tell us his name?" I asked Pete.

"Shazam."

I wondered whether the name was a clue about Shazam's origins. If I recalled correctly, that was the magic word used by a comic book character to transform himself into a superhero, or something like that.

But if this Shazam was magical, he probably wouldn't have wound up abandoned at a shelter, even one as great as HotRescues. At least things would improve for him now. He could count on it.

I called Carlie's veterinary clinic and set up an appointment to bring Shazam in.

Not only did they have a time slot available in an hour, but Carlie herself would do the honors.

We were back at HotRescues, Shazam and I. He had been given a relatively clean bill of health by Carlie—just needed a good bath to deal with a flea issue and some better, more regular food.

I'd had him checked for a microchip, too, to no avail. Whether he was a relinquishment or stray, we had no way of finding Shazam's prior human.

The good news was that he appeared to be just a year old and mostly physically fit, and soon should be adoptable. As long as I manipulated the situation right.

I was good at manipulating situations. I knew what to

try with this one—since it had suddenly become common-place.

I was in my office now, with Zoey lying at my feet. I'd left her with Nina, and she'd acted glad to see me on my return—as always when I'd been away from her for a while.

Bev—here today, too—had taken Shazam back into quarantine, where he would remain for a week to ten days as a matter of policy. I'd been a little concerned whether Bev, even more senior a citizen than Pete, would be able to handle the Dobie, but from the moment we had found him here he had been as docile as a smaller dog with a breed reputation for being submissive. Which suggested he had been well trained, wherever he had come from.

Now, it was time for that manipulation. I called Matt. I'd called him before, when the other two dogs had been found in the early morning hours at the HotRescues doorstep. I felt I could ask him for quasi-official advice without putting too much stress on our growing friendship . . . or whatever it was.

The first time this had happened, the pup, a combo of small breeds I hadn't been able to decipher, had come with no indication of an owner relinquishment. I'd called Matt then, too. He'd asked me to have someone drop off that dog at the nearest Animal Services facility, the West Valley Care Center, and I had—with my standing request to let me take him back if no one adopted him soon. He was a cutie, and I'd heard that he'd found a new forever home quickly. As long as the adoption stuck, that had worked out fine.

The second dog to appear had looked more senior, a black Lab mix with gray hair around his muzzle. He had come with a note that claimed his owner had dropped him off, unable to care for him anymore. Of course I was suspi-

cious. Why not bring him in when HotRescues was open—
so I could try to convince the owner otherwise if it was a
genuine relinquishment? As enticement, we could provide
food and counsel and limited veterinary care. But despite
our few cameras outside and our overnight security personnel, the person who'd left Abel—the name on the
note—remained a mystery.

When I'd called Matt and explained the situation, he was
generous enough—and an animal lover enough—to say it
was okay to treat Abel as an owner relinquishment. Not that
there was anything wrong with entering a healthy animal
into the public system—as long as there was enough room
to let them stay till adopted. But an older dog like Abel
might be harder to place. Matt got that, and we got Abel. He
was still with us, and he was a love.

Now Matt and I discussed Shazam.

"You're sure he came with a note like the last one?" I
didn't blame Matt for sounding skeptical. If I were him, I
might think that the administrator of a private rescue organization might make something like this up, to avoid having
to put a stray through the Animal Services system. Would I
do such a thing? Not if I thought he might find out. And I'd
believed he'd come to trust me over the last few months.

"You doubt my word?" I poured all the ice I could into
my tone.

"No. You know I trust you, Lauren. You're one excellent
animal rescuer. But you have to admit it sounds a bit suspicious."

I warmed a bit. "Thanks, and yes. So . . . ?"

"Let me ponder this—including what to do if it happens
again. Tell you what. Why don't you meet me at the Northeast Valley Animal Care Center? Since it has more room,
the hoarded animals were all just moved there, in case we

do wind up having to hold on to them for a while as evidence." In other words, if Mamie didn't follow through on surrendering them, no matter what she had told me. "I'll fix it so I can bring you up to date on how well our latest guests are getting along. Even let you visit some."

I loved the idea! Still . . . "Can I meet some friends there, too? Other private rescuers, I mean. A bunch keep e-mailing me about the hoarding situation, since I let them know about it on a Web site where we communicate, and they always express concern about the rescued animals." Some had also quizzed me about Bethany's murder and Mamie's possible involvement, but I'd been selective about what questions to answer.

"Sure," he said, "as long as you and I get an opportunity to talk about . . . what's his name?"

"Shazam."

"Abracadabra, too," Matt responded.

It took me a couple of hours to get on my way. I handled a bit of paperwork, and then Zoey and I did our usual walk around HotRescues—including peeking in on Shazam and on Abel, who was in one of our residences for larger dogs toward the rear of the shelter area.

I said hi to our volunteers who were walking some of our dogs—and cleaning their enclosures. I also posted a notice on the Southern California Rescuers Web site. There, I let the administrators of other private shelters who monitored it know that, if they could get away quickly enough, we had an invitation to visit some animals who'd been the subject of the hoarding. I explained that it was too early to pick any up to take back to our shelters, but I was hopeful that the day would come soon.

I doubted many rescuers would see the post, and even fewer would be able to make it on such short notice.

Eventually, I got in my Venza, once again leaving Zoey behind, since she wouldn't be welcome at a city shelter.

Besides, I planned to stop at Gavin Mamo's animal training facility later, to meet with him as scheduled during our phone call the previous week.

I called Matt on my hands-free system while on my way. He was already there.

I parked in the lot, which was more crowded than usual. This care center was not open to the public, due to lack of funding, but Animal Services people worked here and took care of animals that were housed in this shelter for reasons such as being evidence in possible animal cruelty prosecutions.

I walked up the path, glancing up at the poles holding pictures of dogs and cats. The building wasn't open, and I noticed some familiar people on the patio, including friends who also ran private shelters. They hurried over to me.

My notice posted on the Web site had had more reach than I'd anticipated, a potentially good thing. In the event the official shelter didn't have room for all the rescued animals, the more private facilities interested in taking some in, the more that could be saved.

"Hi," I said to Kathy Georgio, the first to reach my side.

"This is so great, Lauren!" Kathy was a fiftyish lady who had a pudgy face bisected by a huge smile. I had seen her last at the meeting about hoarders that Bethany had held. Today, she wore jeans that were too tight on her zaftig body, and a T-shirt that seemed an equally bad fit. But her looks weren't important. How she treated her charges was, and from all I'd gathered, she was one of the better rescuers in the area—besides me, of course.

Another Southern California Rescuers regular was there as well. Ilona Graye, whose rescue organization mostly placed animals with fosterers, had come, too. She was a youthful secretary at a small Valley law firm that specialized in entertainment law, so she occasionally got celebs to take in pets she had saved.

I noticed then that some of the people I'd met at Bethany Urber's hoarding seminar were there, too—a group of six people, including Cricket and Darya. Interesting, that they were at least lurkers on the Southern California Rescuers Web site. But I'd learned that Bethany had been, too. It wasn't much of a stretch to think she had encouraged the members of the Pet Shelters Together to follow her lead.

As I said hi to them, I noticed Matt inside the building, dressed in his Animal Services uniform. He opened the door. "Ready to visit some formerly hoarded rescuees?" he asked.

"Absolutely!" I smiled at him warmly, then said to the rest, "This is Captain Matt Kingston of L.A. Animal Services. He's the head of SmART, D.A.R.T, and Emergency Preparedness." I didn't think I needed to translate to this group of pet rescuers that SmART stood for Small Animal Rescue Team and D.A.R.T. was short for Department Air Rescue Team. "Even more important right now, he's supportive of our private facilities' ability to take in any of the hoarded animals that Animal Services can't care for."

A cheer went up from the crowd, eliciting a sweetly bashful grin from the subject of their applause. Matt wasn't the kind of guy I'd consider to be shy—not with all his muscles and his no-nonsense leadership skills. I thought his reaction was pretty adorable.

He led us inside the shelter area of the center. "The cats are inside," Matt said, "and most of these dogs came from that Beach Rescue facility."

All the pups clamored for well-deserved attention. At least here, the conditions weren't as crowded as they'd been at the West L.A. center, since this was a nearly empty facility. Once we were given the go-ahead, the private shelter administrators, including me, should be able to save every one of these dogs.

Once more, I thought I recognized some of them—a Great Dane mix, a couple of bulldogs, and—yes, that terrier mix had to be Herman, the dog Mamie had claimed was her own.

"Whenever these animals are ready for private shelters to take them in, I'd like dibs on that one," I told Matt, pointing at Herman. His dark brows rose in a quizzical expression. "I think he's Mamie's special pet," I explained.

"I'll do what I can."

My shelter administrator posse members seemed every bit as taken with the dogs here as I was, talking baby talk to them and reaching in to pat them.

"How about the cats?" Kathy Georgio asked. She sometimes signed her e-mails and group posts as Kat, so I figured she was more partial to felines than canines. Matt soon took us to the area where cats were housed, and he pointed out the ones from Mamie's.

Again, all looked well.

Matt's cell phone rang. He pulled it out and looked at the display. "Sorry, got to take this. I'll be back shortly."

I decided I could use the opportunity to take the two women aside I was sure had known Bethany and ask a few helpful questions. "Would you mind coming with me for a minute?" I asked Cricket and Darya. "I've got some questions about Pet Shelters Together." Not exactly, but I figured that would at least spark their attention.

Leaving the other shelter administrators oohing and

aahing over the kitties, I walked out of the feline neighborhood and into a canine area.

"Are you interested in having HotRescues join Pet Shelters Together?" Cricket asked right away. "I'm in charge
now that poor Bethany isn't around, at least until the board
of directors tells me otherwise . . . and I think they'll want
me to stay."

"You do have a lot of experience," Darya confirmed. "I'll
bet you'll do as good a job as Bethany. Maybe even better."

Cricket flushed slightly and bobbed her head so that her
short, curly hair waved a little. "No one could be as good
as Bethany," she said modestly.

"Of course," Darya agreed. "But she was your mentor,
wasn't she? That's what she used to say when I helped out
by working around the office there now and then. She was
so proud of you."

This could go off into a love-fest for Bethany instead of
the direction I wanted to aim. "I'm sure you'll both miss
her," I said. "The rest of the people at Better Than Any Pet
Rescues and Pet Shelters Together—and the animals will,
too. Everyone but . . . well, there's no delicate way to say
this. There's a good possibility that Mamie will be arrested
for killing Bethany, and maybe she did it. But I'd really
love your opinions about anyone else who might have committed the crime, just so I can feel sure that the real guilty
party is found. Like Bethany was your friend, Mamie is
mine." To some extent, at least. "If she did it, then that's
that. But if it isn't her, who would you bet on?"

They both stared at me as if I was nuts. Cricket was
shorter than me and heavier, and her grayish eyes narrowed
in disbelief. Darya was tall and thin, and looked as if she
could blow away in a puff of doggy breath. Her brown eyes
looked equally incredulous.

"I'm sorry she's your friend, Lauren," Cricket said. "But she has to be guilty."

"That's right," Darya agreed.

"Just humor me. If Mamie had been having drinks with the cops that night, or had another perfect alibi, who would you think might have had it in for Bethany?" I looked expectantly at Cricket first.

"Well, she'd been married twice," she said reluctantly. "She always talked about her exes like they're dirt. She said they hated that they hadn't had an opportunity to participate in all her wonderful success. But—"

"Great!" I interrupted. "Anyone else?" I asked Darya. "Like, was Bethany married now?"

"No," Darya said. "She has—had—a boyfriend. A really cute one. I'd seen him at a meeting of Pet Shelters Together. He's younger than she was."

"And did they always get along?"

"I'm not sure," Darya said. "I only just joined Pet Shelters Together, and I didn't know either Bethany or—what's his name? Miguel, I think. Miguel Rohrig—very well."

I looked at Cricket. "You spent some time around Better Than Any Pet Rescues, I assume. Did you know Miguel? How were Bethany and he getting along?"

She bit her narrow lips grimly. "She wanted him to spend more time helping out at the shelter. He's an actor, and it wasn't like he was busy with any movie or TV roles lately. But he's a nice guy. He'd never have hurt Bethany."

Maybe not. But I now had three people I could look at as possible murder suspects.

Chapter 13

Matt returned soon and showed the whole group of us to the rest of the animals that had been at Mamie's, including those I'd visited before at the West L.A. center. As he'd said, all appeared to be well, and most seemed to be thriving. Plus, fortunately, none of them seemed especially aggressive.

Unlike many hoarding situations, this one had the potential for a happy ending for all the rescued pets. I'd told the group, though, that I knew there were legal issues to be worked out before these critters became available for adoption, and Matt had seconded that—but neither of us had given any specifics. I wasn't sure how long it would take for Mamie's surrender to become effective, even if she didn't change her mind.

Eventually, we were ready to leave, a dozen or so pet rescuers all with thrilled smiles on our faces. A bunch of animals whose welfare concerned us all were definitely going to survive.

"You'll let me know, won't you, Matt, when those of us with private shelters can pick up some of the animals that Animal Services can't take care of any longer?" asked Cricket, standing beside him. "No need to euthanize any for lack of space. We'll take them in and rehome them, once those pesky legal issues Lauren mentioned are worked out. I'm your best contact. I represent a lot of private shelters, since there are quite a few of us affiliated with Pet Shelters Together and I'm in charge now."

She was stepping on my toes as brutally as a rogue elephant.

"Thanks, but I'll let Lauren know," Matt contradicted. Sweet man. "She'll remain my primary contact. She can tell you how things progress, and then you can let shelter administrators in your system know. In fact, when the time comes, you should coordinate any pickups with Lauren first. No sense having too many people come here to take whatever animals are available to leave."

Cricket looked bent out of shape as she glanced toward me. Too bad. "Well, maybe Lauren will choose to have HotRescues join Pet Shelters Together." Her tone suggested that her statement was a demand instead of a possibility.

"Maybe," I said, in attempt to be tactful—never my strong suit. But it wasn't in the animals', or Matt's, best interests for Cricket and me to hash this out here. "In the meantime, it's fine for you to call me, Matt."

"But—"

"It'll be okay, Cricket." Darya's voice brooked no contradiction as she opened the door and the other administrators started filing out. Darya glanced back at me with an unreadable expression, then she hurried after them.

Cricket was the last to leave. "We'll talk, Lauren," she said in a tone that suggested she wouldn't take no for an answer—either about talking or getting HotRescues to join her rescue network. What had happened to the shy woman I'd thought I'd met before?

"Of course we will," I said sweetly. "I'll let you know as soon as there are animals ready for rescue by Pet Rescues Together network members instead of independents like HotRescues."

"But—"

"Have a minute, Lauren?" Matt said smoothly. He took my arm, and we both turned our backs on Cricket.

"Thanks," I said as we walked toward one of the care center offices. I enjoyed his answering grin as I smiled up at him. "That could have gotten nasty."

"I figured. Now, what's the story with that dog you found this morning? The one who might be a stray—or may have been an owner relinquishment in partial disguise?"

I reached into my shoulder bag and pulled out a photocopy of the note that had been left. "Pete Engersol and I found the Doberman tethered in the HotRescues parking lot this morning. He looked healthy but sad, and this note was left with him."

Matt looked at the note and smiled. "It does say Shazam. Not that I doubted you."

"He responds to it, so I assume it really is his name."

"So whoever left him knew him. Maybe it really was an owner relinquishment."

"Will Animal Services give me the benefit of the doubt?"

"Sure, if I have anything to say about it. But this is what—the third similar relinquishment of a dog in just a few weeks?"

I nodded. "The first one didn't have a note, though. I took him to the East Valley Shelter. He was adopted nearly immediately, or we'd have gone back to pick him up. But—"

"But I'd suggest you figure out what's going on as soon as possible."

"I agree."

He opened the shelter door for me. "You interested in joining me for a drink later?"

"Sure," I said, "if you'll be in my area. I'm stopping on the way home to meet with that trainer you recommended, and I can tell you what I think about him then."

Gavin Mamo's Alpha Training Center was on Melrose. It took me a little while to get there from the Valley.

I parked at a meter along the street and gazed at the place. It looked like a store with a large glass picture window, and when I stared inside I saw a whole pack of dogs apparently undergoing a lesson on the shining wooden floor. Each was on a leash, with a human—probably an owner—attached.

In the center was a large man in cut-off jeans and a loose T-shirt. He had a fringe of black hair around his head and a round, friendly face. He barked orders, not at the dogs but at the people. Mostly, they were told to encourage the dogs with goodies. When the pups were told to sit, they did—and then they got their treats. Same thing regarding, "Down." Then "Stay." And "Up."

This apparently wasn't their first class. I was favorably impressed by the order I saw.

I quietly walked inside. The work area was surrounded on three sides by seats, some of which were occupied by people watching the session. I sat on the nearest vacant chair.

Soon, the guy in the middle told everyone to demonstrate the "Heel" command, one at a time. He pointed to a person at one end to start. That dog balked, remaining seated instead of following orders. Instead of luring him with treats, the woman holding his leash kept pulling and straining and getting more and more upset.

"Okay, let's stop," the man in charge said. He walked over, took the leash. "Remember what I've said. Don't acknowledge bad behavior. Encourage good." He looked down so his eyes met the dog's. He held out a treat. "Up," he said. "Heel." With no further ado, the dog, a golden retriever, obeyed. The good boy got his reward.

The woman looked relieved as she smiled—until the man handed her the leash. "Now, do it again. And this time, show him you're in charge . . . of his treats."

She issued the command while holding out a couple of goodies she extracted from a small bag. This time, the pup obeyed her, too.

I was impressed. But I had also been interviewing other dog trainers recently to try to find the best fit as a part-timer at HotRescues. Was Gavin Mamo the one?

Whoever we chose had to be smart and in charge, leader of the pack and alpha—yet feel compassion for our residents who'd gotten there for many reasons, including, sometimes, an owner's foolish disregard for a dog's size or power or drive to be pack leader. Those dogs needed to be shown, gently but firmly, who was really their boss—not abandoned forever. Even if it took a lot of treats to train them to change.

Sometimes even the smartest, best-trained dogs required an extra helping of obedience to get chosen by the most appropriate new owner.

HotRescues needed someone to ensure that our residents had the best possibilities of finding new homes. That included learning how to behave as people expected.

When the class was over, I watched the human students

thank Gavin, shaking his large hand, smiling at him. He seemed more relaxed and often smiled back.

His being pack leader was no longer an issue, at least not for this training session.

As the group poured out the door, he approached me. "You're Ms. Vancouver?"

"Lauren," I said, nodding. I held out my hand, and felt his firm grasp as he shook it back. He was definitely a powerful guy. A good thing, I supposed, for training people to train their dogs—making it clear that he was in charge.

"Please, come into my office." He nodded toward a couple of open doors at the back of the training area.

His office was small, but the walls were covered with plaques from various municipalities and organizations, recognizing his excellence in dog training. Apparently he'd even worked with some smaller police departments to help train their K9 operatives.

He sat behind his compact desk with nothing littering the top. The chair where he waved me was one of two facing him, tall-backed wooden ones with no cushioning.

"So," he began. "Matt Kingston told you about me? He's a good guy. Encourages the members of the teams that report to him, even helps in other ways."

A point in Gavin's favor, since I liked Matt, too. A lot.

"Yes, Matt recommended you highly," I said. "I watched you teach your class, too. I like your attitude with the dogs and their owners."

"Much of what I do is appearances, Lauren. I can teach by example how owners need to behave around their pets if they really want them to learn to follow commands. Firmness, yes, and kindness and repetition, all encouraged by rewards. Basically, though? I'm cool." He smiled, revealing shining white teeth behind the deep tone of his skin. "In case you were wondering how I'd do as one of your consultants. You hire me to do something, I do it—and I don't give you a hard time. Unless, of course, you deserve it."

"Never!" I said, earning an even broader grin. "So . . . let me ask you a few questions, and then we'll talk terms."

The terms he quoted were reasonable. As I drove back to HotRescues, I felt pretty certain that I'd give him a try.

I could always fire him if he didn't work out.

Nina was behind the counter in our welcoming room when I walked in the door. She stood immediately. So did Zoey, who dashed over to greet me, her tail wagging effusively.

"Tell me," Nina said, smiling.

"About which piece of breaking news—how well the animals rescued from Mamie's place are doing, or the new dog trainer I'm likely to hire?"

"All of the above." She looked as if she was ready to start dancing around the room.

"You tell me first," I said, noticing her giddiness. "What's going on to make you so happy?"

She blinked. "It's that obvious? Well, we had a busy day, Lauren. Four—count 'em, four—adoptions waiting for your approval. Three cats and a dog. Mona was here, so the potential adopters all got official counseling already. Plus, there's a family who called, and they're on their way to see who's here for them to bring home soon."

"It has been busy." I mirrored her smile as I looked up from where I knelt beside Zoey. "Which'll be a particularly good thing if we wind up being able to grab up any of the former hoardees. I couldn't tell for sure during our visit, but I had the impression that Animal Services was glad

I got so many private rescuers on board to take in some of those guys."

A thought wafted through my mind about Cricket Borley and her attitude about my being first on the contact list. The heck with her. The animals came first, not her ego, undoubtedly unchained by the loss of her mentor. Or maybe Cricket just assumed that she had to emulate Bethany now that her former boss couldn't assert her own narcissism any longer.

"Anyway," I concluded, "show me to the paperwork and I'll start reviewing those potential adoptions. Were any so obvious that you wanted to let the people take their new babies home?"

"All of them. I think Mona liked them, too."

"Great!"

Nina picked up a stack of files from the table where she'd been sitting. They contained adoption applications and contracts from the people she'd been talking about. "Oh, one more thing," she said. "Brooke called. She wanted to hear how things went at the Northeast Valley Center. Please give her a call."

Perfect, I thought as Zoey and I retreated down the hall to my office, the files in my arms. I wanted to talk to Brooke, too. I called her first thing. "Hey, security lady. I thought this was your time to sleep, since you were here last night."

"I'm always awake enough to talk to you, boss lady. So . . . how are all the animals you visited at the city shelter?"

"Thriving amazingly well," I said.

"Any coming to HotRescues soon?"

"Funny you should ask. I'm not sure, but I intend to push a little bit more this evening. I'm meeting Matt for a drink."

"If you meet him for more than a drink, I'll bet he'll find a way to let you take all the animals you want out of the danger system."

I just laughed. I'd no intention of discussing my personal relationship with Matt . . . although I'd also considered what Brooke had suggested. Not the bribery part, but spending a little extra time with Matt sounded good to me. And if it did result in a quicker release of the hoarded brood . . .

"There's something you can do for me about the Mamie situation," I told Brooke. "I talked to a couple of her former associates today about who else might have wanted Bethany dead."

"Yeah, I was going to ask you if there was any further unofficial investigating you wanted me to do. Who'd they say?"

"Bethany had a couple of unfriendly ex-husbands. Plus, her current boyfriend and she had apparently had some recent disagreements. I don't have names for the exes, but the boyfriend's evidently a wannabe actor named Miguel Rohrig—I think I remembered that correctly. I'm not sure what you can find out about any of them, except maybe to ask Antonio unofficially whether the cops are looking at them as potential suspects. They sound as logical as Mamie, at least."

"They do as long as their arguments were around the time of the murder," Brooke amended.

"True. Anyway, anything you can learn would be helpful."

I called Mamie a while later, just to say hi. She sounded sad but was able to hold a relatively normal conversation, perking up for only a moment as I told her about how her animals were doing.

"Mr. Caramon is putting together the paperwork for me to surrender them." I heard her sob.

"This is so wonderful of you, Mamie," I said. "The animals would thank you if they could."

She had little to say after that, so I ended the call.

Matt came by around six o'clock. Nina had already left, as had many of our volunteers. Pete Engersol was still around, helping the remaining volunteers serve dinner to our residents.

And, yes, the family Nina had mentioned earlier had come in and fallen for one of the toy dogs in our center building, a little Maltipoo—a mix between a Maltese and a poodle. Their answers and paperwork had seemed impeccable, but they promised to come back to be interviewed by me before taking home their probable new family member.

"Can I see Shazam?" Matt asked after Zoey and I greeted him in our welcome area. He'd called me on my cell to let me know he was here. We walked him through the shelter area right away to the enclosure where our newest arrival, the sweet-tempered Doberman, was hanging out. Shazam reveled in the attention and the petting we both lavished on him.

"Okay if I feed this guy?" Pete Engersol asked. "He's next on my list."

"You found him, didn't you?" Matt asked.

"Joint effort." Our handyman nodded at me.

"Sure, go ahead and feed him," I told Pete. "Still no indication of who left him in our parking lot?"

"Nope, but I'd like to meet them sometime." Pete's expression was grim. He was always such a nice guy, but I sensed he wanted to wring the abandoner's neck.

He could stand in line behind me. At least whoever it was should have had the guts to dump the poor dog in person.

"But he'll be okay here," Pete went on, his eyes on Matt as if daring him to say we had to turn Shazam over to a city shelter.

"Good thing he was an owner relinquishment," Matt said with a nod. Pete visibly relaxed.

I felt pretty good about it myself.

A short while later, Matt and I sat at a table in a local British pub. We both had ordered beer and shepherd's pie.

He'd followed me home first, and I'd left Zoey. Matt would drive me back when we'd finished our dinner and drinks.

"So you and Gavin got along okay?"

I hadn't so informed Matt, which meant he'd undoubtedly spoken with the trainer. "Remains to be seen, but I think we reached an understanding. I liked his technique, and his attitude. We'll see if he works out."

We chatted about the pet rescuers who'd met up with me at the Northeast Valley care facility earlier, and Mamie's soon-to-be-former wards.

We also talked about Mamie. "Have you heard anything about what's going on with her?" Matt asked.

I told him about our earlier conversation. "She's inching closer to signing documents to surrender the animals, even with everything else going on with her."

"I hope, for your sake, that she's innocent," Matt said.

"My sake?"

"You seem to be taking her on as a cause, Lauren. That's one of the things I like about you. Especially when your cause is animals. But people are okay, too."

I smiled at him. He smiled back.

"The food's pretty good here," I said, taking a bite of the rich shepherd's pie.

"The company's even better," Matt replied, keeping his eyes on mine.

I'm not the kind of person who blushes, but I felt my cheeks redden. "I can't argue about that," I said. I straightened in my chair. "I enjoy trying out different places to eat, especially with you. We seem to have similar tastes."

"In a lot of things," he agreed.

I thought about what Brooke had said earlier, implying that I might bribe Matt with my middle-aged body to secure the release of some of the hoarded animals faster.

But there were no strings attached when, after Matt drove me home, I found myself in his arms—and he found himself in my bed. Definitely not for the first time since we'd met a few months earlier.

And, I hoped, not for the last.

Chapter 14

Matt left around eleven o'clock. I wouldn't have minded if he'd stayed the night, but I was okay with it this way.

He had to go home to take care of Rex. And I had to stay here and think—more than I wanted to—about where we were going with this growing relationship. If it was, in fact, a relationship. I pondered it while I lay in bed, alone, before falling asleep.

As I considered often, I'd been married twice. My dear Kerry had died when the kids were young. My second husband was a disaster. Charles Earles had no interest in my children, only in accessing my already meager bank account—to help pay for his flings with younger women. Our divorce had been a huge relief, in more ways than one.

And now there was Matt. He'd made no demands, but he'd started being there for me when I'd needed guidance regarding the official L.A. Animal Services system. Plus, he'd found the perfect rescue dog for me—Zoey.

He hung around for dinner and drinks and some fooling around that took my breath away—even though, initially, I hadn't wanted even that, despite how tempted I'd felt. Now, I lay there in bed, wondering. I guessed it was okay. I wasn't leading him on. As we spent more time together, I'd been honest with Matt, that as attracted as I was to him, I wasn't looking for a deep, meaningful relationship.

I'd had that with Kerry. I know logically that there's no loyalty required to a dead man, even my husband. Kerry would probably have wanted me to find someone to care about in his absence. And I had come to care for Matt. More each time I was with him.

But I wasn't looking for something permanent. Not now. Not ever. Probably.

Somehow, I finally drifted off to sleep.

The next morning, I arrived early at HotRescues. When I let Zoey out of the car, I watched her with some trepidation. Had another pet been abandoned on our property?

But Zoey didn't pull on her leash as we walked to the side door to the main building. All was well, at least for now.

No one was in the welcome area, which wasn't a surprise at this hour.

Zoey and I took our first walk through the shelter. Our presence caused some of the dogs to bark in greeting, and to let their unofficial pack know the area had been invaded—even though, by now, they surely recognized the scents of both Zoey and me.

We ran into Pete Engersol nearly immediately. He always arrived early and stayed late. He considered it his responsibility to make sure all our residents were well fed, and I didn't suggest otherwise. Instead, I relied on him.

"Good morning, Lauren," he called from the far end of the main pathway. "Everything okay with you?"

"Sure thing." I joined him. "Is Brooke still here?"

"No, she left about the time I arrived."

I heard a hammering noise from the adjoining property. "Sounds like the contractors are already at work."

"Yep, I saw them, too, when I got here. The guy in charge said they're putting finishing touches on the exterior and working on the interior today. He said they should be finished there soon and ready to take on the remodel of the center building." He nodded toward the structure near where we stood.

"I hope so. I'll be glad when we're all done." Which I knew would be soon, thanks to Dante's paying a lot to make sure the construction would be accomplished fast and right.

"We all will," Pete said. "Got to get back to our hungry horde now." He hurried toward the rear storage building where all the food was kept.

I kept going around our outside enclosure area, then into the back door of the center building where Zoey and I could check in on the cats and toy dogs. Finally, we returned to my office.

My BlackBerry was ringing, and I dragged it out of my purse, which I'd shoved into a drawer. It was Mamie's number.

"Hi, Mamie." I sat as I answered. I watched Zoey do a circling gig on the rug beneath my desk, then lie down, obviously not interested in the conversation.

Silence for a few moments. "I just will never get used to these modern things, like you seeing my number on your phone and knowing it's me."

"I kind of like it," I said lightly. "How are you doing?" Like, have you signed papers to relinquish the animals?

Are the cops still questioning you? Have they said your arrest is imminent?

"I'm okay, I guess. But Mr. Caramon tells me that we have to go back to the police station. The detectives have said they want to talk to me again."

I wanted to advise her not to say anything they could misinterpret as a confession or could otherwise use against her, but she had Mr. Caramon for that.

"Interesting," I said. "Be sure to let me know how it goes."

"Then you're still trying to help me, Lauren?" Her voice had perked up into what sounded like utter relief.

"There's not a lot I can do, Mamie. But if you have any more ideas about who could have killed Bethany and why, you be sure to tell the cops, and let me know, too."

I'd said that before, in different iterations. But I still sometimes felt as if I was talking to a grumpy and forgetful child when I spoke with Mamie. Maybe she wasn't as psychologically fragile as I believed . . . but she had been a hoarder, and she clearly wasn't a normal, sane human being—assuming such creatures even existed.

"Okay," she said.

After another pause, I asked, "Did you get the paperwork yet for giving up the animals?"

"Yes." She sounded despondent. "It came by messenger this morning and I signed it."

"Great!" I exclaimed. "You're super, Mamie." More silence. "So . . . did you call for any particular reason, or just to say hi?"

"Oh . . . There was a reason." Her tone had become hard. "Only . . . I don't want to talk about it now. Bye, Lauren." She hung up.

What had that been about? Would I ever be able to read Mamie's ephemeral moods?

All that ambivalence that had been rocking me lately once again shot through my mind. I'm not an ambivalent person. I always take a stand. And yet, helping Mamie was driving me nuts.

I wished I could drop the whole idea, but I knew myself better than that. I had taken this on as a responsibility and wouldn't stop until I knew the truth—no matter what Mamie's attitude was.

For now, I assumed that Brooke, after catching up on sleep, would get in touch if and when she had any information on Bethany's exes or her last boyfriend.

Meantime, I had to do something positive toward finding Bethany's killer—for my sake almost as much as for Mamie's. I decided to do what I always did with problems, how I kept track of all of our rehomings and all other administrative details.

I would come up with a detailed plan—as I had not long ago when I'd been the one suspected of committing a murder. In fact, I would use that investigative plan as a model.

At that time, I'd started with an organizational chart and added information, as I'd found it, about other potential suspects. It had worked to help me clear myself.

It would also help me look into Bethany's murder and figure out whether unpredictable Mamie was guilty . . . and, if not, who was.

I booted up my now-ancient desktop computer. We'd been friends since I helped to start HotRescues six years ago, and though I could have talked Dante into funding a newer one, I didn't want it. I had Internet access, and I had usable word processing and accounting programs. That was enough.

I opened, then copied, the main file I'd made. I went through it and cleared out all the items relating to the other murder and its suspects. Oh, did that bring back memories.

Not that I'd forgotten that really awful time. It had only been a few months ago. But now that it was over, I'd stopped focusing on it and gone on with my life.

I started the plan with a brief description of Bethany, what I knew about her and her businesses. About her officiousness that had so grated on me, and her egotistically bragging about stopping Mamie's hoarding. I added what I recalled about her actually quite helpful program on hoarding, and Mamie's appearance there.

Then I started subfiles on everyone whose names I remembered from that night: Mamie, of course, and Cricket and Darya and a few others. I'd get the rest from Cricket, if she decided to cooperate. If not . . .

I didn't actually have to wait, as it turned out. I Googled Pet Shelters Together and found the Web site that had been created for Bethany's network. It mentioned about a dozen pet rescue organizations besides Better Than Any Pet Rescues and provided links to their Web sites.

It was easy enough to find out who their respective administrators were. But on the main PST site, there were all sorts of testimonials about Bethany, attributed to each of the other administrators. Would any of them have had a reason to hurt her?

Maybe, maybe not. But even if they didn't, each might have other suggestions about who could have hated her that much.

I'd finish devising the beginnings of my plan today. And then the first person I would call would be the new administrator of both of Bethany's organizations—Cricket.

But before I got very far, my BlackBerry rang again. It was Matt.

"How are you today?" he asked first thing, and the sweet gruffness of his voice reminded me of last night.

"Full of happy memories," I said.

"Which we'll add to one of these nights soon," he said with a laugh. "But I need to talk business with you now."

"What's wrong?"

"Nothing you can't help with. Mamie's lawyer called to say he has the signed document for her surrender of the animals. Their relinquishment will be official today. I've gotten word that some of the animals will be available tomorrow for private rescuers to take in."

"Are they in immediate danger?" My tone must have reflected my concern, since Zoey sat up and put her head on my lap. I petted her distractedly as I waited for Matt's response.

"No, but unless you hear otherwise from me, you and any others you choose should come to the Northeast Valley Animal Care Center tomorrow afternoon to pick up the first batch."

Chapter 15

Needless to say, I was thrilled. I'd had no idea it could happen this quickly. I wondered if Matt had pulled strings to allow private rescue facilities to start taking some of the animals—or was it simply the best way to ensure their safety?

After hanging up with Matt, I hurried down the hall to our welcome area. "Nina, I need you," I called.

She leaped up from her chair behind the counter. "What's wrong, Lauren?"

"Everything's right!" I countered. "Well, not everything. But I need you to do a resident count and let me know how many enclosures we can make available right now to bring in new dogs, and also how many cats we can fit into our kitty rooms. Both after quarantine, of course."

Her eyes widened. "What's—Oh, I get it. Are some of your friend Mamie's animals getting released from city care?"

"Sounds that way. I've no idea how many yet, but I need to know numbers that we can take in. Meanwhile, I'll get in touch with administrators of the other rescue organizations who said they could help out."

Which was an even better thing. It gave me a really great excuse to call Cricket Borley.

"Too bad the timing worked out this way," Nina said later.

"It could have been worse," I responded.

We were back in the welcome room. She'd given me a rundown of enclosures that could be made available, and then I'd gone with her to confirm.

We had room to take in about half a dozen dogs, since they mostly had to be housed individually until we could test compatibility with others. The cat situation was perhaps better, if we got our current inhabitants to squeeze a little—maybe eight or so.

With the stable of friends I could contact via the Southern California Rescuers Web site, I wouldn't need to overdo taking in animals, despite how much I wanted to save them all.

Maybe a situation as emotionally compelling was why Mamie, already fragile, had started hoarding.

Could I start hoarding?

I shrugged off the question. I knew better.

I'd post a request for help if I needed to. But first, I waited for Cricket to return my phone call.

She could be genuinely busy. She could also be avoiding me as a result of her being miffed that I'd been the rescuer chosen as the primary contact when any hoarding subjects were ready for new rescue locations.

That could mean I'd need to use another way to get her to talk to me about Bethany and her friends and enemies.

"In a few more weeks," Nina said, "just think of all the extra room we'll have." That would be when the new building was finished, and new enclosures were added to its remaining property.

"It'll be great. Meantime, though, we'll make do as we always have—including getting other rescuers involved to the extent we need them." My BlackBerry rang. "Here's one now." I recognized Cricket's number from the caller ID.

"Tell me what time to be at the care center," she said. "I'll have a whole bunch of our network people there to be sure no animal is left behind."

I couldn't help smiling as I hung up. Cricket might have been trained in egotism by Bethany, but when it came to animal rescue, she was evidently an administrator after my own heart.

The next day, Pete and I stood outside the Northeast Valley Animal Care Center a few minutes before the time Matt had told me. I nevertheless sent him inside to be sure we were the first from the private rescue organizations to arrive. I hadn't contacted anyone outside Pet Shelters Together, since Cricket had promised that her network could handle as many animals as were available.

Pete and I had brought the large van, filled with crates for more animals than we were likely to be picking up here.

We'd also stopped at a HotPets on the way, after I spoke with Dante. Thanks to his ongoing generosity, the van was filled with food, bowls, bedding, and toys to be meted out to the organizations who also took on some of the animals.

The media had heard about the situation, too. I didn't know how, but I suspected that, once again, Cricket had followed her mentor in snapping up publicity for their organization in as many ways as possible.

If that was the worst evidence of her inherited self-centeredness today, I'd live with it.

And with the publicity. I do anything I have to when notoriety can help find homes for our residents.

"It's nearly the scheduled time, Lauren," Pete reminded me. "I told the people staffing the place that we're here, but maybe we should go inside."

"Just another minute." I'd wanted to greet people, maybe even have an opportunity to talk with Cricket first. I couldn't control their timing, though. Since saving the animals was paramount to everything, I didn't want to ruffle any feathers of the city shelter's personnel. Even if they cooperated now, I didn't want them to think bad thoughts about HotRescues or me the next time there were animals we needed to pick up fast to keep them from being considered among the expendables.

In less than a minute, Cricket; Darya and her husband, Lan; and a few others I recognized from Bethany's meeting strolled around the corner. I had the sense they were making a grand entrance, a show of strength and unity, whatever. If so, I didn't understand why they thought it necessary.

Maybe another holdover from Bethany and her ostentatious ways.

"Hi," I greeted them.

They stopped near the door—a photo op for the media photographers milling in the area. A pang of guilt shot through me. Maybe I should have told my friend Carlie about this situation. But I didn't think she'd be particularly interested, for her show, in private-shelter administrators picking up rescued pets from a city facility. It happened every day.

"Hello, Lauren." Cricket was dressed in blue jeans decorated with embroidery beneath a shiny gray blouse that would have done Bethany proud. Facing the cameras as she smiled, she continued, "Let's go save some animals, PST people!"

The crowd around her, all Pet Shelters Together members, yelled, "Let's do it!" and they flowed inside, leaving Pete and me in their wake.

I gave him a look, shrugged my shoulders, and followed. Even if I was theoretically the rescuer in charge, I had a feeling that Cricket, in her rebellious way, had taken over.

But inside, Matt was already there. Smiling, he gestured for me to follow him. I maneuvered around Cricket and the PST gang, feeling their leader's spiteful glare searing my back—and, I admitted to my own officious self, enjoying it. Pete stayed behind me.

The media folks stayed right behind him.

Matt took us not to the same area we'd seen before, but into a back room where a dozen or so cats and dogs of various sizes were in crates. It was a place the media wasn't welcome, and he shut the door behind us.

"Here are the animals that are ready to leave with all of you," he said. "Their health has been checked. I'll make sure you get the paperwork on the ones you take, including veterinary clearances." He looked over my shoulder toward the other administrators, then back at me. "I'll leave it to you to figure out who's taking which animal."

I glanced at Cricket. I conceded that she might have authority over the others in her network, so I said, "I could fit most at HotRescues, but I'd be delighted if, instead, you and the rest could take as many as nine or ten."

"Done." Cricket nodded vigorously and motioned for

the others to join her. I listened cursorily to their discussion as I walked over to Matt. From where I was, it sounded as if Cricket was telling her minions which animals each would get, like it or not.

"I'm not sure I ever heard a final count on how many animals, total, were rescued from Mamie's. Will there be any more relinquished to private hands?"

"Probably, but the ones today not only have health clearances but are also those that our folks decided might have less of a chance of being adopted in time." I read between his lines—and in the grim yet official way he looked at me: *In time* not to be euthanized to provide room for more inmates in the system.

Cricket moved away from her group. "We've got it figured out."

"Great," I said.

Matt nodded. "Go into the office, and we'll do the paperwork."

I walked beside Cricket, with Pete again trailing behind. Matt was in the middle of the other rescuers, who peppered him with questions about the animals whose custody we were about to take over.

"Let's exchange information," I told Cricket. "That way, if any of us gets any potential adopters that might work out for animals in the custody of someone else, we can send them to the right spot."

"Fine with me."

I'd also find time to visit as many of the other shelters as possible. I'd no reason to believe any of these pups and kitties would be mistreated, but I wanted to assure myself of their well-being.

The paperwork took a little time, especially since there were five people from Pet Shelters Together besides

Cricket, but we soon had it completed. I asked Pete to load the three pets we were rescuing—a senior Rottweiler mix that had checked out as nonaggressive, a medium-sized dog of unknown heritage, and a skinny gray cat—into the van. I stayed with Cricket, ostensibly to help her load the three cats she was taking to Better Than Any Pet Rescues into her SUV.

"I'm just so glad all the animals from Mamie's appear to be thriving now," I said. I carried one of the three small crates, and Cricket carried the other two. "I just wish . . . well, I may be in the minority, but I still doubt that Mamie hurt Bethany. Do you know of anyone besides her exes and her boyfriend who might have been upset with her for any reason?" Like yourself, I thought, or any of the animal rescuers who might not have adored prima donna Bethany and her attitude.

But that would hardly have been a good motive to kill her.

Cricket shook her head as she looked at me. By now, we were outside, and the media was snapping pictures and shouting questions about the animals and how they were doing and where they were going. We ignored them. So did the group of Cricket's affiliates who trailed behind us.

"Friendship's a nice thing, Lauren. I can understand why you want to help Mamie, but she's a bitch. You heard her yell at Bethany."

I couldn't believe that Cricket didn't have other suspects in mind, but she obviously wasn't about to reveal them to me.

"Maybe," I said neutrally. We had gotten into the parking lot, and she'd popped the back door of a silver SUV. "Now, let's get these sweethearts inside, and we'll be off."

I helped her arrange the crates. One of the cats started meowing, and I pulled the top off the crate and patted it.

"I need to get out of here," Cricket snapped. I closed the lid again, and Cricket slammed the door closed. She got into the driver's seat without another word.

I stood there watching. Darya and Lan Price joined me. He held a leash attached to a golden Lab mix, and she had the leads for two small terriers. The media had mostly left, but I saw a flash or two from a couple of remaining cameras.

Much taller than me, Darya leaned over and spoke softly. "I'm sorry, Lauren. About Cricket, I mean. I know she means well, and it's got to be hard to try to take over everything after Bethany, but . . . Well, I heard you asking about whether Cricket knew of anyone else who might have wanted to hurt Bethany. A few adopters got angry with the way Bethany pushed them about how to take care of their new pets, but I doubt any of them did anything drastic about it. And I know we told you about Bethany's boyfriend, Miguel, and her two ex-husbands?"

I nodded.

"Well, then. That's it. Except . . . I know I shouldn't even mention this, but at some of our recent PST meetings, there were times that . . ." She tapered off. "Never mind. I don't think it's important."

"Even so," I said, "as I told Cricket, I want to eliminate other possibilities, if just to satisfy myself. Who else did you think of who might have wanted to harm Bethany?"

"Well . . . Cricket and Bethany mostly were really close friends. Bethany was in charge, of course, but Cricket was her second in command. But lately . . ."

"Lately?"

"Lately, they seemed to be arguing a lot—nothing serious, you understand. But Cricket was second-guessing some of Bethany's management decisions, and you can imagine what Bethany thought about that."

"Fireworks?" I suggested.

"Kind of. But if either of them was going to hurt the other, I'd have guessed that Bethany would have fired Cricket."

Unless Cricket instead had fired at Bethany in a preemptive maneuver . . . ?

Chapter 16

Pete and I stopped on our way back to HotRescues at my buddy Dr. Carlie Stellan's clinic in Northridge—The Fittest Pet Veterinary Clinic. I'd called ahead, and Carlie, fortunately, had been there. She'd told me, last time we'd spoken, that she would be heading off soon to Oregon to film a segment of her *Pet Fitness* show. She'd asked me for some pet shelter contacts there, since it seemed that, in Oregon, more rescued animals got adopted per capita than in Southern California and she wanted to explore why.

I loved Carlie's pink stucco veterinary building, wrapped around a parklike setting where the vet techs could take dogs outside for light exercise and air—those who were well enough, and those being boarded. Inside, as always, it was bustling with activity.

Thanks to the Internet and personal contacts, word was out already that we had just picked up a few animals who'd been saved from the hoarding situation last week. Both staff and visitors made a fuss over the two pups and kitty we brought in, who seemed a bit overwhelmed by all the attention.

We were soon shown to an examination room, and Carlie came in a few minutes later. She wore one of her usual white veterinary jackets, and her blond hair just skimmed its shoulders.

"Pete, how good to see you!" she effused. The tall man looked a little awkward as she hugged him. "And Lauren, you sly devil. Not only do you get Animal Services to save a bunch of animals from being hoarded, but you talk them into releasing the babies so quickly into the hands of private rescuers."

She knew the details of getting Mamie to relinquish them, so she was purposely making it sound easy—and my doing. "Not all of them," I said solemnly. "At least not yet. But I feel relatively sure that none will be euthanized for lack of room. I'll at least be called first."

"Good girl!" My turn for a hug. Then Carlie knelt to look at the two leashed dogs on the floor beside us. I'd lifted the crate holding the cat onto the examination table. "Hi, fellas." She looked up at me. "Do they have names?"

"If so, we don't know them. We'll give them temporary monikers once we get back to HotRescues."

"Let me. This one"—she pointed to the Rottweiler mix—"is Hale, and this one"—the unknown middle-sized pup's turn—"is Hearty. The cat will be Fitzwalter, a take-off on fit, and therefore my show. Assuming, of course, that they're all as healthy as they should be after being released by Animal Services."

"That's what we're here to find out, but the names are

fine by me." I looked at Pete, who nodded, too. The guy was indispensable to HotRescues, and I always listened to his opinions.

Carlie called in a couple of techs, who took the animals to get them weighed. Meantime, she glanced over the paperwork I'd brought and sent it out to have copies made. In a few minutes, the animals were back. She noted their weights on charts she had started, then examined them.

"I've looked over the results of the blood tests and other samples taken by Animal Services," she said when she was done. "All looks fine to me, but I'd suggest you keep them in quarantine for a while like always."

"Of course." Pete and I got ready to leave. "How's Max, by the way?" Carlie's spaniel mix had always been a favorite of mine—and not just because he'd been the first dog ever adopted at HotRescues.

"As adorable as ever. So . . . when are you going to let me interview you on my show about the hoarding situation?"

"Around the same time I let you interview me about the puppy mill situation." That had occurred a few months ago, and Carlie was still waiting.

"I figured. Well, let's do lunch soon. My next trip's in three weeks, by the way."

"Let's aim for before then."

"Fine. Oh, and one more thing."

Her tone, and how she phrased her apparently casual comment, made me wince. I knew her well enough to figure that she really gave a damn about what she was about to say. "What's that?"

"How's your investigation into the murder of that Bethany person going?"

Too bad I'd already winced. Now I felt like shriveling

under her amused gaze. "What makes you think I'm investigating?"

"Because I know you. And I know that you somehow feel responsible for Mamie Spelling—even though you shouldn't. Who's your best choice of a suspect now—Mamie or someone else?"

I glanced at Pete. He was grinning, too, the louse. He found this amusing.

"I honestly don't know yet. Mamie's not off my list, and I've barely scratched the surface of looking at other possibilities. But I'm really hoping to find the truth."

"Before the cops do?"

"*If* they do."

"Well, just remember the thing you learned the last time you got involved in an investigation that shouldn't have been your problem."

"It *was* my problem. The cops suspected me."

"Whatever."

"And what do you think I learned?"

"That you can't ever cross the least likely suspect off your list."

Of course I didn't know who the least likely suspect was. I pondered that as Pete drove us all to HotRescues. I wasn't certain who the *most* likely suspect was, either. Mamie, I supposed.

Pete and I discussed the care of these new residents, how long they'd be in quarantine, and the likelihood of when, and if, we'd get more of the hoarded pets to take care of. The discussion occupied my mind during most of the drive.

I also had no time to think more about suspects when we reached the parking lot. Dante DeFrancisco's car, a late-model silver Mercedes, was parked there. Why had he come? He hadn't called first—or at least he hadn't spoken to me.

No need for me to get all angsty. It could just be a social visit. Or, he might be here to check out where all his money was going, since he largely funded HotRescues. And the purchase of the adjoining property and the construction going on there . . .

That had to be why he was here—to check on the progress of the new building.

Turned out that was correct. Nina, in the welcome area, told me that Dante had stopped in, said hi, then went next door to examine the work.

I'd sent some volunteers to help Pete bring our new residents inside to the quarantine area. I was free to rush over to say hi to Dante.

I heard voices as I slipped through the gate dividing the two properties. Sure enough, one was Dante's.

He was dressed in a crisp blue shirt and black trousers, which told me he'd come from his office and had doffed the jacket and tie from his suit. Dante was a tall, good-looking guy with dark hair and a darker expression if people crossed him. Which I never did if I could avoid it. I might be in charge here when it came to everyone else, but Dante, our chief benefactor and chairman of our board of directors, was my boss. Period.

He now seemed engrossed in conversation with Halbert, the chief construction contractor for the new building. Big contrast there. Halbert wore jeans and a ratty blue T-shirt. But Dante wasn't wielding a hammer that day, far as I knew. Halbert probably was—or at least holding one over the heads of his employees charged with finishing the building as quickly as possible.

I strode toward them. "Hi, Dante and Halbert," I said

cheerfully. "How are things going with our new building?"
Like, had Dante made it clear exactly how much longer
Halbert and company had to finish up?

"Fine, Lauren," Halbert said. "I was just telling Dante
that we're pretty much done with the exterior, and a lot of
the interior, too."

Amazing! They'd only started a few weeks ago. But
Dante's money obviously dictated their speed.

"Want to join us on a tour?" Dante asked.

"Absolutely!"

It really was amazing. The building had a lot of similar
amenities to our current central building. The offices
upstairs were nearly complete except for details like paint-
ing walls and finishing floors. Downstairs, the kitchen and
areas to house toy dogs, cats, and other small animals were
still mostly just framed in so far.

I especially liked, upstairs, the balconies we'd added into
the architectural detailing. That way, we could bring some
cats outside in crates to get them fresh air. Smaller dogs, too,
when they weren't being walked. It would be easier on the
wide patio areas, even lugging them up the steps, than it would
be to take them outside to our park a couple of times a day.

There were belt-and-suspender safety measures as well,
including folding screens that could be secured to ensure
that, even if any animals got out, they'd be confined on the
balconies till someone came to put them back. The screens
were still boxed, though—not yet installed.

The place looked wonderful. But I didn't offer an opinion until Dante, too, gave a verbal pat on the back to Halbert. "Good job. Just step it up a little, will you? I want you
to get to the remodeling of the existing central building on
the other property as soon as possible."

"Sure thing, Dante," Halbert said.

We returned downstairs. "Do you have a few minutes?" Dante asked as we headed to the main HotRescues facility.

"Sure."

We talked over the hoarding situation. He didn't seem upset that I was in the news because of coordinating private facilities to take in the hoarding victims that Animal Services gave up. "I want to meet your three new residents," he said. I led him toward the quarantine area, on one side of the downstairs area of the central building, far from where toy dogs and cats were currently housed. I assumed that Pete and the volunteers would have situated them there already, which they had.

Dante was one really nice guy, not only because he gave us all the money we needed to keep HotRescues going, but also because he genuinely loved animals. He opened their enclosures. While petting them, he talked fondly to our new rescuees, welcoming them as much as if I were the one speaking to them.

In a few minutes, he secured the locks again, used the hand sanitizer we always kept in the area, and turned toward me. "I've got an idea to take advantage of the publicity you're getting for bringing these guys to HotRescues. How about a fund-raiser—not that we need a few extra bucks, but that kind of thing often brings people in—where the public will be invited to come in, meet our residents, and maybe see some kind of show."

"Show?"

"I don't know—do you have a new trainer yet who can perform something with some of the dogs?"

"I'm just hiring someone, but it's premature to have him show off our current residents."

"Well . . . Think about it. Maybe there's some other kind of event we can hold. We'll give out free food for pets.

People can pay for theirs, but I'll donate the proceeds. We'll also give special prizes to those who decide that day to adopt a pet—as long as they meet with your approval, of course."

"Of course." His tone was teasing, but I knew he liked my attitude—and wouldn't have left me in charge here if I'd done things much differently.

"Anyhow, I'd like to have something going on here that'll attract as many people as possible."

I smiled. "Love the concept. Let me think about possibilities." Something had just crossed my mind, but I wasn't sure whether it would work—or even be a good idea.

I'd have to ask Matt.

We went out the back entrance and took our time before heading back to the main building. Dante knew Pete and some of the long-time volunteers, like Bev.

Ricki was there, too. Her veterinary tech school would not start until fall, and the recent college graduate was spending more time at HotRescues for the summer. Wanting to branch out from just walking and cleaning up after animals, she was brushing teeth, grooming, and performing basic health assessments in anticipation of her soon-to-be new career.

Dante and she greeted each other and started talking about a new line of dog food Dante had recently begun to stock at HotPets stores. We all slowly walked by the outside enclosures where our middle- and large-sized dogs were housed. A few barked greetings, which started others responding. Noisy, yes, but usual. And heartening. All our charges were healthy and normal.

Eventually we reached the welcome area. I heard voices from inside and hoped that Nina was speaking with some possible adopters. I always liked to impress Dante that way, although he knew how successful we were. I sent him reports weekly in addition to those we discussed at monthly board meetings.

I was surprised, though, to see that the person standing at the tall reception desk facing Nina behind it, and barely able to see over it, was Mamie.

Nina caught my eye, and her expression was a combination of irritation and frustration. Mamie must have noticed it, because she turned. She appeared upset, until she saw it was me.

She hobbled over, threw herself into my arms, and said, "Lauren. I did it. I made it over the hill without driving on the freeway. I heard that you have some of my babies here now, and I want to see them."

"Okay, Mamie. But you—"

"And now that I know I can get here by myself, even though it takes forever—Lauren, I want you to give me a job."

Chapter 17

Okay, what should I do now? A confirmed hoarder who undoubtedly loved animals—and just might be a people-murderer—had just asked me for a job.

At least she'd come here at a reasonable time during the day to make this pronouncement—rather than early in the morning, as she had done the day Bethany had been murdered.

Yes, she had been stable enough to give up the hoarded animals for their sakes, and for her own. And, I wanted to help Mamie. To clear her name, if it turned out she hadn't been the one to kill Bethany.

But have her here? Around all the creatures I love, when she was definitely someone who'd abused pets in her care . . . intentionally or not?

I glanced at Dante. He stood behind me, arms crossed, looking amused. With his eyebrows raised that way, he also appeared as if he wanted to know how I'd handle the situation.

So did I.

Of course Dante had met Mamie before, when she had interviewed for running HotRescues. She looked different now, but I was certain he knew who she was—if for no other reason than her picture had been on the news a lot lately.

"Let's talk about this," I said to Mamie. I turned my gaze on Nina at the other side of the counter—entreating her nonverbally to find me a distraction—then back on Mamie. Mamie was smiling, but her gaze looked challenging, as if daring me to say no. What would she do then?

I heard a "woof" from down the hall. The distraction I needed! Nina had shut Zoey into my office while I was gone, and I hadn't let her out yet. I'd wanted to take the tour of the site next door without bringing her. Now, I wanted to hug her. Of course, I always wanted to hug her.

"Tell you what, Mamie. That's my dog, Zoey, calling me. Why don't you come along on a quick walk, and we'll discuss whether it's a good idea for you to make a commitment now to work here."

"Okay." She didn't follow me, though. I turned back to see her standing in front of Dante. "Hello, Dante. Remember me?"

"Yes, I do, Mamie." He held out his hand formally, for a shake.

She complied, but her hesitation suggested it was an effort to touch him. With dignity, she said, "I know things don't look good for me now, but I love animals. I'd have been a real asset here if you'd chosen me to run HotRescues. I really . . . Well, since you didn't, maybe you could convince Lauren to hire me now."

"We'll see," he said. "Lauren and I can talk about it." He shifted his gaze toward me.

"You'll say no." Mamie sighed. "But I'm not a hoarder, wouldn't have looked like one if . . . I can show you here, I promise. It's so lonely at home—my shelter—without any of my babies around. Someone who didn't know what happened tried to do an owner relinquishment yesterday, and I was so tempted . . . but until I know I won't get arrested for killing Bethany—which I didn't do—I can't try to get my shelter back."

"Mamie, you know you're still subject to prosecution for animal abuse," I said gently. "You can't even think about starting your shelter again. Not now. Maybe not ever."

"No babies, no fur babies either . . ." She stopped and closed her eyes. When she opened them again, they were wet and mournful. "Please, Lauren, let me work here. I can't be alone."

I wasn't sure I understood all she'd said, and I absolutely felt sorry for her. But this wasn't a good time for her to start working, or even volunteering, here. Not until all the issues surrounding her were resolved—if they ever were.

"We'll talk about it," I said, repeating Dante's comment. "Right now, let's go walk Zoey."

We soon passed through the welcome area again, with Zoey prancing beside me. Dante was still there, talking to Nina. "I'll be taking off now, Lauren," he said. "Let me know your ideas for some kind of event here." He smiled at Mamie. "I hope everything works out well for you."

"Thanks," she replied in a tone that suggested she wasn't optimistic.

He exited through the door to the parking lot. I gestured for Mamie to join Zoey and me as we headed for the nearby door to the shelter area.

My old mentor oohed and aahed over each of the residents as we passed their enclosures, including Babydoll, Dodi, and Hannibal. She reached in to pet them, and every one of them closed their eyes in apparent ecstasy at her touch.

She'd always had a way with animals . . . until she wound up abusing them with her love.

Zoey danced at my side until we reached the visitors' park at the far end of the rear storage shed. There, she fulfilled her restroom duties, and I used one of our recyclable bags to pick it up.

"Good dog." Mamie patted her again, too.

I knew how lonely she was, and how the absence of pets around was hurting her. Even so . . .

I waved her to a seat at a picnic table where our visitors could sit and watch their prospective new pets romp and play and, with luck, win their hearts. Mamie sat down across the table, looking at me expectantly.

"Mamie," I said, "I don't think it's wise for you to commit to be here any particular days or hours, but you're welcome to visit, and to help us take care of our residents, whenever you're able. I have a budget for regular employees, though, and don't think I can hire you under these circumstances, but—" Okay, I might be able to squeeze a small hourly rate out of our funds, thanks to Dante's largesse. But I wanted to see how things worked out first.

Things like how often Mamie would actually show up. And whether she was about to be arrested.

"But I can come here to help? Whenever I want?" She sounded thrilled. "And I can pet the dogs, and hug the cats, and there'll be plenty of food for them, and—"

She looked almost childlike in her glee, clapping her hands enough that some of the dogs nearest us started to bark.

I laughed. "Yes to all of that." I had to ask, though. "You

do collect Social Security, don't you? I mean, you have enough money on your own to survive, right?" Otherwise, I'd rethink everything.

"Of course, dear. It's enough for me. I just couldn't stretch it enough to make sure that all my sweet rescues had enough to eat. That's part of what led to my difficulties. That, and not many donations. But you don't have that kind of problem, do you?" Her gaze turned shrewd. "Not with Dante's money."

"No, thank heavens." Was she blaming me again for her problems? Or just reminding me?

"Oh, coming here often—it's wonderful! Thank you, Lauren." The shrewdness left her face, and her eyes, among all the surrounding wrinkles, seemed to glow.

All right. Maybe she had no hidden agenda. And I had planned to keep an eye on her anyway. This could be a good idea. Maybe.

"Don't thank me yet," I said. What she'd said earlier kept circling through my mind, and I had to ask. "What did you mean before by, 'no babies, no fur babies either'?"

"I shouldn't have mentioned it. I was hoping to make you feel sorry for me, but . . . did I tell you, back when you helped me at my shelter, about my failed marriage?"

I shook my head. I also held my breath. I'd heard that when people became hoarders, it was sometimes the result of a highly emotional event in their lives. I'd assumed, if that was true with Mamie, it was because she hadn't been chosen by Dante to run HotRescues. She had apparently started bringing in more animals to her shelter after that. But maybe it wasn't the only reason. And maybe I'd had nothing to do with it. Or at least not much.

"It wasn't too long before I met you." She tried to keep her tone casual, but her voice hitched and I knew it was something that had affected her significantly. "I'd had two miscarriages and was told I probably couldn't carry a baby to term. My husband and I had been married for a few years, and I started talking adoption. That's when he told me he was divorcing me to marry a woman he'd been sleeping with. She was pregnant. She didn't miscarry." Mamie's laugh was forced. "I didn't care about him after that. But I had a lot of love to give somewhere. That's when I really started concentrating on pet rescue."

"I'm so sorry, Mamie," I said.

"I'm not. Or at least I won't be, when I can start taking in my own fur babies again."

I didn't reiterate that her wish might be impossible. I understood that the recidivism rate for hoarders was astronomical. To avoid being prosecuted for animal cruelty, she and her lawyer might have to cut a deal in which she'd promise never to take in any animals, or maybe she'd be allowed just one or two.

"Well, we'll have to see how things go. Did they recommend that you see a counselor when you were at the facility where the police had you checked out?"

"Yes, and I'll be seeing her, about once a week. When I can."

Which made me think she wasn't seeing the therapist at all.

"But I promise, I won't even think about taking in animals—well, I'll think but I won't do it—till things are resolved about Bethany's death. And as long as I can come here to hug your pets." She bent to pat Zoey, then looked up at me once more. "Are you going to find out who killed Bethany, Lauren? I swear it wasn't me."

I wanted to believe her even more now. I felt so sorry for her—for everything.

"I can't promise to figure that out, Mamie, but I'll keep looking."

She smiled up at me, her expression now one of trust. "I know you can do it, Lauren. I saw the news about how you did it before, how someone was killed right here and you helped to catch that murderer."

"Well . . . yes. But that doesn't make me an expert. Let me ask you a couple of questions. Who do you know that also knew Bethany and, in your opinion, is the least likely to have killed her?"

"Besides me?" I nodded. "And you?"

I laughed. "Yes, besides us."

"And besides Dante?"

"Yes, besides him. I don't think they were really acquainted anyway." Although I remembered that Dante said Bethany had contacted him.

"Oh, but Bethany knew everyone. Especially everyone with money and power and anything else she thought she needed to be the most important person in the world." She nodded knowingly. Even though she acted ditzy and confused at times, I suspected that was an act. She clearly still retained a lot of insight.

"I gathered that," I said. "In any event . . . who, among all the people you think she knew best, was the least likely to have killed her?"

"Well, I think she really loved her boyfriend, Miguel. I heard they argued a lot, but I think he loved her, too. So, maybe he's the least likely." She leaned over the table toward me. "Especially since I heard that she was supporting him, but she didn't leave him much in her will."

I couldn't help laughing. Insight. This woman was one shrewd and perceptive senior citizen . . . sometimes.

"I get it," I said. And I did.

I intended to have a little conversation soon with Bethany's main squeeze before her death, Miguel Rohrig.

Mamie stayed long enough for me to treat her to dinner at a nearby family restaurant. She ordered meat loaf. If she always ate as little as she did then, she'd be able to dine on the remainder, boxed for her to take home, for the next two evenings.

I'd been virtuous and ordered a salad. Even so, it was large enough that I, too, got a doggy box for the remainder.

What did we talk about? Pets, of course. I'd left Zoey at HotRescues, and Mamie waxed eloquent about how wonderful she was. I, of course, agreed.

Which got Mamie sighing over how much she missed her own special pet, who'd been taken by Animal Services along with the rest of the hoarded animals.

"I just wish they had left Herman with me," she said sadly as we walked to my car. "Just one dog, that's all. I could have taken perfect care of him, especially if he was the only animal around. I always treated him specially, which was most likely unfair to all my other babies."

"I know he's special to you," I said sympathetically.

She looked at me with a hopeful expression lighting her face. "Was he one of the dogs that you could pick up before?"

"No, but I'll check on him again."

"Thank you so much, Lauren! For everything. You are the absolute best." She hugged me again, then got into my car.

Back at HotRescues, I saw her to her own automobile, which looked as elderly as she was beginning to appear—an old Chevy sedan with lots of dings, its red paint faded and scratched. "A vintage car," I said, half in jest.

"It's my baby, too, like Herman. It's gotten me where I've needed to go for years."

"Well, I'm a worrier. Why don't you give me a call when you get home?"

"You think this senile senior citizen can't drive worth a damn?" She said it lightly, as if she wasn't offended at all if that was indeed what I thought. Close enough.

"I worry about everyone I care about, Mamie. You sound like my kids—except for the 'senile senior citizen' part."

She laughed. "I'll call you," she promised. "Count on it."

Which she did, maybe an hour later.

I was still at HotRescues. I'd received a message on my office phone from Kathy Georgio, asking why I didn't contact her and the usual gang from the Southern California Rescuers loop to help take in the hoarded animals released that day by Animal Services. I called her back and explained that I was motivated by hoping to appease some of the shelter administrators involved with Pet Rescuers Together, without going into detail—like, I wanted information from them to help clear Mamie.

Kathy wasn't mollified. "That prima donna Cricket seems as self-important as her former boss, doesn't she?"

"I'm not arguing with that," I said. "For now, though, I'd like to maintain a cordial relationship—with everyone. I'll contact you next time, okay, Kathy?"

"I'll consider that a promise."

When I left my office with Zoey for our last walk of the day around the shelter area, Brooke Pernall showed up with Cheyenne. At her urging, I gave her a rundown of my so-far useless and disorganized investigation into Bethany's murder.

"I'll have some more information for you tomorrow about the men in her life—from Antonio and also the Web. I'll get a better rundown on Miguel before I hand it over to you. That seems a little too obvious, though."

"You're a believer in the least likely suspect as the killer, too?"

She laughed. "Not always."

When Zoey and I returned to the main building, Mamie called on my cell phone. "I'm home safe and sound," she said. She paused. "Any news about Herman?"

"Not yet," I said, "But I promise I'll ask after him."

I called Matt right after we hung up, but had to leave a message. "I'd like an update on the dog Mamie particularly considers hers—the one I pointed out to you before," I said. I nevertheless described the terrier mix.

If I did get Herman turned over to me, I'd tell Mamie that it was under the condition that he stayed at HotRescues for a while. Even if she could take care of a single dog adequately, doing so might mess up her defense in any prosecution for hoarding.

Zoey and I drove home then. Matt called me a little while after I arrived.

He still didn't know when or if Herman might be available for pickup by a private shelter, but he'd ask again—and tell me about it tomorrow night, when we met for a drink and dinner.

Fine by me. That was when I would ask him about the idea I'd had to satisfy Dante with a demonstration to take place at HotRescues.

Chapter 18

I got to HotRescues early the next morning, in time to see Brooke—but not necessarily the way I wanted to see her.

Dressed in her black security T-shirt and jeans, she was stalking through the parking lot, carrying two small red-dish pups—probably Pomeranians—one under each arm. Pete was following her, looking equally stormy.

I caught up with her. "Are those—?"

"Supposed owner relinquishments," Brooke muttered so low that I could hardly hear her.

"Found 'em out back like the others." Pete waved some paper that I assumed was a note like the one left with Shazam.

"Then did you—?"

Brooke stopped in front of me at the doorway into the welcome area. "I'll double-check, but whoever left them managed to stay pretty much out of range of the new secu-rity camera."

After we'd talked about how Shazam and the others had

been left here, Brooke had said she'd take care of it—at least so we could identify whoever was leaving the animals, owner relinquishments or not. She'd mounted a new security camera outside, then camouflaged it with decorative trim that was being used on the new building.

Apparently the supposed relinquisher had seen through the disguise—although that was what Brooke would be checking out. Me, too.

Zoey stayed beside me, obedient as always, but her nose was in the air as we neared Brooke and the dogs she held. "Cute," I said. "Why would an owner relinquish them?"

"They were most likely abandoned," Brooke contradicted, "no matter what the damned note says. No microchips. I scanned them." We'd recently gotten a scanner to keep here. "And you know better than to ask anything like that, Lauren. Why would anyone abandon, relinquish, or abuse any animals? Because some people are crazy. And because they can."

I couldn't argue with that.

We all trooped into the welcome room, and the little dogs began squirming in Brooke's arms. "Want me to take them to the vet to be checked out?" Brooke asked. "I can drop them off on my way home, and someone can pick them up later if the visit will take much time."

"Fine." I looked at Pete. "So, what are their names?"

"Pint-size and Tiny, according to this." He waved the piece of paper, then leaned toward Brooke and the pups she held. "Hey, which one of you is Tiny?" Neither stopped squirming. "Pint-size?" Still no change. "What do you want to bet that whoever found these two made up the names to make this look like a relinquishment . . . again?"

"Not a bet I'd take," I said. "But I still think it's better for them to stay here once their health is checked out. I'll call Matt to let him know about these latest 'relinquish-ments,' though, to make sure he's okay with our hanging on to them."

I helped Pete find some standard leashes with loops at the end for dogs that weren't wearing collars, and we attached Pint-size and Tiny—or whoever they were—to them back in the welcome area. "Let me know what hap-pens. I'm not sure whether Carlie will be at the clinic, but—"

"All the vets there are good," Brooke said. Another state-ment I couldn't argue with. "I'll let you know who we see and what the results are."

They left, and Zoey and I followed Pete back into the shelter area. He continued toward the storage building at the end of the path to get our residents' breakfasts ready. Zoey and I took our stroll, making sure everyone looked healthy, although most of the dogs appeared lonesome and in need of a pat. Then we went inside the center building, and after greeting the toy dogs in enclosures there, I looked for an empty cage where our new dogs would eventually stay after their quarantine, assuming they were healthy. Also assuming that Matt wasn't as tired of this scenario as I was and used it as a reason to insist that I turn them over to Animal Services. I'd fight it—but I didn't dare fight too hard. I had to stay in their good graces, for the sake of our residents.

I preferred staying in Matt's good graces, too—but if it came down to having to end whatever relationship we had entered into, or helping more pets, the animals would win. I felt sure he had the same attitude, too.

At least we had room here for these two new ones, since I hadn't taken on many of the pets made available from Mamie's surrender.

Back in my office, I saw that Brooke had been busy last

night, even before she'd rescued those two Poms from our back alley. There were printouts on my desk from research she had done online about possible suspects in Bethany's murder.

She had also left a list she'd gotten from the police about people they were considering as suspects. Presumably Antonio had been her source, although that wasn't obvious from the paperwork. The list included nearly everyone I'd met, and many I hadn't, who'd known Bethany.

Mamie was, unsurprisingly, at the top, although it wasn't stated to be in the order of who was the most likely candidate. Bethany's guy, Miguel Rohrig, was next, then her two ex-husbands, Cricket, all administrators whose shelters were part of PST, some people who'd adopted pets from Better Than Any Pet Rescues, and others who'd been involved with her cosmetics company.

There were a lot of possible murderers out there.

A thought crossed my mind. I'd already booted up my aging computer, and it had chugged to life. I did an online search for Bethany Urber's obituary and learned that her funeral would be on Saturday, two days from now, at Hollywood Forever Cemetery, the resting place of many stars. I figured that Bethany must have left instructions for an ostentatious send-off that she would love. Too bad she wouldn't be there to watch.

Could be that most of those on the list Brooke had obtained would be present. I'd be there, too, I decided on the spot. But I was unlikely to do much more than observe the suspects who also attended. Long conversations about their relationships with Bethany were unlikely to be feasible.

So . . . I flipped through the papers that Brooke had left. When I'd glanced at them before, I'd seen she had located Miguel Rohrig. Though I'd heard he was an out-of-work actor being supported by Bethany, he was apparently an in-work waiter at the moment, at an upscale Westwood restaurant.

Good excuse for me to call Matt. That, plus our new upcoming residents.

First, though, I got a call from Brooke. The pups needed to stay there for a few hours till they got the results of some blood tests, but the initial vet exam suggested they were fine. I arranged for Nina to pick them up later that day.

I then placed my call to Matt, but just reached his voice mail. I left a message inviting him to dinner.

I heard back from him nearly immediately. "It's a date, Lauren," he said. "Got some stuff to talk to you about, too. And I'll be interested to hear the reason you chose Esplendido as our restaurant for the evening."

Like his former girlfriend, Miguel apparently enjoyed milking any situation for all the publicity he could. Maybe he thought it would help him get his next film role.

I'd been concerned that he might be taking some time to himself after Bethany's death, not working, staying in seclusion to mourn. But Googling him yielded a majorly pretentious Web site, linked to Twitter and a Facebook page. He'd let the world know he was facing his loss bravely, still maintaining his job, missing Bethany, the works. And if anyone wanted to have him serve their table at Esplendido, they just had to ask—and, of course, leave a big tip.

Well, he didn't really add that last sentence, but I felt certain that was his intention.

His Web site also linked to Esplendido's, and I swallowed hard when I saw the prices. I'd invited Matt, so it should be my treat. I wouldn't argue much if he suggested paying for it.

Maybe we could go Dutch, but even so I was still in for a large tab. The price of helping Mamie, I supposed.

I departed early from HotRescues, changed clothes, and left Zoey at home. Matt and I were meeting at the restaurant at seven.

I found a metered parking spot along a neighboring street, avoiding the cost of a valet, at least. I'd thrown on a rather nice dress, black with sequins decorating the neckline, and thought I looked pretty good, even as I took my time walking on my not-quite-stilettos the two blocks to the restaurant.

Catching Matt's sexy gaze when he first saw me, I figured I'd made a good choice.

I took his hand and we walked inside. Esplendido had large picture windows to the street, overlooking a series of tables of different sizes covered with pristine white tablecloths and surrounded by patrons. I loved the spicy odor that greeted us as we entered, but I could have done without the loud buzz of conversation.

The place was brimming with people. We were met nearly immediately by a maitre d' dressed in an attitude of subservient responsibility: white shirt, black trousers, and a small black apron. "Dinner for two?"

"Yes. And we'd like to sit at a table where Miguel Rohrig will be our server." I'd spotted the guy I believed to be Miguel about halfway down the long room, talking to some patrons. He looked like the wannabe-star photos on his Web site, and everyone was looking at him with interest and concern.

"I'm afraid he is quite busy already. You could wait for one of his tables, but it might be a while."

I did see a couple of empty tables not far from where he stood, but that didn't mean he was assigned to them.

"Oh, but I really want him to be our server. We have some friends in common, and I especially want to convey my condolences on his loss." I stared into the maitre d's eyes. He seemed to know what I was talking about, but he didn't budge.

Until Matt pulled a twenty-dollar bill out of his pocket and slipped it to the guy. "We really don't have much time to wait," he said. "Could you possibly seat us now?"

"Of course, sir."

I glanced at Matt, who only smiled. I should have figured that was the answer, but I didn't eat out at this kind of place very often.

Did he? There was a lot about him that I still didn't know.

The table to which we were shown was only one away from where Miguel stood still conversing. I wondered whether any of the patrons he was serving would actually receive any meals that night. Like us.

"So that was your ulterior motive," Matt said as we took our seats and lifted menus that had been placed on the table. "That guy's Bethany Urber's former boyfriend?"

I looked over Matt appreciatively. He cleaned up well, too. He wore a charcoal suit with a burgundy tie, and his dark hair seemed to be getting a bit longer than I'd seen it before. He mostly wore it in a short military cut. It looked great on him either way. In fact, I'd concluded from the moment I'd first met him, at the puppy mill rescue, that he was one handsome guy.

"Yes, he is," I said as Miguel approached us.

"Good evening." He appeared to be in his early thirties, younger than Bethany had been. He had long, gleaming black hair, an obvious five o'clock shadow, and thick, dark brows. A Latin lover sort? A gigolo? Probably all of the above. He wore an outfit similar to the maitre d's. "My name is Miguel, and I'll be your server this evening. Can I get you anything to drink first?"

I ordered a glass of the house wine, and Matt ordered beer. Then I said, "Miguel, I was a friend of Bethany's. Or at least an acquaintance. We'd only recently met. I'm very sorry for your loss."

He looked at me, and his eyes welled up with tears. "Thank you. She was a wonderful woman. I will miss her, and I'm sure you will miss that you didn't get an opportunity to know her better. Are you coming to her funeral?"

"I plan to."

"Thank you," he repeated. He seemed to fight genuine tears. Oh, yes, this guy did appear to be someone unlikely to have murdered Bethany, if he'd cared for her so much.

On the other hand, he was admittedly an actor.

I ordered chile verde, and Matt ordered a gourmet burrito. Miguel served us chips and an utterly delicious salsa to start with. He was surprisingly attentive, considering the crowd of people he was serving.

But I realized that this was hardly a better locale than the upcoming funeral to get any real information from him, only an impression of what he felt.

Matt and I talked shop a bit—and I did ask if he had found out anything about Mamie's Herman.

"He had some medical issues—strange to think he was Mamie's favorite, since he was even more emaciated than some of the others. Even so, he'll be fine now. You want to take him to HotRescues?"

"Can I?"

"Sure, as long as you don't let Mamie take him home."

"That'll be difficult. You mean permanently?"

"At least until we have some assurance that she won't starve the poor dog again—or take in any others."

"Of course." I told him then about our two new drop-offs. "I really thought, with the measures our security expert, Brooke, put in place, that we'd be able to catch whoever's been doing it, but not yet. We got the same kind of note, that these were an owner relinquishment, but you know I can't guarantee where these two came from. No microchips. Is it okay if we hang on to them?"

"I'll see what I can do."

When we'd finished, I didn't allow myself to gasp at the bill, but after arguing with Matt, who wanted to treat despite the magnitude of the amount, I tendered a credit card to pay my half when Miguel had it split.

"I'd really love to talk to you some more about Bethany," I told Miguel as we got ready to leave. "I'm a pet rescuer, too, and her ideas of creating a network the way she did, and her telling the world so much about rescuers . . . we've really lost a wonderful person."

Yes, I was gushing. Maybe I could get an acting role, too. Maybe I'd even be better at it than Miguel.

But whatever I'd done, it apparently worked. He reached into the pocket of his small apron and drew out a card. "I'm always pleased to talk about my Bethany," he said. "Call me any afternoon, before I come here. Maybe one, two o'clock? It will be my pleasure, Lauren."

Lauren? He'd obviously read my credit card, which worried me.

On the other hand, I was looking at him as a potential murderer. Identity theft? I'd know who to come after.

But was he the one who'd killed Bethany?

Chapter 19

Matt walked me to my car. The sidewalk outside the restaurant was crowded with other people, and there was a substantial amount of traffic on the street despite the hour. Or maybe because of it. The west side of Los Angeles attracted people who liked to have a good time.

"That guy did seem to be in mourning." Matt moved slightly behind me to let a couple going the other way get by.

"Yeah. I don't know how much was genuine. I'll have to find out."

Matt was right beside me again, his arm around my shoulder. "Be careful. Genuine mourning or not, he still could have killed her."

"Duh." Humor filled my voice.

He laughed, then said, "Okay, Lauren, I know you're not stupid. Foolish, sometimes, maybe—but not stupid. You'll still keep me informed about what you learn about him, and anyone else you think could have killed Bethany?"

Repetitious, yes, but at least he'd phrased it as a question this time. I also knew he was only behaving this way because he gave a damn about me. "Sure." It was time to change the subject. I hadn't forgotten what I wanted to ask him at dinner but hadn't found the best time to mention it.

We'd reached my car after turning a corner onto a quiet side street. I was hoping for a goodnight kiss. He took my arm and gazed down at me beneath the illumination of the streetlight. Looked as if we shared that intention, which gave me the perfect opening for what I wanted to say.

"So . . ." I cocked my head slightly as I looked up at Matt. The cragginess of his features was emphasized by the shadows created by the light's energy-saving bulb. "Is this a good time to ask you for a favor?"

He laughed again and hugged me. "You do know how to play a guy, don't you, Lauren?"

"You don't even know what I'm going to ask," I said defensively.

"No, but the answer is yes."

I stared up at him. "Are you nuts?"

"No, but I'm coming to know you. I trust you. If something's so important to you that you think you have to play a game with me about it, then it'll be important to me, too. Unless—" He paused. "You're not going to ask me to do something against Animal Services policy, are you—at least not something I can't easily get around?"

"Nothing like that. But it's something to help HotRescues, and to help me impress the chairman of our board of directors."

"You want to impress Dante DeFrancisco? How can I help?"

"He's planning some kind of fund-raiser at HotRescues in conjunction with showing off our new building. It's more of a public relations thing than for bringing in a lot of money."

"And I can help how?"

"Could you get SmART to do some kind of demonstration?" The Small Animal Rescue Team was an amazing group of Animal Services personnel who volunteered to save nearly any kind of small animals, pets or not, from life-threatening situations. They were the ones who had saved the puppies tossed down a storm drain recently to hide them from a puppy mill raid, and I was really impressed with them.

I always felt awed that Matt was their commanding officer, along with the Department Air Rescue Team that brought in helicopters to save horses and larger animals from danger, as well as strategic planning for handling animals in area-wide disasters.

"Sure, we can work something out," Matt said. "Do you want them to save MARTE from a fictional situation you put together?" He'd told me before that MARTE stood for "Mock animal for training exercises"—a fair-sized stuffed dog that the team "rescued" for practice.

"Maybe, especially if they do something sexy like rappel down the side of one of our buildings."

"Let me think about it, and give me some choices on dates. But you can count on something, Lauren. Especially if it helps call attention to the great job HotRescues is doing as a private no-kill shelter."

I didn't hold back then, but threw my arms around him. He bent down, and our kiss was wonderful.

"That's one nice thank-you." Matt sounded a little out of breath when we finally unlocked our lips.

"And you're one nice captain, Captain."

"All in the interest of saving animals. Oh, and impressing one certain animal rescuer."

"You can definitely consider me impressed." I pushed the button to unlock my Venza and slipped inside, waving to Matt as I drove off . . . and wishing he was following me home.

Soon, I promised myself. It had been long enough since our last time together.

I was thrilled to hear from my kids that night, and to learn that Tracy and Kevin both had plans to come home for the weekend. Not that I anticipated seeing a lot of them. Their reasons for the visit, in both cases, involved get-togethers with some of their high school cronies that would occupy much of their time.

On the other hand, I'd get to see them as they moved around our house and maybe they'd have some time for dinner with their mom. They'd both arrive tomorrow night—Friday.

I awoke early the next morning, took Zoey for a neighborhood walk, then we both took off for HotRescues. I held my breath as I drove into the parking lot, but I saw no abandoned—or relinquished—pets lying around anywhere. Brooke had had someone else sleep there at night as our security force, and that person, Karen, was chatting with Pete inside our welcome room when Zoey and I entered.

"Everything okay?" I asked.

"No new pets dropped off, if that's what you're asking." Our senior handyman looked much more at ease this morning than he had yesterday.

Karen was nearer my age than Brooke's. She'd stayed here before a few times. Her light eyes appeared bleary, as if she missed her sleep, and she wore a backwards cap over her dull blond hair. She bent to pat Zoey, then looked up at me. "Rather boring here overnight, Lauren. I'll have to create some excitement next time."

"Please don't." I matched her smile.

That day turned out to be fairly routine in all ways. Our residents were thriving—and I assured myself of that with my first walk around the shelter. No new drop-offs. No frantic calls from any public shelter volunteers asking us to bring in some endangered animals from their facilities.

Matt called only to let me know he was still trying to get an answer on when I could pick up Mamie's dog Herman. Plus, he'd spoken to the SmART team leader about what kind of demo they could perform at HotRescues and when, but nothing was certain yet.

Mid-afternoon, I pulled Miguel Rohrig's card out of my purse while I was alone in my office, but he didn't answer. Nor did he return my call, though I left a message.

Eventually, I was able to dash home—in time to see Kevin before he ran out to meet his friends. We got together in the kitchen, where he'd taken a glass of water from the fridge dispenser and sat on the floor teasing Zoey with an ice cube.

My handsome eighteen-year-old son, a freshman at nearby Claremont McKenna College, made my heart stop as always, since he looked so much like his dad. He was tall and slender, with intense brown eyes beneath straight brows. His hair was unmanageable, the deep red of an autumn leaf about to turn brown. He smiled a lot, too, with the greatest, upbeat personality—unlike his serious mom.

"You doing all right?" He eyed me up and down as if trying to find something off that he could fix. "I mean, if you need me for anything—"

"You've already given me what I want just by being here," I said. "But . . . what are you up to tomorrow?" It would be the day of Bethany's funeral, and I wanted to go, to observe everyone who attended, but if it was a choice between seeing my kids and going to a funeral, guess which would win.

Kevin had plans. So did his sister. Tracy arrived about half an hour after Kevin left. A friend had picked her up at Bob Hope Airport in Burbank and would return for her soon.

"Hi, Mom." She gave me a quick kiss, then hurried upstairs to leave her carry-on bag in her room. In a few minutes, she showed up in the living room, where I'd turned on TV news. She looked more like me—medium height, relatively slim, with green eyes. She wore her dark brown hair shoulder length, though, while I kept mine sheared into a manageable cap.

Their reunions with their high school friends had different origins—some ball games for Kevin, and an extended engagement party for one of Tracy's friends—but both would be occupied tomorrow.

I could follow through with my plans, too. But mine were far different from the kinds of celebrations they were attending.

It was late Saturday morning. I'd left Zoey at home, since she would get attention from the kids when they woke up. I'd headed to HotRescues early and once more held my breath when I arrived, but again there were no unanticipated drop-offs.

Eventually, leaving the place under the control of Nina and some volunteers, I left to face the ordeal of the day.

I hate funerals, even when I don't know the deceased person very well. The surroundings never fail to remind me of my dear Kerry's funeral. We'd held it in a much more

modest location—Forest Lawn of Hollywood, not Hollywood Forever Cemetery. Even so, interments are interments.
Though rhetoric suggests their purpose is to celebrate the
life of the deceased, they're in fact burials of the dead. A
final ceremony in a life that has ended. Period.

Okay. I'd gotten past Kerry's funeral. I'd certainly be
able to deal with Bethany Urber's. She wasn't a close
friend. She wasn't really a friend at all.

It was an ordeal nevertheless. I arrived early, since I
needed to see who else was there and, if possible, talk to
some of them. Cops were already present, some in dress
uniform, I supposed, and others in suits whom I recognized
as detectives. But I felt certain they were observing the
attendees with the same goal I did: to see if anyone jumped
up and confessed to murdering Bethany.

Which, unsurprisingly, didn't happen.

The Hollywood Forever Cemetery was actually quite
impressive, with its mausoleums and tall obelisk commem-
orating some of those interred there, its mostly flat green
grounds, shallow pools, hacienda-style chapel, and palm
trees.

Right now, though, it was bereft of the serenity that I
assumed it usually displayed in honor of the many Hollywood stars and others buried there. The media had turned
out in droves, which was probably just what Bethany wanted.
If nothing else, her murder had catapulted her into her five
minutes of fame. I recognized some newscasters and paparazzi, including one I'd met several times before, Corina
Carey of *National NewsShakers*. She was a sort-of friend
of Kendra Ballantyne, Dante's significant other.

I'm not usually a mingler. At parties or whatever, I find
people I know and hang out with them. But at this event, I

wanted not just to pay my respects to Bethany, but to get further ideas about who might have hated her.

I started by edging my way through a crowd that had formed around Miguel Rohrig from the moment he walked onto cemetery grounds. A lot appeared to be paparazzi, although others included scantily dressed young women who might just have shown up to hang out with the would-be film star.

I managed to get near him, earning not a few dirty looks. Quizzical ones, too, like what would some broad my age be thinking, trying to get near this young hunk?

"Hello, Miguel," I finally said when I was right beside him. "Remember me—from the night before last?" The way I'd phrased my question earned me a lot of curious— and jealous—stares.

"Of course, Lauren. Sorry I didn't get an opportunity to call you back yesterday. Let's get together for a drink one of these days, shall we? I'll call you."

Except for the last, what he'd said was exactly what I was looking for. I couldn't be sure he actually would call. But, as determined as I was to talk with him, I'd keep phoning him till we got together.

I moved out of his sphere of hangers-on and headed toward the group of people who looked familiar from Bethany's presentation on hoarders. Most were probably administrators from the shelters included in the PST network.

Cricket was at the forefront, dabbing her eyes with a tissue. She had worn an over-the-top black dress that would have been something Bethany could have chosen as she presided at the Better Than Any Pet Rescues plantation house—a full length black gown that looked like something from a history film. Since Cricket was on the short side and a little plump, I couldn't say the attire was especially flattering. It nevertheless made a statement about her grieving for Bethany.

As I approached, Cricket dashed over and embraced me soggily. "Oh, Lauren, thank you so much for coming. Bethany would be so happy to know you're here."

I doubted it but just said, "My condolences again, Cricket."

She released me and paraded among some of the others. Though she appeared sad and perhaps a bit vulnerable, I didn't think she was off her guard enough to admit it if I asked if she'd murdered Bethany.

Coming here was turning out to be as helpful in finding Bethany's murderer as if I'd tried to hold a séance. And, no, I don't believe in paranormal stuff like that.

I glanced around to see who else I could chat with. Darya Price was there with her husband—what was his name? Ran? No, Lan. I made my way over to them.

"My condolences," I repeated to her. Darya looked pale and drawn, and if I'd thought her fragile enough not to withstand an exuberant jump from a large-breed dog before, I now thought she might be in trouble even with a friendly moderate-sized one. She clung to her equally slim husband's arm. They both wore suits, Darya's charcoal and Lan's black. "I wish I'd gotten to know Bethany better," I continued. "She must have been quite a wonderful person to draw this kind of crowd at her funeral."

"Wonderful? Of course." Darya's voice sounded distant, as if she wanted to be anywhere but here. She wasn't alone in that. I empathized.

"That's what she wanted everyone to believe." Despite his harsh words, Lan sounded sad. "She did try to help a lot of animals," he continued. "That's what she should be remembered for."

He looked down at his wife with obvious fondness in his eyes.

"You know," I said, "I've been considering, in Bethany's memory, the possibility of looking into some affiliation of HotRescues with Pet Shelters Together. First, though, I'd really like to meet more of the administrators who joined. Could you introduce me to some who're here?"

That was when I noticed that some dark-suited guys who must be part of the funeral staff were herding people into the chapel. The service must be ready to begin.

"Later," I amended. "Okay?"

"Of course," Darya said. "Although—"

There was a note of distress in her voice, but Lan took her arm. "We'd better go in." He looked at me. "She can introduce you to people, of course, but you know that Cricket is in charge of PST. You'll need to talk to her."

I started to follow the crowd inside.

"Hi, Lauren," said a soft, sad voice from beside me.

I looked down.

"Mamie!" I had to force myself to keep my own voice low. "What are you doing here?"

Chapter 20

Mamie wore an appropriate black dress, a shirtwaist with its hem below her knees. She also wore a somber expression befitting the occasion on her age-wrinkled face. Her reddish hair was combed into submission, despite its unmistakable waviness.

"I'm here to pay my respects," she said quietly. "And to show everyone I have nothing to hide, nothing to be ashamed of. I didn't hurt Bethany."

You did hurt a lot of animals, I thought, and might have wanted to hide that from this group—and your behavior was certainly something to be ashamed of. But that wasn't what she meant. Since I'd already promised myself I'd try to learn the truth about Bethany's death, and hoped that Mamie wasn't the killer, I should have felt happier to see her there. She was right, wasn't she? Showing up at Bethany's funeral was a positive gesture and a moment of holding her head up instead of slinking away in guilt.

Maybe.

I glanced around. People had begun wending their way into the chapel. A couple I recognized from the hoarding meeting at Bethany's glanced our way, and Mamie, obviously knowing who they were, nodded a solemn greeting to them.

"Are they members of Pet Shelters Together?" I asked her.

"Yes, poor things."

We joined the throng heading for the service. "I'd like for you to introduce me to them later," I said, "if the opportunity arises and you don't feel uncomfortable talking to them." Even though she might not know all the members of PST, I figured I could count on her more than on Darya to introduce me to those she was familiar with.

"Why would I feel uncomfortable?" She looked puzzled.

Because they're animal rescuers, and you're a known hoarder, I thought but didn't say it out loud. Apparently my concerns about her discomfort were unfounded.

"No reason," I lied. "But if you happen to see anyone else you know, I'd like to meet them, too."

"In case one of them killed Bethany?" Her voice sounded eager. Although she kept her eyes down as we walked, she glanced sideways at me. She might have no sense of reality about her hoarding, but she otherwise appeared fairly astute at times.

"We'll see," I answered.

I stayed with Mamie for the service in the small, crowded chapel, with its arched ceiling and gorgeous chandeliers. We found seats in a row of pews near the back of the room.

It was most likely the kind of rite Bethany would have wanted, except for the lack of celebrities. But she was eulogized by a whole bunch of pet rescuers who'd signed their facilities up as part of PST. I still wanted Mamie to introduce me to them, but as I sat in the pew, I wrote down names of the people and the shelters they ran so I could follow up later.

The chairman of the board of directors of the group who'd bought Better Than Any Cosmetics from Bethany also praised her—her creativity, her foresight, her business acumen, and her generosity of spirit for selling out and taking on pet rescue as her cause.

Miguel Rohrig spoke, too. As he had before when we'd talked briefly at the restaurant, he truly appeared to mourn Bethany's loss. He talked about how sweet and generous she was. And how, to the extent he could, he would try to continue her work.

Cricket Borley echoed those thoughts. She was certainly in a better position to do so, given that she was Bethany's apparent successor as the head of Better Than Any Pet Rescues and Pet Shelters Together. She waved some photos she said were of dogs and cats for whom Bethany had recently found new homes, and tearfully chatted about Bethany's high pet adoption rate, talking about how the animals would miss her most of all. I found my eyes tearing up, too.

Mamie must have noticed. "I admit she did some good," she whispered, "but she made other shelters in her network take in a lot of the older or otherwise less adoptable animals, so her own record looked good."

I glanced at her. This was something I needed additional information about, but not just then. "I want to hear more later," I whispered back.

"I guess her exes aren't going to say anything," Mamie murmured later as the service drew to a close.

"Are they here?" I asked in a low tone, surprised by the possibility.

"Sure. There's John Jerremiah and there's Sam Legroote." Mamie pointed off to the left, to two guys sitting not far from one another toward the front rows of pews. "I'll bet they're here to cheer her passing." She spoke right into my ear. "But knowing Bethany and her love of publicity, she probably left them something in her will if they showed up at her funeral. If so, she'd have told them in advance."

I wished it was appropriate for me to set up interviews with all the people here who I thought might have disliked Bethany, but it was, after all, her funeral.

Even so, when the service was over and Bethany's remains were placed in a vault in an ornate structure nearby, I looked around. Miguel, instead of being surrounded by fawning women, was now talking with Bethany's ex-husbands. I found that interesting. Were they comparing notes about the exes' divorce settlements, and how they stacked up against anything Bethany had left Miguel? Had Mamie guessed correctly, and they were being paid to show up?

Had she left anything to Miguel—like, enough to constitute a motive to kill her?

And what about the shelter administrators she'd recruited into PST and then, perhaps, used to suit her own blatant needs?

I had a feeling that my speculations and more might get answered—correctly or not—on some of those celebrity-following TV shows, since the media reps were snapping pictures from the fringes of the crowd still milling on the cemetery grounds.

The LAPD detectives kept looking in our direction, and I believed they were scoping out Mamie and what she was doing here.

I did get some of my wishes fulfilled when Mamie took my arm and led me toward where a group of pet rescuers milled around. Cricket was there, and Darya Price and her husband, plus others I recognized from Bethany's hoarding discussion and the visits to Animal Services centers to see, then pick up, some of Mamie's animals. Mamie walked right up, joining them as if she was a member of their group.

"Lauren," Cricket said, ignoring Mamie. "Thanks so much for coming. Do you know everyone here?" At the shake of my head, she said to the group, "This is Lauren Vancouver, administrator of HotRescues. She may be interested in joining our network."

The group, mostly women and nearly all dressed in dark colors, seemed to each start talking at once, welcoming me, thanking me for coming, and also pretending that Mamie wasn't there. Interesting. Whatever authority Bethany had exerted over the heads of the rescue groups in her network, Cricket had apparently taken it over easily. Too easily?

At least I didn't have to count on Mamie's introduction to these people. They mostly introduced themselves. I was glad I'd jotted down some of their names and shelter affiliations, since I wouldn't remember them all, even the ones I'd seen before. Now, though only a few names sounded familiar, a lot of their rescue organizations' names jogged my memory, such as Redondo Rescues, Amazing Animal Rescues, Pet Home Locators.

"Thank you all," I said. "I appreciate the invitation to join. I'd love to hear more about the organization, so if you don't mind, I'll be in touch with some of you soon."

Everyone seemed to welcome that possibility. And if I managed to ask a few subtle questions about Bethany, how everyone liked her, and who might not have adored her quite so much and why—well, I'd just have to see how that went.

In a short while, I walked outside the cemetery with

Mamie and stood beside her at her car. "Did you figure out, from all the people who showed up, who might have killed Bethany?" she asked.

We'd been shadowed here. A couple of the suits I'd noticed before stood nearby and weren't subtle about watching us.

"I think the police still suspect you." I nodded in their direction.

She closed her eyes for a second, and when she opened them again, her expression blazed. "It wasn't me. How about . . . Cricket? She had a good reason. Why aren't they after her?"

"I don't know that they aren't," I said. "If they thought they had enough evidence, they'd have arrested you by now, I'd imagine. That may mean they're still checking into other people, too. Just like you, Cricket's an obvious choice—although taking over a shelter and organization like she did? That might be a reason to protect someone's life instead of taking it."

There was no humor in Mamie's laugh. She got into her car. "I'm going home now," she said sadly. "My empty home. The place I hope I can keep living, instead of prison." She closed her door and started driving away.

"Lauren?"

A flash from a camera blinded me for an instant when I turned to see Miguel, and behind him some of those damned paparazzi. They must have followed him to take his picture, and now I was memorialized, too.

"Hi," I said. "It was a lovely service, Miguel."

"Yes. Thanks." His handsome actor's face scrunched into a grimace of a smile. "Even Bethany's ex-husbands were impressed."

"It's great that you get along," I prompted. "And also

very nice that they came to her funeral." Okay, I was getting tired of following rules of etiquette—I wanted some
answers. "Why did they come?"

"Money," he said briefly. "My dear Bethany put in her
will that they, and I, would get paid to appear at her funeral,
if she passed before we did. She made sure to tell us all—
although it wasn't enough for any of us to kill her, of
course."

I was flabbergasted—not only that Mamie had guessed
that possibility, but that it was true and that Miguel dis-
closed it.

"Before you accuse us of anything, they both assured
me they didn't kill her. And I know I didn't."

But I didn't really know that. I couldn't cross the others
off my list because of what they might, or might not, have
said to Miguel. And just because he'd seemed to really
grieve for Bethany didn't mean he hadn't killed her.

"So," he continued, "are you going to make HotRescues a part of Pet Shelters Together? I just heard from some
of the members that you're considering it. That would be
great. And smart."

His tone, when he said the last, made me wonder what
his underlying meaning was. Would I somehow be in danger if I chose not to sign up HotRescues?

Enlisting wasn't my intention. But using the possibility
as an excuse to ask a lot of questions was.

"So you're still affiliated with Pet Shelters Together?" I
blurted that out without thinking.

"It's part of Bethany's legacy," he said. "So, yes, I still
intend to help out in any way I can."

Did that mean he considered it his mission, in memory
of Bethany?

Or, like being here, was he going to be paid by her estate to stay involved?

Yes, I still had a lot of questions.

And, no, I hadn't yet eliminated anyone from my list of murder suspects.

Not Mamie. Not Miguel. Not Bethany's exes.

More research to come.

Chapter 21

I don't ever consider attending a funeral, even for someone I'd hardly known, an enjoyable way to spend a day. I always like being in charge, but not solving murders—and this investigation was getting nowhere fast.

Even so, I wouldn't give up. Not if I might be able to help Mamie. I'd made the decision to help her, taken it on as a responsibility. That meant I'd continue trying.

But I'd nevertheless have to stop if it took all my time. At the top of my to-do list, now and always, was to take care of the animals at HotRescues and make sure that as many as possible were adopted into appropriate households.

Okay, that was second on my list. First was to ensure that my own kids were doing well—especially since they were in town and I might be able to check on them in person. I called each from my car before getting on the road. Both answered right away, which made me smile. Unsurprisingly, both were in the middle of the plans they'd already made.

So, their take-charge mom wasn't going to be able to take charge of them just now. But the good thing was that they had compared notes, and both planned to join me for brunch tomorrow before heading back to their campuses. Mom would get a couple of hours of their time. Mom's treat, of course.

Mom was delighted.

So, next on that ever-growing list? A home visit—one I'd undertaken a week ago without giving notice to my target household, and had not found anyone around. Today was Saturday. I'd brought the phone number along, and the call was answered right away.

Consequently, I would make a stop in Northridge before going to HotRescues.

After heading up the San Diego Freeway and taking surface streets into Northridge, I returned to the house I'd popped in at last week after checking on how Carmen Herrera was doing with her new adopted kitty, Queen J. Again, no dogs greeted me from the large fenced yard, but they barked from inside.

When I rang the bell, Margie Tarbet answered the door immediately. Both Beardsley and Moe sat behind her, wiggling on their butts as if they wanted to leap up and greet me. Obviously, she had trained them well.

Which made me feel even better that they'd found a home with this organized and caring lady.

"How wonderful to see you, Lauren." She squeezed my hand, and then I entered her small but pristinely maintained house, and was led into her neat, compact living room. That must have been her signal to the dogs, or they took it that way. Both leaped over to me and butted me with their heads, demanding that I pet them. I complied, of course.

Margie, short and a little overweight but dressed nicely in a blue shirt tucked into gray slacks, was a nurses' aid at a nearby hospital. That had been her profession when she had adopted the medium-sized, black, long-muzzled pup Moe, whose heritage I hadn't been able to guess, and the gray cat Nemo, whom I hadn't seen yet today. She'd entered it on our application then, and had done so again a few weeks ago when she'd dropped in and fallen in love with large, red Briard mix Beardsley. A born caretaker. One who loved pets.

A perfect adopter—at least in theory. I had to make sure all was going well.

"Would you like some lemonade?" Margie asked. "I don't have much around in the way of people treats, but I may be able to find some of my son's cookies."

Speaking of whom, a gawky human form came barreling down the hall from the area containing first the kitchen, with a couple of bedrooms in the back. I'd checked it all out on previous visits.

Including the gawky human. He was Margie's son Davie, a high school student, although I didn't remember which grade. A senior, I believed.

"Lauren . . . Ms. Vancouver. It's so nice to see you!" He stopped in front of me, and I saw that Nemo the cat was in his arms, not looking especially thrilled about it. "Mom told me you were on your way. I'll show you what good care we're taking of Nemo, Moe, and Beardsley. How are things at HotRescues? Are all your animals okay?"

I knew Davie was a chatterbox. He'd talked nonstop when he'd come with Margie first to look at our residents, then pick the latest one to take home. He had something positive to say about each animal. I had the sense that, if he'd been able to, he'd have taken every one of them home with him. The only time I managed to get him to keep quiet was when I answered his questions about how animals got rescued.

Margie's round cheeks had turned pink. "Calm down, Davie," she said in a no-nonsense tone that I figured she must also use while training the dogs.

I just smiled. "Everything at HotRescues is fine," I said. "You're welcome to visit anytime."

"I sent a neighbor to see you," he responded. "Mrs. Herrera, a few blocks away. She adopted a cat, too, didn't she? I love to send people to HotRescues. You take such good care of the animals, like Nemo. Animals rock." He looked down at the bored cat in his arms, hugged her, then put her down. Then he knelt on the floor beside Beardsley and Moe, and the three of them started to wrestle.

I accompanied Margie into her kitchen and sipped some lemonade, just to be friendly. But I'd seen what I needed to here. The two previously adopted animals were thriving, and now so was Beardsley. Margie obviously cared about them, and Davie adored them.

I wished all home visits yielded such positive results.

On my way to HotRescues a little while later, my mind only stayed briefly on the house I'd just visited. Mostly, I thought again about the funeral. And Mamie. And how she hadn't been arrested, though the cops appeared to be watching her. But they were watching others, too.

Since my intent was to help Mamie, which primarily meant ensuring that she wasn't railroaded, maybe I didn't need to focus as much on looking for whoever killed Bethany.

Or maybe I did. I never gave up, and the matter hadn't

yet been resolved. An idea for continuing my investigation had started to germinate in my mind.

It might not lead to anything but discord in my life, but what the hell? If anyone could handle it, I could. Hadn't I survived my horrendous second marriage—and in fact become a better person for it?

But I'd have to lay a little groundwork first.

When I arrived at HotRescues, I said hi to Bev, who was in charge of the welcome room. Nina had gone off to volunteer at one of the city animal care centers.

Next, I took my usual walk through the shelter area, patting all the residents and assuring them that I was looking for the right homes for them and hoped to place them as soon as possible. I'm not sure that Junior, Dodi, or Hannibal, some of our longest-term rescues, still believed me, but I was serious.

I went upstairs in the center building to check in with Angie, our vet tech. Dr. Mona was with her, and I gave them a recap of our latest adoptions. I always liked it when Mona was there to meet prospective adopters in person, but because she was part-time, I relied both on what she had taught me and on her talking to people by phone. If she wasn't available at all, I felt comfortable approving adoptions on my own, of course, but that wasn't my preferred way.

Next, I went to my office and called Dante. He answered his cell phone right away. Never mind that he was the CEO of the largest pet supplies retailer in the country, or the benefactor of HotRescues and the wildlife sanctuary Hot-Wildlife. Big, important honcho that he was, he remained accessible.

"Hi, Lauren. What's going on? I heard on the news that Bethany Urber's funeral was today. Were you there?"

"Yes. It was definitely a grand affair. She'd have approved.

That's partly the reason I called." I laid out my plan. "So you may hear that I'm doing something completely out of character, not in HotRescues' best interests. But it's not what it'll sound like, and I have a good reason."

"I get it," he said. "That's one thing I've always appreciated about you, Lauren. You take on problems head-on and find solutions. Even when they're not *your* problems."

When we hung up, I took a deep breath, pondering if I really wanted to do this.

The answer was both yes and no, but I'm not a wishy-washy person. My mind was made up, and I knew I could control the situation even if it became unpleasant.

I called Cricket Borley next. She, too, answered right away. "I've been thinking," I said, "especially after poor Bethany's funeral. I'm intrigued by what she started. I'd like to sign HotRescues up for Pet Shelters Together." My teeth involuntarily clenched after I spoke that lie. I didn't truly like the idea, but I was following through for other reasons.

Cricket didn't know that. "That's wonderful, Lauren! Bethany would have been so pleased. We're having a planning meeting on Monday night, and it'd be great if you could attend. It'll be at the Better Than Any Pet Rescues shelter."

"See you then." I shook my head as I hung up. It wasn't a mistake. But it wasn't something I was proud of, either. Would I come to regret it even more?

Good thing I'd decided to do it, though, since that evening Mamie called me, hysterical—and sounding as confused as the first time she had called me after all those years I hadn't heard from her.

"Mr. Caramon says those detectives want to talk to me again, Lauren. I don't have anything else to say to them. Tell him, please."

"Tell who—a detective?"

"No. Mr. Caramon. Then he can tell the police, and they'll leave me alone."

Poor thing. The latest phone call may have driven her nearly over the edge again. "It doesn't work that way," I said softly. "You just do whatever Mr. Caramon says, okay?"

"But you'll still help me, too, won't you, Lauren?"

"Yes," I said. "I will."

Chapter 22

Zoey was eagerly awaiting me when I got home that night. The kids had been in and out of the house, but she'd been alone most of the day. I gave her a big hug, then took her for a nice long walk.

I'd gotten a call from Matt on my way home. We met for a drink after I fed Zoey and myself, but only a drink, since my kids were in town. Matt told me about the kind of demonstration he was working out for HotRescues. "But before we schedule anything, I need to take another look at the new construction, and how it's progressing."

Since he wanted to see it during daylight, I arranged to meet him there the next day, after I had brunch with the kids.

Brunch, by the way, was outstanding—and not just because Tracy and Kevin picked out one of my favorite family restaurants to have it at. The company couldn't have been better. Summer classes were going well for both of them. They enjoyed their jobs.

And they both seemed happy to spend some time with their lonesome mom.

Both were eager to pop in at HotRescues, so I brought them along for my session with Matt. I took the whole group over to see the progress on the new building. I even led them up to see the outer balconies on the second floor.

"This is cool, Mom," Kevin said, walking outside and leaning over the short concrete wall to gaze toward the ground below. Which made my heart stop. Eventually, there would be safety railings out there, but for now it looked like too easy an area to fall from.

"It's perfect!" Matt said, earning a confused look from Tracy that probably resembled mine. "For the demo, I mean. You know that the SmART team practices sliding down mountainsides on ropes, using all kinds of mountain rescue equipment. The idea is to be prepared for any kind of small animal rescue, no matter how difficult."

"They did a great job rescuing those beagle puppies from where they'd been tossed down a storm drain," I remarked.

"Their preparedness training definitely helped with that. So why not give them an exercise in sliding off a building? They could start right here, and you could have a crowd below watching them. They'd be able to rescue MARTE just fine from this location." He looked at my kids. "That's their little stuffed animal who's always getting into a lot of trouble and needing to be rescued in training sessions."

"Cool," Kevin said. Tracy just smiled. They had both met Matt before, knew we were seeing each other, but I'd made it clear we were just friends. I didn't want them to think I was about to present them with another father substitute, even though Matt was a whole lot nicer than Charles had ever been.

"I like the idea," I said. "When could they do it?"

"I'll talk to the team leader a little more about dates and times, then you and I can coordinate it."

"Perfect." I'd let Dante know right away that his fund-raiser-publicity event was going to be awesome.

The kids left to return to their schools a few hours later. I'd gone home with them to watch them pack, and I even drove Tracy to Bob Hope Airport.

I felt pretty lonesome as I headed back to HotRescues. Matt had left at the same time the kids and I did, so I didn't have his company. I did, however, visit with our residents and a few dedicated volunteers for a while, not even heading to my office to address mounting paperwork.

Good thing I didn't. A lady around my age, in fraying jeans with a nice umber-colored shirt tucked into them, arrived wanting to pick out a cat to adopt. "I live in North-ridge," she said. "Near the Tarbets. They told me that the best place in the area to find the ideal pet is right here."

"They're really nice people, aren't they? Oh, and by the way, they happen to be right."

She laughed, and I accompanied her personally into one of the cat rooms in our middle building—where mostly young adult kitties were housed. One of our volunteers, Sally, a student who only worked on weekends, came along. The woman—Trix, she said her name was—laughed at the felines' antics on the miscellaneous stands and other recreation equipment we'd obtained from HotPets and installed to keep our cats exercised and occupied. In only a few minutes, she'd narrowed her choices down to two: a calico and a yellow kitty.

"Maybe . . . do you think it's a good idea to adopt two at the same time?" She looked at me with troubled brown eyes. "I just lost my only cat about a month ago, and it's been so hard adjusting. If I get two, I might not wind up all alone this way—but only if it's okay for them, too."

"Let's let them help with the decision, okay?"

With Sally's assistance, I moved the two she was considering into an otherwise empty room. We put them down on the floor and watched them. They didn't exactly bond right in front of our eyes as lifelong friends, or if they were they didn't show us. Neither did they display hissy fits.

"Here's what we'll do," I said to Trix. "If you're interested in adopting them, come back to our welcome area and fill out the paperwork. I require an application so I'll know the kind of environment you'll provide—a house or apartment—and a contract where you'd make some promises about how you'll treat them. Also, you'd give permission for someone from HotRescues to drop in and visit now and then to be sure everything is going okay. I may want to see your place first, but if you could bring back any pictures of your home, that would be fine, too." The knowledge that she was another in a list of referrals from the Tarbets worked in her favor. "Assuming everything pans out, you can adopt them both, but if there's ever any trouble between them, or otherwise, you can bring one or both of them back."

I went into my office and called Margie Tarbet while Trix filled out the forms. "Oh, yes, I know her, Lauren," Margie said. "Not well, though. She lives a few blocks from me. I wasn't aware that she'd lost her cat, poor thing. I didn't refer her to you, but I would have if I'd known she was looking. Must have been Davie. Hold on a sec."

It was over a minute before Davie got on the phone. "I'm the one who sent her there, Lauren," he said. "I hope that's okay. I take Moe and Beardsley on lots of walks, so I know

what's going on with people and pets around here. Sometimes I—I mean, I stopped to talk to Trix the other day and
she really seemed to want a new cat after losing hers, so . . .
I knew you'd do a great job of helping her." He paused for
a moment, then said, "She seems like a nice lady to me. I
know you check references and all that. It's one of the
really great things about HotRescues."

I smiled at his enthusiasm, said goodbye, and hung up,
then went back into the welcome room.

Trix's paperwork passed muster with me. She invited
me to go with her right away to her place, but I declined—
instead just looking the house up on Google Earth as she
watched and pointed out its features. She promised she
would keep both kitties indoors—a major consideration
before I permitted any cat adoptions.

I called and made an appointment for her to talk to
Mona the next day. Assuming our shrink had the same
opinion I did, this lady would be able to pick up her new
kitties within a couple of days. She seemed thrilled.

When she left, after hugging her prospective kitties, I
went back into the shelter area, found Sally, and we high-
fived. More HotRescues residents had most likely found
what I hoped would be a good home.

A little later, I called Dante about Matt's idea. He loved it.
I called Matt with some dates and times Dante suggested.
We picked a couple that he thought matched SmART's
availability, but he'd double-check.

He also told me that a few more animals rescued from
Mamie's were finally available to private shelters. Otherwise, due to an influx of other animals at city facilities,
their lives might be in danger. Fortunately, no euthanasia

would occur at least for another couple of days if no one took them in.

"I'll take some," I assured him. "And I'll be meeting with other rescuers tomorrow. One way or another, I'll make sure to find a place for all of them."

"Somehow, that doesn't surprise me." I heard a note in his voice that suggested more than relief.

Turned out that neither of us had any plans for that evening . . . until we spoke. We decided to grab a light dinner together. Brunch was still taking up room in my stomach, so I didn't want anything heavy.

We rented a DVD of a movie we'd both missed, a romantic comedy, and he accompanied me back to my home.

The rest of the evening? Well, it turned out not so lonesome after all.

The PST meeting wasn't until seven the next evening, which gave me a lot of time to anticipate what would happen.

After getting to HotRescues that morning, and doing my first walk-through, I phoned Cricket to confirm I'd be there, and also to ask that she put into the agenda a request that everyone take in more rescues from the hoarding situation.

She sounded thrilled. "Of course, Lauren. I'm sure we'll be able to accommodate all of them. That's what a network like this is for."

I intended to use it to try to find a murderer, but I didn't tell her that.

However, the conversation reminded me of the number one suspect, and if I'd understood correctly, today was when her next police interrogation was scheduled. I'd no idea what time, so I called Mamie.

"It's at eleven o'clock this morning, Lauren." Her voice was soft and choked and scared. "Mr. Caramon is picking me up soon. Have you figured it out yet?"

"You mean what happened to Bethany?"

"She was murdered."

"Yes, I know," I said patiently, although I was a little confused. "What do you want me to figure out?"

"Who killed her. I didn't like her, I yelled at her, but I didn't kill her. So, who did?"

"I'm still working on that," I said. A thought occurred to me. "But if you really want me to try to help, you can't tell the police I'm doing anything. It's our secret, okay?" I wasn't sure she even knew what a secret was, at least with her once more befuddled state of mind.

"Okay," she said.

"I'll call you later," I told her.

Which I did, mid-afternoon, but got no answer. Nor did I reach her an hour later. I went out to the welcome area, where Nina was holding down the rescue fort, and asked her to check on the Internet to see if she could find a "Mr. Caramon" who was most likely a public defender in L.A. She did, with no trouble. I called his office and was told he was out with a client, and had been all afternoon.

That didn't bode well for poor Mamie, or so I figured.

Which made what I intended to do that evening potentially more important. Could I preserve her freedom?

Could I prove her innocence by figuring out who killed Bethany?

Or was Mamie in danger of imminent arrest—for something she had actually done?

Chapter 23

Once again, I felt as if I'd relocated to the southeastern United States of a century and a half ago as I walked up to the huge, ornate gate at Better Than Any Pet Rescues. I arrived at the same time as a couple of other people who looked familiar both from Bethany's funeral and my visit here for the hoarder discussion, but I didn't recall their names. Even so, since I was here under somewhat false pretenses as one of them, I smiled and held out my hand. "Hi, I'm Lauren Vancouver."

"We know," said a young African American woman with light-toned skin and a solemn expression I couldn't read. "I'm Sylvia Lodner. I understand you've decided to join PST."

"That's right."

"Why?" asked the other woman, taller than me with puffy golden hair. "You run HotRescues, don't you, and you're funded by the guy who owns HotPets? I'm Raelene

Elder, by the way. I'm the chief administrator of Redondo Rescues."

I'd already thought of an answer, but the gate opened and all three of us headed inside.

Instead of Bethany greeting visitors from the top of the stairs leading into the plantation house, Cricket stood there. She didn't look as fashionable or elegant as her predecessor— and didn't wear the antique-looking gown she'd had on at Bethany's funeral—but she seemed to be an enthusiastic hostess, smiling and ushering us all inside. She wore a peach-colored suit with a floral blouse, business-like yet not especially formal.

"I'll address your wonderful news first, Lauren," she told me after waving us all toward the first-floor conference room where the prior meeting had been held.

Which item of news? I wondered, but I didn't have long to wait.

I slid into an aisle seat halfway down the group of mostly occupied chairs, and saw I was right behind Darya and Lan Price. They both turned to say hi, just as Cricket took her place at the front of the room and began speaking.

"Welcome to the regular monthly meeting of Pet Shelters Together, everyone. Some of you already know her, but I want to introduce you first thing to Lauren Vancouver. She's the head of HotRescues, and she is interested in joining our network. Please stand, Lauren."

I tried not to roll my eyes as I complied. Being singled out and applauded wasn't something I enjoyed, but I could understand why she did so.

"Lauren also has some other good news for us. A bunch more of the animals rescued from that"—she made a face that probably curled my hair as much as hers—"terrible hoarding situation need to be rescued from the city shelter system within the next couple of days. I've assured her that our network will find room for every one of them. Right?"

"Right!" came the enthusiastic reply. Okay, I'm not a particularly emotional person, but their response made my eyes tear up.

"I'll pass around a sign-up sheet. Everyone write down your shelter and how many animals you could take in, if necessary." Cricket waved a spiral notebook in her hand, opened it to the first page, and handed it to a person in the first row.

I wondered how many rescue organizations belonged to PST. Judging by this group, there had to be nearly two dozen.

Unsurprisingly, some of the people I wanted to hear more dirt about—the men who'd been part of Bethany's life—were not here.

Cricket next gave a short eulogy of Bethany, although I thought that most, if not all, of these attendees had been at her funeral. This would have been a good time for me to talk, but I didn't want to interrupt whatever program Cricket had devised for this evening. My intent wasn't to incur her wrath—at least not any sooner than necessary.

She moved into some business items that sounded as if they were left over from Bethany's tenure.

Discussion ensued. Some of it was interesting, including the suggestion that their current provider of supplies might need to be replaced with a more reliable source of good food and other items for less money. Perfect opportunity for me to jump in to show I could be a valuable member of the group. I raised my hand.

"Lauren?" Cricket called on me with a smile. "Are you going to suggest HotPets as our supplier?"

"We know you have an in with the owner," Raelene said dryly. She'd taken a seat in the front row and had turned to look at me. "Will he sell us great stuff cheap?"

I laughed. "I can't guarantee anything other than the quality of the products I get from HotPets, but I'd definitely suggest that you get a proposal from them along with whatever other sources you're looking at. I'll put in a good word for Pet Shelters Together."

That earned a group laugh in response.

Other discussion ensued, including suggestions on other pet rescue organizations people knew about that might be good fits as new members. That earned me a number of glances, too—as if some of these people welcomed me, and others were questioning my attendance. Oh, well.

Finally, the meeting appeared to be drawing to a close. "Is there any more old business we should discuss?" Cricket asked.

Silence.

"Any new business?"

My turn. I raised my hand.

"Lauren?" Cricket sounded surprised as she recognized me.

"May I join you up there?" I asked. "I have something I'd like to discuss with everybody."

She didn't say no, so I joined her at the front and turned toward the crowd.

"I may be speaking out of turn, but there's something I'd like to do, to recognize and thank Bethany. If it weren't for her, I wouldn't be here. And"—I didn't need Mamie's approval or forgiveness for what I was about to say, and I intended not to criticize her here . . . too much—"a lot of animals would want to thank her, too, if they could, especially the ones recently saved from a terrible hoarding situation."

That earned me some applause again. These people were definitely enthusiastic. Maybe that would help with what I was about to do.

"In recognition of Bethany, I'd like to do something special. What I have in mind is to create a Web site in her honor, or maybe just a separate Web page for the Pet Shelters Together and Better Than Any Pet Rescues sites." They were separate, but already linked together. "I want to collect any photos all of you have of her, and have some of the best posted. Also any recollections you have of her. I'm going to pass out my e-mail address for HotRescues, and I'd like for every one of you to send me at least one quote I can use, preferably more."

I paused but made sure my expression didn't waver— even though the crux of my request was pending.

"It doesn't have to be all pats on the back," I continued. "I'd like to know your recollections of her, good and bad. I'll edit them, but I want to include a genuine snapshot of who she was. How did you meet her? When did you join Pet Shelters Together? Which seemed to be her favorite member shelters and why? Which of you administrators did she seem to favor, and why? Did she give you any directions to change your approach to pet rescues? Did you know her personally? Did she ever talk to you about her love life?" I laughed at that, even though I was serious. "Did you meet people she'd selected for adoptions of animals from Better Than Any Pet Rescues, and what did they say about her?" Did any complain . . . enough to sound as if they had a motive to kill her? "Whatever."

Their responses, and attitudes, might give me a lot to look into . . . but these people, as a group, probably knew

Bethany well. At least a few might have disliked her, or have valid suspicions about who disliked her more.

"Should we throw in anything about how we saw her get along with your friend Mamie Spelling?" Sylvia called. Her snide expression suggested that she was determined to become a thorn in my side. On the other hand, facing issues head-on was always my style.

"Why not?" I responded. "I don't want to libel anyone with what I put together to remember Bethany, but if you have an interesting anecdote, send it along." Even if it was about Mamie. I couldn't rule Mamie out. If I got enough evidence against her, I'd let her lawyer know, at least, before turning it over to the cops. I turned to Cricket, whose smile looked thin as she watched me. "Thanks," I said.

As I'd hoped, my request generated some comments as we all trooped out of the room. Sylvia Lodner was the first to join me. "Bethany wasn't always easy to get along with," she said. "You know that your attempted pat-on-the-back to our deceased leader may bring up a lot of bad stuff instead."

"I think it'll be a good thing to get a full perspective," I said. "I may even write a biography of her. She was certainly an interesting person, with her starting and selling a successful cosmetics company, then taking charge of pet rescues that way." I stopped on the porch. "I'll bet you'll have a lot to contribute about her. I'd love to quote you on the site and, maybe, in the book."

The face I'd considered unreadable before now looked as pleased as if I'd offered to write a flattering biography of her. "I'll be in touch," she said, waving one of the business cards I'd handed out.

Good, I thought. She didn't seem the type to mince words.

I noticed the Prices exiting the door, talking to one another. "How about you?" I asked. "Can I count on you to send me some quotes about Bethany?"

"Good or bad?" Lan laughed. "I don't get why you'd want anything less than happy stuff, but I'll bet that, if people are honest, the bad'll way outweigh the good."

"Lan!" Darya sounded upset. "Bethany was a nice enough person. She had a kind heart for animals, at least."

Her attitude was the same as I'd heard before. Nevertheless, I'd follow up with this couple to learn more about their time with Bethany.

I talked to some of the rest, too, as they left, including the other person I'd walked in with, Raelene.

As the place emptied out, I found myself standing on the porch with Cricket. "Great meeting," I said. "I'll look forward to many more."

"Will you?" she asked, much too shrewdly for my comfort. "What's that Web page thing really about, Lauren? Are you still trying to help that lunatic Mamie?"

I didn't try to defend Mamie. Didn't even want to, since she genuinely might be a lunatic. She'd definitely harmed animals, which made her repugnant to everyone who'd been here tonight. Even, in that respect, me.

"I'm not trying to help anyone," I said, which was largely true, since all I might do is underscore all the evidence against Mamie. "But I feel bad about my attitude toward Bethany before she died, and this is the only way I can think of to make up for it." Especially if I happened to figure out who killed her.

Cricket shook her head slowly, but even so her curls bounced around her face, looking too perky for the sorrowful expression she wore. "Bethany was a complicated person, Lauren. I suspect that, once you start receiving the quotes you asked for, you'll drop this project for lack of nice things to say about her."

I couldn't resist—especially since I deemed Cricket to be one of my best suspects. "How about you?" I asked. "Will you have anything nice to say about her?"

"Me?" She looked shocked. "Of course. She was my friend. My boss. She taught me so much about pet rescues. I just hope to do an adequate job of filling her shoes." I thought this lady did protest too much.

"And is there anything not so nice you can add to that?"

Cricket just glared at me. "No one's perfect. Good night, Lauren."

She nodded in the direction of the parking lot, obviously intending that I head that way.

Perversely, though I didn't want to hang around, I walked slowly, not wanting her to feel in control. Never mind that I'd encouraged her somewhat by indicating I would join the network of pet rescuers she now ran. Before I descended more than a couple of steps, I heard a noise behind me. I turned back.

Miguel Rohrig was there. Where had he come from?

Once I'd learned that Bethany had lived in an apartment upstairs, I'd assumed Miguel stayed there with her . . . while she was alive. I'd no idea where he lived now. Here, still?

And where had he been on the night of Bethany's murder?

He suddenly joined me on the step I'd reached. "Lauren. Hi. Got a few minutes? I'd like to chat with you."

I glanced up toward the porch where Cricket remained. She glowered at me, her look stating that she wanted me gone. Immediately. Just as her words and actions had suggested only a minute ago.

Only one response I could make. "Of course, Miguel. I'd like to talk to you, too. Where—here, on the porch?"

He glanced at Cricket. "Why don't we go grab a drink?"

His meaning was obvious. He didn't want her to listen in.

"Fine with me," I said. "See ya." I waved to Cricket and walked down the steps more spiritedly, Miguel beside me.

Chapter 24

I agreed to drive, since my car was right there, in the parking area near the walkway from the porch. Miguel said his was in a garage behind the building.

I'd hoped to do another walk-through of the shelter area while I was there that day, not because I figured any animals were being mistreated, but because seeing residents was always important to me when I visited a rescue facility. It hadn't worked out this time, but I'd probably be back. Soon.

Plus, I needed the final count of how many animals the members of PST could take in from the hoarding release. Kathy Georgio had already promised to take in as many as five dogs and an equal number of cats.

"Nice car," Miguel said as he got into the passenger seat of my Venza.

"Thanks." I wondered whether he was just trying to put me at ease before he killed me, as he'd done with Bethany.

Yes, I was suspicious of him, but levelheaded as well. If he wasn't trying to kill me, he might help me narrow down suspects, assuming I could subtly move our conversation that direction. Besides, he was aware that Cricket knew we were planning on getting a drink. It'd be stupid to harm me when a witness could tell the cops we left together—especially a witness who didn't seem to like him.

Unless it was an act, Cricket and Miguel were lovers, and they'd both planned to get rid of me this way . . .

I don't usually have a murderous imagination. I doubted that either of these people believed I had zeroed in on them as favored suspects in Bethany's murder. My stupid musings were getting me nowhere.

I pulled the car onto the road. "Where are we going?"

"An Irish pub okay with you?"

It was fine, and the only speaking we did for the next few minutes involved his guiding me to our destination, O'Henry's on Century Boulevard, located inside a shopping center. I parked and we headed for the small bar.

Although it was busy, the crowd seemed tamer than I was used to seeing in pubs—or maybe it was a time that there were no sports of interest that could be shown on the TVs mounted high on the walls. The lighting was muted, and nearly all the tables were occupied. We sat at a small table and both ordered Guinness beers imported from the host country, Ireland. Miguel, despite being a waiter by profession, seemed quite at home as a euphemistically called "guest" instead.

"So," Miguel said when our server had left. "You still think I killed Bethany, don't you? But you're wise enough to check into other possibilities, in case the cops don't ultimately see things your way."

I felt myself blink at him, as if he'd suddenly found a

way to copy a page of my thoughts onto a computer and print it out. "I haven't drawn any conclusions yet," I told him, then added honestly, "and I find it really frustrating."

He laughed. I could see why Bethany had chosen this younger man as her boyfriend. He wasn't just cute and sexy, with his dark, wavy hair and handsome appearance, but he seemed smart. Direct in what he had to say, in a disconcerting but charming way.

"I'm not sure trying to set all those women on each other will get you what you want to know," he said, "although it's a good approach. At least most are female. More women than men appear to run shelters in this area—or maybe it's because Bethany was more inclined to invite women administrators to join her network." At my wary gaze, he said, "I was cavesdropping, of course." His smile was disarming. "Bethany got me involved with it when she was alive—maybe more than I wanted to be, then. I thought it took too much time from my auditioning for film roles. That was one of our main bones of contention—appropriate term for someone involved with saving dogs, don't you think? She also wanted me to do more to help manage BTA, too. We argued about it, yes. Now that she's gone, I'd like to do more, in her memory, but Cricket wants me to butt out—which gives me even more incentive to stay involved. Somewhat, at least. I like animals, don't want to see them suffer, but I leave the rescue stuff to people like her. And you." His smile deepened.

Did he suggest that we get together tonight so he could try to convince me of his innocence? If so, was it because he was guilty?

I'd ask him. What was the harm? We were in public, and I was interested in his response.

Our server placed our filled glasses on the advertising

coasters that were already on the table. When he had left again, Miguel raised his drink in a toast.

"Here's to finding the truth. May it not be any more painful than the loss of Bethany."

I noticed the dampness sparkling in his eyes despite the dark atmosphere in the pub. I remembered his emotionalism before, too, and how I'd not been certain of its veracity—or if it was just a sign that he was a good actor.

"I'll drink to that." I sipped my lager. It was good and dark and cold, and it went down smoothly. Seemed appropriate, considering who I was with.

I didn't need to pose my question. He directly addressed what I was curious about. "So here's my take on it, Lauren. I assume you want to hear it?"

"Why not?"

"I've already told you that neither Bethany's ex-husbands nor I killed her. Have you talked to either of them?"

"No, but I intend to."

"Good. Then you'll know I'm right."

"Maybe."

He smiled again. "Of course. You don't take anything for granted." I felt my eyes dart toward the table, in case that elusive computer printout of my thoughts was there . . . "Okay, then. My opinion? If it wasn't Mamie, I'd choose Cricket as the murderer. If not her, there are a few members of PST who argued with Bethany even more than I did." A fond expression softened his hard features. "She really loved being in charge and telling everyone what to do. It was part of her charm."

Everyone to his own tastes, I thought. That would be a big turn-off to me in a relationship—someone even more demanding than me. But I said to Miguel, "Who else did she argue with?"

"There was one person who adopted a dog from BTA who was always calling to complain. She asked for Cricket a lot. She loved her dog but nitpicked about things like food and training he'd been given while he was there. She also claimed she wanted Bethany to leave her alone, not call her all the time and give orders about how to treat her own dog."

"Who is she?" I asked.

"Her name is Nalla Croler, I think. Strange name. Stranger woman. She adopted a pit bull mix—a really sweet dog she renamed Pitsy."

"Have you spoken with her? Do you have any contact information?"

"I doubt she's the killer, but, yes, I can e-mail you her data if you give me your address."

I pulled a HotRescues business card from my purse and handed it to him.

"And who did Bethany argue with most at PST?" I asked.

"Most? Probably Raelene Elder of Redondo Rescues. Darya Price was new with the group, and I know she and Bethany had some disagreements, too. Then there's Sylvia Lodner, another member. I'll try to come up with some more. If Bethany didn't argue with someone, there was probably something wrong with them."

"Got it." I tried to think of a tactful way to address what I wanted to ask next, then gave up. Tact wasn't really necessary anyway. "I gather that you lived with Bethany. Were you home on the night she was killed?"

He laughed. "I figured you might ask that. The police sure did. The answer is no. There was a huge private party at Esplendido that night. It lasted way into the wee hours, and those of us who worked were put up in a nearby hotel for what was left of the night. I didn't have a roommate, so

I can't prove I didn't leave and come back. But I swear to you, I didn't kill Bethany."

"Okay," I said, as if I completely bought into his alibi. I soon finished my beer, and so did Miguel. On our way back to BTA to drop him off, I pretended to be teasing as I asked more about his disagreements with Bethany. He parried all with humor—and ease.

Sure, he could be the killer, but I tucked him at the bottom of my list, just above Mamie.

Even so, I remembered well what the detective who'd been after me for murder a few short months ago had said. Detective Stefan Garciana had confided his investigation methods to me. He did an exercise with every case he was assigned, analyzing how each of the least likely suspects could have done it, then erasing them as he eliminated aspects like genuine opportunity and realistic motive. I'd told Carlie, and she'd recently reminded me of what he'd said.

I couldn't wholly discount Miguel as a suspect, nor the people he believed couldn't have killed Bethany.

As a result, I made a couple of calls the next morning, after arriving at HotRescues. Not first thing, though. I had to check my e-mail, see what kinds of praise and accusations the members of PST had sent along to me about Bethany.

There were already quite a few. Most were tactful, starting out by saying how much they appreciated Bethany and all she'd tried to do for the pet shelter community. Few said anything about what she'd done for the animals, though.

As I'd already figured, whatever Bethany had done, it had all been about her.

Several administrators described how rosy they thought the future of PST would be under Cricket's auspices.

Then there were a few I decided to follow up on. Interestingly, those people included Raelene, Sylvia, and Darya. Maybe they'd been more honest than the rest, since I'd actually spoken with them. But even when they said good things about Bethany, the way things were phrased suggested an undercurrent of distaste for at least something in the way she'd handled situations. I needed to know more.

After printing out the interesting e-mails, I called and made appointments to meet with Bethany's ex-husbands. Both surprisingly agreed when I explained who I was. The second I talked to, John Jerremiah, clarified why: Miguel had been in touch.

I got together with John first. He was a film executive who'd gotten to know Bethany in her cosmetic sales days. I went to his Hollywood office, off Sunset Boulevard, to chat.

I'd noticed at the funeral that he was much older than Bethany had been, maybe in his seventies. Interesting that she'd changed her taste in men so much. Or maybe she'd needed someone with more age to guide her until she reached the level of success she had.

In any event, John was tall, gray-haired, and dignified. He shook my hand firmly and motioned for me to have a seat. His office was small but poshly decorated. It wasn't within one of the studios, but ornately framed posters on the wall indicated he had been affiliated with a lot of successful movies—as a producer, I gathered—which meant connections and money.

"Good to meet you, Lauren. I know Dante DeFrancisco and his connection to HotRescues."

Interesting, I thought. If, when I left here, I still considered John a suspect, I'd have to ask Dante his opinion.

"Thanks for seeing me." I went through the brief litany I'd used in our phone conversation about recently having met Bethany and been impressed with her—and also being a friend of the person who was most likely her murderer. "I just wanted to check with other people she knew for ideas to throw at the police, to make sure they've considered all possibilities."

He laughed. "Very politic, Lauren. But I know you're here checking me out as a possible suspect. I'd figure that out even if I hadn't talked with Miguel. Nice guy, but a bit pushy. He's using this as an excuse to sound me out about a film role one of these days."

"Really?" I hadn't thought of that angle, but in some odd way it made sense.

"I'm sure that everyone you're talking to is assuring you they're innocent. Add me to the list. And let me be clear on this: In this instance, at least, it's true. Bethany and I parted on affable terms—profitable terms for her, I might add, but she gave me some really enjoyable years, so it was worth it. I hadn't seen her for a long time, and I thought of her with affection. There was something in her will that she had mentioned to me long ago, that she left me money to go to her funeral if she died before me, but I'd have been there anyway."

I left soon after, making notes to stick John's file within my murder-business plan way down at the bottom.

Innocent? I believed so. But he still remained a possibility.

Bethany's other ex, Sam Legroote, owned a card shop franchise in Newport Beach, which was down in Orange County. I hated to spend the time to go there, but Nina and

Angie were in charge at HotRescues and I knew the animals would do fine without me, even if I didn't manage to pop in till late that day. Once again, I'd left my poor Zoey at home alone, but she was sweet and resourceful and would be fine.

Sam was about two decades younger than John, and his attitude sucked. "Yeah, I hated the bitch," he said, his voice low because there were some customers browsing in his store, which was located in a trendy shopping area. He had only a thick fringe of brown hair, and I wondered if Bethany, who'd seemed all about appearances, had dropped him because he was going bald. "She dumped me a few years ago, just before she sold out her cosmetics company. Our settlement didn't allow for me to share in her proceeds." He, too, mentioned that Miguel had called. "He said you're trying to help a friend by pointing fingers at other people who might have wanted to kill her. Yeah, I had a grudge, but if I was going to do her in, I'd have done it way back when I was really mad because she'd screwed me."

Maybe. Or maybe he'd decided to play it cool, and get his revenge when he wouldn't appear on the top of anyone's radar.

I chatted with him a little more, even bought a couple of cute cards to send to Tracy and Kevin to convey my love to them, and left.

My notes: This guy's place in my murder analysis files would stay near the top for now.

Chapter 25

The next day, Wednesday, I intended to accomplish a lot, and not just my official duties at HotRescues. I woke up early, and Zoey and I headed to the shelter after grabbing quick breakfasts.

We arrived even earlier than Pete usually does. I parked and started toward the entrance to the front building . . . just as Zoey started tugging on her leash.

Uh-oh. The last time she'd done that, we'd been the ones to find one of the supposed owner relinquishments, outside camera range. But Brooke had done a lot more to enhance our observation capabilities—or so we'd discussed.

As I let Zoey lead me toward the end of the parking lot, around the corner, and into the alley behind the storage building at the back of HotRescues, I called Brooke.

She answered right away. Her voice was groggy. I'd awakened her, but that was part of our deal with her running security at HotRescues. "What's wrong, Lauren?" she demanded. "Karen was there on duty last night, not me. I can be there in twenty minutes."

"I'm not sure, but we may have . . . Hello." Zoey had stopped beside a large cardboard box near one of the doors in the fence where we could haul in supplies. She didn't have to tell me what she smelled. I could hear a cat meowing. "I'll check with Karen to see if anything was caught on camera," I told Brooke, "but it sounds like we had a feline dropped off last night. I'll have to open the box to confirm it, though."

"I'll call Karen, and I'll be there fast," Brooke said.

I knelt beside Zoey and hugged her, glancing up at the commercial buildings across the alley. I didn't see any movement. It was probably too early for the office workers to get there. As I looked around for the nearest visible camera at the top of our storage building, a minivan drove up. Pete had arrived. He parked fast and ran over to us. "What's that, Lauren?"

"I'm about to check." I still held my car key. After gently maneuvering Zoey to a spot behind me, I used the key to rip open the tape sealing the box, careful not to let the point drive too far inside in case what I suspected was true. Not that I had much doubt. The critter inside was meowing louder now, obviously knowing that something was going on around him—or her.

Unsurprisingly, when I peeled back a flap, I saw a gray, furry cat head. The poor little guy started moving frantically inside the box, and I was afraid he'd jump out and disappear before we could help him. I pushed the flap back and held it.

"Let's get him inside," I told Pete, who picked up the box. I used a key to open the nearest gate, and we went through the rear entrance.

"Should we check him out here?" Pete asked over the loud barking of a crew of dogs now on alert.

"There's an empty enclosure down there." I pointed to one beyond several filled with indignant, noisy canines. "Let's see what we've got before we decide what to do with him."

Since we were inside the fenced HotRescues grounds, I released Zoey's leash as soon as I shut the gate. Not that I was overly concerned that my smart pup would run off. But I always expected those who adopted pets from our shelter to take extra care of their new family members, and I always tried to practice what I preached—especially when failure to do so could endanger an animal.

Zoey dashed toward the front of HotRescues, as if she wanted to take the first look of the morning at our residents. She passed Karen, who had just emerged from the center building. Her blond hair was mussed, and her black security T-shirt was crumpled. She looked bleary-eyed, so I felt sure she'd been sleeping. No problem with that, as long as she'd done her scheduled walk-throughs. I asked, "Did Brooke reach you?"

"Yes. I'll check the camera footage right away to see if we captured anything interesting, but I wanted to see first if there was anything I could do to help."

"Please go grab a crate, so we'll have someplace to hang on to this kitty till we decide what to do with him," I said, and she hurried back into the center building.

Pete had taken the box inside the enclosure, and I shut the gate. He opened the top. The meows increased by several decibels.

"Let me get you some gloves," I said to Pete— unnecessarily, as it turned out, since our handyman was, as usual, ready for anything. He yanked a pair out of his back pocket and covered his hands before removing the kitty from the box.

He lifted him and checked underneath, hanging on despite how frenziedly the little cat squirmed and protested. "Well, he is a he, so we've been right about that." Pete stroked him in a manner that assured me that he was confirming there were no broken bones or other obvious problems.

Karen joined me again, this time holding a crate.

"Let's put him in there for now," I said, carefully entering the enclosure to join Pete and our new guest. "Angie's due here pretty soon, and after she checks him over, I'll have her run Mr. Kitty in for an official veterinary exam."

Once the cat was crated in a more substantial and comfortable container, I opened the box he'd arrived in.

Unsurprisingly, there was a note inside. This was another drop-off by someone alleging to be an owner relinquishing a pet. The note, printed on computer paper in a large, common font, said, "This is my good friend and pet Lionheart. I am sorry I can't keep him anymore, but I have heard that HotRescues rocks as a great place to find animals new homes. Please take good care of him."

I started to shake my head, then froze. And smiled.

Yes, I'd contact Matt yet again, but this time I had an idea—flimsy, maybe, but I just might be able to locate the someone who could explain these supposed relinquishments.

Something else to put on my busy agenda.

Angie arrived on schedule about half an hour later. Our vet tech checked out Lionheart, scanned him for a nonexistent microchip, proclaimed that he appeared healthy, and agreed to take him to The Fittest Pet Veterinary Clinic. "Say hi to Carlie for me, if she's there," I said. "Tell her I haven't forgotten that we're to grab a lunch together soon." Assuming my busy veterinarian friend wasn't heading off early to film her next *Fittest Pet* TV show.

By then, Karen had checked what had been recorded by the cameras in the area where Lionheart had been dumped. Notwithstanding the infrared capabilities that didn't require any light for the pictures to be taken, the screen showed only some off-camera shadows and motion, and an occasional shot of a person who kept his back to the camera and also wore a jacket hiked up to obscure his face. Apparently whoever had left the cat was once again smart enough to mostly stay out of the way of any potential filming—despite the fact that Brooke had upgraded the system again. Not only were the mechanisms camouflaged, but they panned back and forth.

Smart—yes. Even so, I intended to follow up with the clue that had been left.

Zoey and I took our first walk through the shelter for the day. Nina had arrived by the time we got back to the main building, and I filled her in on what had happened. But not what I had guessed.

It was past nine o'clock by then. Leaving Zoey with Nina, I went to the rear storage building and put some stuff into a paper bag. Then I headed—where? To Northridge, of course.

To the Tarbets' home. Under normal circumstances, I'd have called first. But I didn't want to alert my prey to my upcoming visit.

After parking and grabbing the bag from the passenger seat, I walked up to the fence surrounding the small house and carefully unlatched the gate, making sure none of the animals waited there to escape. Seeing no one, neither human nor pet, I approached the cottage's front door and rang the bell.

The two dogs started barking. I wasn't sure what Nemo the cat's reaction to hearing the bell was—observing curiously or deciding to hide. In a minute, I thought I heard someone behind the door, which had a peephole in it.

I smiled and held up the bag. "Hi," I called. "Sorry to bother you, but I forgot something the other day." Like asking Davie if he was dumping animals at HotRescues—only, I didn't suspect that was true four days ago.

The door opened slightly. Margie stood there, holding back the dogs, whose tails were wagging. Her presence was a bit of a disappointment. I'd figured the nurse's aide would be at work, and I would be able to talk to her son. But maybe this was better. He was a minor. I shouldn't just face him down without his mother being around.

"Hi," I repeated. "I meant to bring this bag of supplies from HotPets to you the other day. I was in the area for another home visit, so I thought I'd just drop it off." In case she'd just want to grab it and close the door in my face, I continued, "Of course now that I'm here, I'd love to visit with Beardsley, Moe, and Nemo again." I bent and patted the dogs' heads. "Check on their well-being. I'm such a worrywart, but I do love all the animals we place."

Yes, I was prattling, but I wanted to put Margie off guard.

"Well, sure, Lauren. Come in." She backed away. Her round cheeks were pale, and she'd put on no makeup yet. She wore a ragged but frilly bathrobe and apologized for it.

"You look fine. Besides, it's not like I warned you I was coming."

She showed me into the living room and offered me a

cup of coffee, which I declined. I continued to pet the dogs and asked about the kitty, and Margie offered to go find her for me.

"Soon," I said. "Is Davie here? I really enjoy talking to him, too."

But her son had gotten a part-time job for the summer at a kids' day camp held in a nearby park and had already left.

I was sure poor Margie wanted to throw me out, but she was gracious despite my continuing to talk about nothing. Or at least she probably considered it nothing. But I spoke of animals, and how we got them to HotRescues and how we took care of them.

While I was chattering, I managed to work in some questions, like inquiring whether Davie had his driver's license. He did. And about any strays that might have shown up lately around this neighborhood—dogs, cats, or both.

Margie professed to be aware of none. Yes, she, too, thought Davie's love for animals was cute. She fortunately didn't appear concerned about the reason for my blathering.

But Davie had been the one, when I'd been here last, to say that HotRescues rocked. Not an uncommon expression these days, of course, but to have something similar turn up on the note left with Lionheart had ratcheted up my suspicions.

Nemo poked his gray head into the living room, as if assuring himself that the intruder wasn't anyone worth checking out more closely. I just laughed.

But I didn't find the situation very humorous. My questions were only partly answered. Margie didn't seem to know about it if Davie was the one who'd been taking animals to HotRescues. Nor could I be sure he wasn't my target.

Margie walked me to the door a little while later. "Thanks for the supplies," she said.

"You're welcome. You know, I'd love to talk to Davie about—" I stopped. If she told him I wanted to see him, he'd realize I was on to him, assuming he was our dumper. Inspiration struck. "We're planning a demonstration by the Small Animal Rescue Team sometime soon at HotRescues. A fund-raiser. I'll let you know when it is. I'll bet Davie would enjoy it."

"Oh, yes," Margie said. "Thanks, Lauren."

And once I was in his presence again, I might have a few questions to lob at him.

Chapter 26

I'd received the e-mail I'd expected from Miguel Rohrig late last night and printed it out. He had checked and confirmed that the pet adopter who'd argued with Bethany a lot was Nalla Croler, and he recommended that I add her to my suspect list. He'd sent along her phone number—and her place of work. It was in the area where I'd hoped to go later that day anyway.

I wear my dark hair short, and it had been a few weeks since I'd had it cut. Nalla was a hairstylist. Before I drove away from Northridge, I called the salon where she worked.

I was pleased to learn that she did indeed have an open spot that morning, about forty-five minutes from now. I'd get there in plenty of time, traffic along the western side of L.A. permitting—which was always iffy.

Once again I lucked out. I even got there enough in advance to find a relatively cheap parking spot, at a meter.

The salon was in Westwood. It was likely to charge less

than a similar establishment in nearby Beverly Hills, but I figured my haircut, even a no-frills one, wouldn't be cheap.

I walked into the Hair Today salon on Hilgard Avenue right on time. From behind a desk, a smiling young woman with streaked brown hair asked my name, then showed me through the door behind her into a long room that smelled of fragrant shampoos and the chemicals associated with hair dyes and permanents. The cubicles on both sides were separated by decorative half-walls, resembling those in a high-end commercial office.

Nalla's was the third cubicle on the right. The chair I was shown to was royal blue and upholstered and appeared very comfortable, which proved to be true.

Nalla looked as if she'd just had her own blond hair styled. She was probably mid-thirties, buxom, and wearing a black apron similar to the ones I'd noticed on other stylists. Her eyes peered from behind small-framed glasses. "Hello," she said, and introduced herself.

"Hi. I'm Lauren Vancouver." I watched her face, but there was no reaction. She apparently didn't know who I was, nor should she. Good. It would be easier that way to get the information I sought.

I told her how I wanted my hair trimmed. With its cap-like style, there wasn't much way she could ruin it, even if she wanted to. I only wanted it shampooed and cut, no dying or streaking or anything else.

She was friendly, but wasn't one of those stylists who appeared to believe the world would end if she failed to keep up a running conversation with her customers. That left it up to me to get her talking.

After she finished my shampoo and studied my hair before cutting it, I chatted about the weather and hair in general, then told her what I did for a living. "I'm a pet rescuer," I said. "I run a private no-kill shelter in Granada Hills. Are you a pet person?"

"Yes, I am." She smiled. "In fact, I just adopted the sweetest dog—a part pit bull."

We talked briefly about how she believed the breed is maligned a lot thanks to some of them being bred for dog fights—which was a form of cruelty. And how owners still have to train them to be sure they wouldn't attack other dogs—and keep them under control. Not always easy.

Then I asked where she'd gotten her pup.

I watched in the mirror as her face clouded over. "At a shelter that I thought would be perfect. The woman who owned it was so well known around here—used to be a star among those of us in the beauty community. She'd started, then sold, her own high-end cosmetics company. Her stuff is really great—I still buy a lot of it. She died recently, though. The bitch." She met my eyes, then looked abashed. "Sorry. I know I shouldn't speak ill of the dead, but the way she acted . . ."

"Toward the animals?"

"No." Nalla began sectioning my hair and using clips to keep some out of the way. "Toward people. She made me come back three times before I could take Pitsy, and even then she kept giving me a hard time about how to treat my sweet dog. Telling me over and over how to train her and feed her and love her and . . . Did you know her? Her name was Bethany Urber. I know she started this whole network of other pet rescue organizations, Pet Shelters Together. Does your shelter belong to it?" She started trimming, and I became concerned suddenly that her emotionalism might lead to a really horrible haircut.

"No." I kept my tone even as I watched every snip. "But I've heard of her. How did you handle her demands?"

Unspoken meaning: Did you start hating her enough to want to quiet her by shooting her?

"I thought about just leaving the first day I visited her place, but I'd fallen in love with Pitsy. There were some other people around. I guess one was her assistant . . . Cricket? She tried to smooth things over. There were a few other women there—I gathered they all ran shelters, too, and were part of that network. One even suggested I might want to visit her shelter, that she had some pit bull mixes there, too. I figured, from the shocked looks the other two gave her, that recommending another place was forbidden around Bethany. If it weren't for how strongly I already felt about Pitsy, I'd probably have just walked out, maybe even gone to that other person's shelter."

"Who was that?" I asked. "Which shelter?"

But she didn't know.

She did, however, after adopting Pitsy, prevent Bethany from the home visit that was so important to many of the best private shelters. They'd argued about that, too. Also about Bethany's many phone calls still telling her what to do. Nalla stopped taking Bethany's calls and would only talk to Cricket.

I couldn't fault Bethany completely. I acted similarly at times, in the interest of protecting the animals we adopted out. But I probably came across a lot more tactfully—something that didn't come easily to me, either.

"I did go back there one more time, just to tell her off," Nalla admitted. "Stupid, maybe, but I was pretty damned mad at her for her attitude. I accused her of abusing the animals under her care, in a way. If she turned off other potential adopters like she'd turned me off, how many of the animals she cared for wouldn't get the right homes? She was so mad that she threatened to take Pitsy back, which is why I wouldn't let her come see us. Fortunately, we live on a middle floor in a condo with a great security system, so she couldn't just barge in. I've got a dog walker who takes Pitsy out days I'm not home, and I warned her to watch out for Bethany. And I threatened Bethany right back." Nalla shrugged. "Even more stupidity? Yes. And the thing was, some guy was hanging around. He heard it all. He must have told the cops about it, because they came to talk to me after Bethany was murdered."

I assumed the guy was Miguel, and that was why he'd told me to look at Nalla as a possible suspect.

"But," Nalla said, flourishing her scissors as she gave what appeared to be a final snip to my hair, "I didn't do it. If someone had to get murdered, I can understand why it was Bethany. But as long as she left Pitsy and me alone, I'd have had no problem letting her live forever. Here, want to take a look?"

She passed me a hand mirror, twirling my chair around so I could check the reflection of the back of my head.

The cut looked good.

The information she had provided gave me additional food for thought.

So when I saw the amount on my bill, I swallowed my gasp and even added a nice tip to my credit card receipt. This killer inquiry was costing me a lot, and it wasn't the sort of expense that I could get back from HotRescues or Dante, even though he was very generous in bonuses and raises that helped me keep my kids in school. I'd better end my investigation successfully.

I'd add a section on Nalla to my find-Bethany's-killer computer file.

Eliminate her as a suspect? Not really.

I'd place her toward the end, though, near Miguel and Mamie.

But thanks to her, I now had additional questions to ask a few people who were already in that growing file.

At the same time I'd printed out Miguel's e-mail about Nalla that morning, I'd also sorted through the correspondence I continued to receive about Bethany. As I'd hoped when I requested that people send me their memories, the members of Pet Shelters Together still dissected and vivisected Bethany and their relationships with her. She'd been a saint, trying to help people help animals. She'd been a thorn in many sides as she had engaged in some less-than-lovable stunts in her crusade to get people to join and do her bidding. I'd need to spend a lot of time figuring it all out, but in the meantime I knew who I next intended to visit.

Sylvia Lodner, a member of the network, had been the first to tell me that my asking for eulogies over the fruit of Bethany's efforts would most likely dredge up some pretty rotten stuff about her, too.

Sylvia's shelter, Pet Home Locators, was in Torrance, about twenty miles southeast of Westwood. My GPS got me there in about half an hour, since traffic was cooperative, too.

The shelter was on a side street off Torrance Boulevard. I almost drove by it, since its entry was marked only with an inconspicuous sign. I parked on the street and headed up the driveway.

At its end was a nondescript building that people evidently had to go through to reach the shelter area. The exterior resembled a series of ticket windows, where visitors had to check in and talk to someone before going any farther.

I headed for the first window. "Hi," I said to the teenage boy behind it who was thumbing through some paperwork. He looked up, apparently startled.

"Hi." He smiled. "Can I help you choose a new pet today?"

I laughed. "You've been trained well. But I'm actually here to see Sylvia Lodner. Please tell her Lauren Vancouver would like to talk to her."

The boy left, and Sylvia appeared at the window less than a minute later. "What are you doing here, Lauren?" Her voice sounded less than welcoming, and the expression on her face—which had almost always been solemn when I'd been around her—now looked downright suspicious.

Not surprising, the logo on her bright red shirt that contrasted attractively with her light African American skin tone said, "Can we help you choose a new pet today?" Obviously, that was a theme around here. A good one.

"I'd just like to talk to you about what you submitted to me on Bethany," I said. "I had a few questions."

"Ones you couldn't e-mail to me? Never mind. Why don't I show you around this outstanding facility, since you're here, and we'll talk."

She pointed toward a door off to my right. It opened, and she motioned for me to join her.

She showed me through a small but well-kept facility. Dogs of all sizes leaped around in their enclosures, demanding our attention. There was a separate building at the rear where cats were each kept in their own generous-sized crates.

In all, I really liked the place. I told Sylvia so.

"Thanks, Lauren." We had just left the cat building, and she turned to me and gave me one of her rare smiles. "So what is it that you really want from me?"

I laughed. "I'm still trying to figure Bethany out, before I try putting the information together for the Web site I intend to create in her memory."

"Bull-puckey, as we say around here, since we've got a lot of young volunteers. You're still butting in, trying to figure out which of us killed her." We'd reached a small outside sitting and exercise area paved in concrete, and Sylvia pulled lawn chairs up for each of us. "Have a seat, and I'll tell you all I know, which isn't much."

"To clear the air a little," I said, "you're right. I am butting in. But I'm only looking for the truth. Mamie Spelling and I have a long history, but if she killed Bethany, so be it. If she didn't, I'd like to help her. That's all."

"That's enough, isn't it? Never mind. Here's my input. First, I didn't kill Bethany but I can't say I liked her much. I did like her idea of a network of shelters with combined resources. That's why I joined. Not because she pulled any of her stupid stunts on me, though she tried."

"Like what? Your place here is wonderful. She couldn't have threatened you with going to the authorities, like she did with Mamie."

Sylvia sat back on her chair and crossed her arms, as if fending off whatever Bethany had done to her. "No, but she did her homework and figured out my vulnerability, too. Pet Home Locators gets a lot of small donations from people who believe we're hurting for money. That's what we do when we're begging—show how much our animals need the help of everyone out there who loves pets. We don't have the kind of resources I understand you have, with your affiliation with HotPets. But . . . well, I don't want to get into a lot of detail that you could use against me, too, but suffice it to say that, even though this is a nonprofit corporation, it runs on certain—shall we say— underreported profits from some unrelated products a few members of our board of directors make and sell. Some of the proceeds would be tax-exempt anyway for a nonprofit, but not necessarily all of them. And if you ever mention that to anyone, I'll deny it."

"Did you deny it to Bethany?"

"Wouldn't have done any good. She knew and tried to hold it over me. But the main reason I wanted to join her network was to wean our organization away from that less-than-ideal situation. I hated what Bethany tried to do to me, but it was her normal course of operation. Any one of us could have hated her enough to kill her, I suppose. But if hating the way she asserted a nasty form of control over anyone was a motive, we all have one. And tight-fisted? Amazing! She kept detailed records about all sorts of pid-dly things, including how many PST T-shirts were bought, how many pins she gave out to members, everything. When one of the members lost a pin, she almost flipped her lid."

"Give me your opinion, then. Assuming that Mamie didn't kill Bethany, and you didn't, who would you choose as top suspect?"

She looked at me as if assessing whether to hand her beliefs over to me. "This goes no further?"

It was a question. I had an answer. "You don't know me well at all. I could say anything, then tell whoever you sus-pect what you said." Her eyes widened in shock, even as her mouth pursed grimly. "But that's not me. I won't bother giv-ing a list of references. I'd only choose people who'd back me up. I hope that the fact that a businessman as astute as Dante DeFrancisco put me in charge of the shelter he funds, and still has me there six years later, speaks in favor of my reliability. So, I swear on my job and my continuing good relationship with Dante that what you say will go no further."

To my astonishment, she laughed. "You're a character, Lauren, and I'd thought you were just another shelter operator with an agenda of your own. Okay, I'll trust you. What I have to say isn't worthy of your oath anyway. But if I had to choose someone I'd met who also knew Bethany—and I've even met that money-grabbing boyfriend of hers—I'd focus on Cricket."

Not that much of a surprise, but I asked anyway, "Why her?"

"She hasn't bothered me, but I've heard rumors she's playing the same kinds of games that Bethany did—coercing people to join and toe the lines she draws. Lording it over members, and even, in some ways, making fun of Bethany and suggesting that her actions, before her death, were pathetic compared with how Cricket intends to run things. More conservatively, for one thing—so there'll be more money available for those who buckle under to her demands . . . and also for her. A good motive for getting rid of her boss, don't you think?"

"Could be," I agreed. But that seemed too easy. I needed more information. "If she hasn't acted that way with you, how did you hear about it?"

"I heard a conversation between a couple of members."

"Who are . . . ?"

"Darya and Raelene. But remember, I haven't told you a thing."

"Gee, and I wish I could convince you to tell me something useful." I smiled at her, and she returned it.

I left soon afterward, with names of two more people I intended to talk with soon.

Chapter 27

I don't necessarily become obsessed when confronted with a problem, but if I think I can solve it relatively quickly, I do tend to focus on it. A lot.

Like now. I'd possibly zeroed in on Bethany's killer, but I didn't want to tell the police my suspicions of Cricket without at least some evidence to back it up. No doubt they'd looked at her, too. Maybe they still were considering her. That could be why Mamie hadn't been arrested.

But their perspective would be different from mine. Official. I could go places and ask things they couldn't under the law, or might not even think of doing.

Which was why I was on my way to Redondo Beach on Thursday morning.

Raelene Elder was the chief administrator of Redondo Rescues. I'd called to let her know I was coming, something I didn't always do lately with people I wanted to talk to. But at least when I'd dropped in at Sylvia's rescue facility yesterday, I'd been halfway there after my hair appointment with Nalla.

That's why I was musing about obsession. I'd been thinking about helping to solve Bethany's murder ever since she died, created my business plan for keeping track of all I learned, and even researched it in various ways. In the past few days, I'd talked to a lot of people. Felt as if I was making progress—and I wanted to get this thing done at last.

Redondo Rescues turned out not to be especially near the beach for which it was named. In fact, it was closer to Sylvia's shelter in nearby Torrance than I'd realized.

Even though Redondo Beach was considered somewhat affluent, I found Raelene's shelter only a bit nicer than Mamie's on the outside. The fence around it was chain-link and seemed dilapidated, sagging here and there. The one-story building at the side of the property could have used some work, too.

I opened the gate and walked in. Raelene must have been watching for me. She strode out of the building, a smile on her face. Her puffy yellow hair was in disarray, but she obviously wasn't trying to impress anyone here, the way she may have been at the PST meetings. She wore what was a uniform of sorts for all of us shelter administrators, our assistants and employees: a shirt with our facility's logo—hers was yellow—over jeans.

"Lauren, how nice of you to come. Let me show you around."

What impressed me most about Redondo Rescues was the number of people around taking care of the animals. I didn't know how many were employees and how many were volunteers, but there appeared to be a high ratio of humans to residents. The animals were housed in a series of elongated buildings kept clean and mostly odor-free.

The animals could have used more toys and other amenities like I was fortunate enough to get from HotPets, but the dogs were obviously walked frequently, judging by notes posted on bulletin boards in each area, and were played with, too.

I gushed over those residents, a lot more canine than feline, all obviously well cared for. So what if the money around here went into pet care and not so much into aesthetics?

I'm not especially known for tact, nor did I want to spend a lot of time here when I had other people to chat with and, more important, my own shelter to run. As we headed toward the front building again, I jumped right in.

"I'm still collecting whatever information I can about Bethany, Raelene. A lot of what's been sent to me already is kind of what I expected—a combination of good and bad." I looked up, since Raelene was taller than me. Equally slim, though. "Some of it suggests that she was . . . well, hard on people. That she'd do anything to get rescuers to join Pet Shelters Together. Was that your experience?"

She didn't love Bethany, either, but she told me that she'd liked the concept enough to join anyway, as Sylvia had.

"What about Cricket? How is she doing so far as the head of the network?"

Raelene shook her head as our gazes met. "Hard to tell. It hasn't been very long. But I get the impression that she'll be even worse than her predecessor. If she is . . . well, as I said, I like the concept, but it has to work for me in practice. Redondo Rescues may secede. I'm even thinking of starting a different network and seeing if anyone from the group will join me."

"I'll bet they would," I said. "So . . . have you spoken with anyone else about this? I mean, about how difficult

Cricket is." I knew at least a partial answer, since Sylvia had already told me about overhearing a conversation between Raelene and Darya.

"Sure, a few people in PST. I've hinted at my idea of a competitive network but haven't come out and suggested it yet."

"I'd love to know about it when you do." I paused, then asked, "How did Cricket and Bethany get along together?" Okay, maybe I would throw in a dash of tact here. "If Cricket has taken Bethany's positions on how to run the network and run with them, can I assume they were good friends?"

Raelene laughed. "I get it. You're zeroing in on Cricket as doing Bethany in, instead of Mamie. My opinion? It could have been either of them, for different reasons. Hey, maybe you could get the cops to arrest them both, as some kind of conspiracy." At my expression, she shrugged. "Or not. I know you're hoping to clear Mamie. Anyway, keep me informed, to the extent you can. I'm really interested in learning the truth."

So was I. I didn't get the impression that Raelene was a good potential suspect herself. Unfortunately, I didn't have time to stop on my way back to HotRescues to indulge in more gossip about Cricket at Happy Saved Animals. Instead, I called Darya Price and asked if I could visit her tomorrow morning at her shelter.

I had an appointment early that afternoon for Gavin Mamo to come to HotRescues and demonstrate his training abilities on one of our new residents, Flash—a golden Lab that Angie, our vet tech, had wrested from a high-kill shelter in San Bernardino County the day before the exuberant one-year-old was scheduled to be put down. The assessment had been that no one would want to adopt an untrainable dog like him.

My opinion? Take him in, get someone good to start his training, then find him the right home.

It had been more than a week since I'd visited Gavin at his Westwood training center and negotiated possible terms of part-time employment with him, but I hadn't been as diligent as I'd hoped about following up with him—not till Angie called me, somewhat frantic, about her last-minute rescue.

Now, Gavin would have to prove himself to me in an especially difficult situation, a sort of trial by fire.

Seemed appropriate with a dog named Flash.

Before going to see Raelene, I'd left Zoey at HotRescues with Brooke, early that morning. No new drop-offs then, fortunately. That was something else I needed to follow up on—my idea of who'd been our supposed owner-relinquisher. I'd do that in a short while, since I had a thought about how to approach it.

Now, I parked and entered the welcome area—and was glad to see Nina speaking with a couple who sounded interested in adoption. I waved at her and headed to my office to drop off my purse, but she called after me, "Gavin Mamo's here. Bev is showing him around."

"Thanks," I said. Nina had shut Zoey inside my office, and my sweet dog greeted me with such enthusiasm that I laughed and knelt and hugged her. "I need for you to stay inside for now, sweetie," I told her, nuzzling against her soft fur. "I'll take you on a long walk in a bit, just the two of us. I promise." She licked my face as I hugged her again, acknowledging that she understood and forgave me for not making our walk immediate.

I was soon outside in the shelter area, tracking them down. Our outspoken senior volunteer Bev was an excellent choice for giving our new trainer a tour. She'd tell him her opinion on all our residents and their state of discipline and adoptability. Most often, I agreed with her.

Unsurprisingly, I found them at the enclosure around the back corner where Flash now lived. They were outside the gated area talking to the dog, who leaped around in obvious joy at the attention.

Not a good sign, I thought. Shouldn't a skilled trainer encourage better behavior, get him calmed faster?

Bev apparently thought so. Her face was even more lined than usual as she glared, and she drew herself up notwithstanding her characteristic slouch. "Why's he still jumping?" she demanded, her scowl leveled on Gavin.

He looked huge, compared with Bev. I studied him to determine how well he took her criticism, which could be a factor in his longevity here.

He grinned at her, then me, baring gleaming white teeth that contrasted brightly with his deep skin tone. He wore a bright green, blue-and-yellow Hawaiian shirt that day, which emphasized his background. "We're just sizing each other up." He turned his large body back toward the enclosure. "I'm in charge now," he said to Flash. I noticed he'd wrapped a leash around his hand, and he loosened it so it dangled. "Okay if I go in?" He looked at me for permission, and I added a few points in his favor.

"Go for it," I said.

He opened the gate and entered the enclosure. Flash leaped up in obvious ecstasy.

"Sit." The word Gavin uttered was low and brief. Yeah, sure, I thought—and was amazed to see Flash obey.

I looked at Gavin's body language. He towered over the

dog even more than he did over most people. His arm was bent, his fist raised, but not, I thought, as a threat.

"Good dog." He pulled a treat from his pocket and gave it to Flash. Then he snapped the leash on and led the dog out through the gate.

Which Flash evidently took to mean he was liberated. He dashed forward, obviously attempting to run.

Gavin quickly but gently snapped the leash and brought Flash back to his side. "Heel," he said in the same firm voice he'd initially used on the pup. Flash didn't appear to know the command, but at least he stopped pulling. And got yet another treat.

Gavin led Flash to our visitors' park along the side rear of the shelter. There, I heard a lot of muffled hammering and sawing noises from the property next door—an improvement from the louder sound effects we'd heard a lot of during the last few weeks. I supposed that was because most of the outside work on the new building was complete and the contractors were working on finishing the inside.

Bev and I stayed at the outer entry to the park, watching as Gavin worked with Flash. The pup seemed amenable to taking orders at first, then got tired of it and tried again to run away. Gavin kept pulling him back, firmly yet gently, and repeating a few basic commands: sit, stay, down, heel. He continued removing small treats from his pocket and rewarding Flash for good behavior.

Soon, Flash appeared to concede that Gavin was alpha in this small pack. When the two of them started to exit the park, Flash trotted at Gavin's side, the leash slack enough to demonstrate that he wasn't been coerced to stay there.

I smiled at Gavin. He smiled at me.

"Next?" he said.

Chapter 28

I was on the phone a lot at home that evening, which bored Zoey, who slept beside me on the couch. Hey, it was her house, too. I didn't agree with those who kept their pets off the furniture. Fine for them, but it wasn't my way.

I called Mamie first. I had no intention of letting her know I believed I was close to solving Bethany's murder—and, hence, Mamie's biggest legal problem. Not till I was certain, I had some evidence to hand over, and the right suspect was in jail. I worried about her, though.

"I'm fine, Lauren," she said when I asked, but her tone suggested the opposite. The stress couldn't be helping her deal with her already fragile psyche.

"How are you and Mr. Caramon getting along?" I asked in a not-so-subtle way of trying to find out if she was still being hounded by the police.

"Okay. We're getting together again on Monday."

"Oh. Well, take care, Mamie."

"You, too, Lauren."

I almost wished I could send some optimism over the phone airwaves.

My next discussion was with Matt. He'd had a busy week, but tomorrow was Friday, and we'd get together over the weekend. He'd rounded up the members of the SmART team. They would visit HotRescues next Saturday to check out the facilities for the demo I hoped they could do for the fund-raiser that Dante had finally scheduled for that Sunday. They'd even do a practice run.

After confirming it with Matt, I next spoke with Dante, letting him know that everything was a go from my end.

"Great, Lauren," he said. "I've had my HotPets PR guys do what they could to get ready without total confirmation. Starting tomorrow, flyers will be available in all local Hot-Pets and on our Web site, and we'll flood all our online customers. We'll emphasize what a great job HotRescues does, and should get a good turnout."

"How much will we charge for people to get in?"

He named a reasonable figure. "Some of our take will go toward a generous contribution to SmART, since the team members pay for all their own equipment that isn't donated, right?"

"That's what I've been told."

"Some will go toward HotRescues programs—not any offset for the new construction. That's my nickel. Depending on how much we get, any extra will go to whatever rescue groups we decide on later. With my PR guys' input, of course."

"Of course."

"Watch that sarcasm," Dante said, but I heard amusement in his tone.

As I hung up, I decided to invite Mamie to our event. She might enjoy the distraction.

Finally, I called Carlie, let her know that our Sunday fund-raiser was happening . . . and also giving her the contact information I'd gotten from Dante about his PR guys. "If it's okay with them, you can film all or part of one of your *Pet Fitness* shows there, if you want."

"Count on it! Thanks, Lauren."

There was a show about pet rescues in New York on Animal Planet that night. Zoey and I watched it before heading to bed.

Happy Saved Animals, the no-kill shelter managed by Darya Price, was located off Sepulveda Boulevard in Mar Vista, a part of Los Angeles not far from Venice and Santa Monica.

After dropping Zoey off at HotRescues that Friday morning, I drove south toward that general area—again. I'd been doing that a lot lately, ever since Mamie's phone call.

I'd also been visiting more competing rescue organizations that ran shelters in a compressed amount of time than I had since before I helped to start HotRescues. Then, while putting together my business plan, I'd looked at other setups, asked questions without fully explaining my need to know, and stirred together the good while discarding the difficult and adding a dash of my own creativity. The result had impressed Dante enough, which had thrilled me. Still did.

Happy Saved Animals had been one of the shelters I'd checked out back then. I wasn't sure who the director had been at the time, but it wasn't Darya.

As I recalled now, the organization had impressed me as being solid, the fund-raising success impressive, and, most important, the emphasis on taking good care of animals had been wonderful.

I wondered if Darya had kept it all up. Why not? Since it wasn't broken, she was unlikely to have fixed it.

I parked in the lot behind the facility and approached the gate. I entered into an attractive courtyard surrounded by buildings. The one on the right had a "Welcome" sign, and that was where I headed.

I'd called ahead to warn Darya I was coming, but she wasn't the one to greet me. Instead, a friendly dark-haired woman showed me to a seat in what appeared to be a waiting room. "I'll give you some paperwork to fill out," she said, "and then I'll have someone take you back to see our wonderful animals who are waiting to be adopted."

She had a heavy accent, perhaps Middle Eastern, and she might not have fully understood what I'd said when I introduced myself. I gently waved away the clipboard she started to hand me and began to explain again who I was.

Darya walked in then. "Lauren, welcome." She laughed lightly as she gestured toward the clipboard her assistant still held. "Lauren would pass all our requirements with flying colors," Darya told the other lady, "but she's here for another reason." She turned back to me with a somewhat quizzical expression. "Which I'm eager to hear about. Come into my office, Lauren." She waved for me to follow her.

Unlike a lot of administrators and their staff, Darya didn't wear a uniform consisting of a T-shirt extolling her shelter. Nor was she the pinnacle of fashion, as Bethany had been. Instead, she had a business-like shirt and pair of slacks on her lean frame, as if impressing possible adopters with her professionalism might help her place her animals into new homes faster. I'd have to ask if it worked. If so, I might change my style.

Darya's office was located down a short hall. I glanced in an open door and saw her husband, Lan, sitting behind a desk at a computer, his back toward the door.

"Does your husband work here, too?" I asked as we continued walking.

"He helps with a few things, like payroll for employees—not many of them, since we try to recruit volunteers. He's great at giving fund-raising advice. He's actually a CPA and works at an accounting firm that manages the books of a lot of doctors' offices and medical centers."

"Handy guy to have around," I said with a smile, meaning it. Fortunately, Dante had a good accounting firm he dealt with for his HotPets empire who also helped to balance our HotRescues books. That meant I didn't have much to worry about except for keeping track of donations—mostly from Dante himself—and expenses. An accounting program on our computer system helped a lot with that.

"He sure is," Darya agreed. She showed me into the next room. "Here we are."

Her office was smaller than mine. Even if I hadn't had the conversation area, my digs were roomy compared with this. But it was neat, with a desk clear of everything but the inevitable computer, and a three-drawer file cabinet sideways against the back wall.

Darya pulled out a folding chair and set it up for me, wedging it in front of her desk. I sat down, regretting that I hadn't asked for my tour first. Someone must have walked through the shelter, since I heard a wave of dog barks, starting with only one or two, then rising to a crescendo. Made me want to see them and hug a few, too.

Later, I figured.

"Can I get you some coffee or water?" Darya asked.

"I'm fine," I said.

She pulled a bottle of water from a drawer and took a sip. "I'm delighted you're here," she said, "but what did you want to talk about?"

"I'm sure you can guess, at least somewhat. I'm still butting my nose in where it doesn't belong, trying to figure out who really killed Bethany." I smiled, but Darya's return expression was only half amused.

"I understand your wanting to clear Mamie," she said, "but if she's guilty—and it sure looks that way—you're just wasting your time."

"I don't think so." I leaned forward in an attempt to suggest earnestness, but I couldn't go far in this cramped room. "I have an idea who really did it, but . . . Look, Darya, I'm still trying to sort through the e-mails I received from Pet Shelters Together members, but the gist of most of them is that Bethany wasn't a very nice person at times. She did anything she could think of to get people to join PST. Nasty stuff. That's what I'd figured led to her death. Someone fought back. It could have been Mamie, but I've come up with a better possibility. That's why I'm here."

I stopped. My intention had been to describe my new theory, that someone had a stronger motive: taking over the whole organization. Handling it differently. Making more money, and whatever else she chose to do—using what she'd learned from her former boss and running with it, after using Bethany's own gun on her.

That someone would have been Cricket.

But I stopped talking as all the color drained from Darya's face. Her former smile drooped, and her expression became guarded.

"Interesting theory," she said.

Interesting reaction, I thought.

"If you have another one, I'd love to hear it," I said, even as my mind backtracked. I'd been talking about someone fighting Bethany's nasty, coercive actions to get people to join PST. Had that happened to Darya? If so, how?

"Meantime," I continued, "it's surprising how many members of PST shared their reasons for joining with me—and their opinions all seemed to be mixed. They liked the concept. But just being approached by Bethany about joining turned into nightmares for some of them. If they said no, or they'd think about it, Bethany would back off a little, then come back at them with some nastiness that she'd researched and could maybe use against them if they didn't opt in." I paused. "She rubbed it in, too—like she did with Mamie that day she talked to us all about hoarding. Did she do that with you, too?"

"That day? Of course not." She responded awfully quickly, her tone squeaky.

Even more interesting. Had whatever upset Darya about this conversation been mentioned that same day by Bethany? What had it been?

Darya sat back then and laughed. "Okay, you got me. You can add me to that list, but I hate to admit it. Bethany twisted my arm, too. I was reluctant to have Happy Saved Animals join the group, and she knew it. I didn't like her attitude, for one thing. There was a situation where someone was interested in adopting a nonaggressive pit bull from Better Than Any Pet Rescues one day when I was there. Bethany kept making demands of that lady, telling her exactly how she'd have to train the dog, what to feed it, the works. The poor lady was almost in tears."

"Was that Nalla Croler?" I asked. "I know she had an

axe to grind with Bethany, so she's on my suspect list, too."
I had some alternate, hugely growing suspicions right now but didn't want to give them away.

"That name sounds familiar. I had a few pretty calm pit bulls here, too, and suggested she might want to check mine out—and I promised not to give her grief about the one she adopted, although she of course would be advised to train and supervise any dog properly. All the other PST members were horrified that I dared to contradict Bethany." She laughed. "It didn't really matter anyhow. The lady had fallen in love with the dog right there and decided to adopt despite Bethany's edicts."

"And you decided to join PST anyway?" I said casually.

"Well, yes. After that, Bethany came to me and told me she knew about . . . Well, something I didn't want anyone else to know."

It had been a big deal to Darya—enough to get her to join the network. I needed to learn what it was, even if she chose not to reveal it. Or had she already?

"The important thing was that I really liked the concept, and the other people. I decided to join anyway."

"And got a lot out of it, I gathered." A loose end that Brooke had mentioned to me suddenly popped into my mind, and I blurted, "Like that pretty pin?"

Darya's pallor seemed to increase and her mouth opened. Nothing came out at first, and then she said, "The pins are pretty, aren't they?"

Not exactly an admission of anything. Still . . .

"I know you worked in the office sometimes," I continued. "You mentioned that before. Did you do a lot of hands-on work there?"

"Under Bethany's supervision. You know how she liked to be in charge."

I had a suspicion, though, that there were other reasons as well. "Cricket was around a lot then, too, wasn't she? You and she became friends, so I'll bet you're glad she succeeded to the head of PST, with Bethany gone now."

Darya smiled wryly. "Well, that was before. This is now. I've gotten the sense that Cricket is going to become another Bethany, and then some."

The discomfiture that Darya had evinced before was gone now. Maybe I had imagined it.

I also had a new thought about who might have killed Bethany, along with a couple of reasons why.

Before I zeroed in on it—and before I'd have anything potentially useful to turn over to the cops—I had some more questions to ask.

But not here.

Chapter 29

I was jazzed.

I was also convinced.

Now, I just needed proof.

Before I left Happy Saved Animals, I had to take the tour I'd anticipated. Darya was pleased to show me around and introduce me to some of the residents and volunteers.

Her husband joined us for part of the walk-through. He was friendly but quiet.

I wasn't especially talkative, either. I had a lot on my mind. But nothing prevented me from visiting as many dogs and cats as I could.

When I left, I did something I tried not to do during the day. I called Brooke, who'd slept at HotRescues last night.

Unsurprisingly, I got her voicemail. "I'm making one stop on my way back," I said in my message. "If I get the information I think I will, we need to talk about what I should do next."

An obscure communication? Probably. But Brooke would figure out the gist of what I was talking about.

The drive from Mar Vista to Westchester was only around six miles. I had to head south, though, which was opposite from the way I needed to go to return to HotRescues.

I didn't call in advance, which was possibly foolish. If Cricket wasn't at Better Than Any Pet Rescues, my extra miles would be for naught.

Also, my frustration would be astronomical.

Fortunately, she was there. Surprisingly, Miguel was in the office with her. Or maybe not so surprisingly. I'd already figured out that he still lived in the office/house. It might be too soon, on this early Friday afternoon, for him to report to work at the restaurant.

The shelter's office was located on the left side of the building's vast entry hall. Hearing voices, I'd headed in there to find the two of them engrossed in conversation. Friendly conversation.

Very friendly conversation? Like, were these two now an item, with Bethany no longer an obstacle? I'd thought they didn't like each other, but that could have changed— or just been an act.

It could also be a motive for one or both to have killed Bethany. But my untethered mind now galloped in a different direction.

"Hi," I said perkily. Standing together at one side of the room, they broke apart, looking a little guilty.

"Welcome, Lauren." Cricket sounded breathless. "What brings you here?" Her face was flushed. She wore a PST T-shirt with a pin near the neckline—a plain one, without the diamonds Bethany's had.

"Some questions," I said. "Hi, Miguel."

"You here to do more snooping to figure out Bethany's murder?" He sounded amused.

"Working on it," I said. "Not that it should give you any comfort, since I'm nobody when it comes to the investigation, but neither of you is at the top of my list." Cricket was still second, but my suspicions of her were waning. They might fade completely, depending on her answers.

"Go ahead and ask." Cricket plopped down on a chair at the table in the middle of the room. She was certainly different in appearance from Bethany, even if she'd inherited her attitude. Yes, she was shorter and a little heavier—but in some ways more attractive, since she wasn't all about appearance. She ran her fingers through her curly hair, as if deriving Samson-like strength from it.

Miguel pulled a chair up so he was almost shoulder-to-shoulder with Cricket, allied with her against me. "Yeah," he said. "What are your questions?"

"I like your pin, Cricket." I intended it to sound like a non sequitur, not the harbinger of what I was about to delve into. "Once I have HotRescues join PST, when will I get one?"

"Right away."

"Then you keep a bunch around?"

"Yes." She frowned, clearly puzzled about my interest.

"I gathered that Bethany was a real stickler for members wearing those pins to meetings. Will you be the same way?"

"What are you driving at, Lauren?" Her question exploded from her.

"Just interested. Has anyone ever lost a pin?"

"Yes, but not often. Bethany got very upset when the first person did."

"Was there a second person?"

"Well . . . yes. Darya."

Yes! My assumption had been correct. But that didn't necessarily mean anything.

"But we never told Bethany or anyone else about Darya," Cricket continued. "I just gave her a replacement and shuffled the inventory numbers."

"Did Darya find it again?"

"I don't think so. She promised to return the new one if she did. I told the cops that, too, when they mentioned the pins."

If true, that shot a hole in my premise. But Darya might not have returned it. And her reaction suggested she had something to hide about pins . . .

Cricket shook her head. "What is all this about?"

"Curiosity, that's all." I had learned from Brooke, who'd learned from the cops, about the PST pin found with Bethany's corpse. They were apparently asking about pins, maybe casually. Had they gotten the same reaction from Darya that I had?

"I'll bet it's more than curiosity," Miguel said.

I shrugged. "No big deal." Which was a lie. "Actually, I was just in the neighborhood"—lie number two—"and thought I'd drop in to see how you were doing, Cricket. Better Than Any, too. Glad to see that everything looks fine. Right?"

"Lauren—" Cricket drew out my name. "You're not a nutcase. You're a smart lady, and I know this is about something important, right?"

"Honestly," I said, "I don't know yet." I was near the door, and both of them had followed, as if to be sure I was serious about getting out of there. "I'll be in touch again soon. I really like the idea of PST, you know? I may actually see about getting the HotRescues board's"—meaning Dante's—"okay to join. Thanks."

I waltzed out with a big grin on my face. I'd acted like a ditz, or someone utterly cagy. Or both.

The important thing, though, was that I believed I had my answer.

Brooke's the one with the investigation background. Plus, her new guy Antonio is an LAPD detective. When she's feeling well, she thrives on law enforcement stuff. At the moment, her health seemed to be improving all the time.

Consequently, when I called her on my way back to HotRescues and told her what I'd learned, she sounded even more excited than me—a feat that seemed nearly impossible, considering that I was so full of anticipation that I wanted to dance my way to Mamie's former shelter and tell her she was saved—from an unjustified murder rap, at least.

But that would have been foolish. And premature.

I could be wrong . . . as infrequently as that happened.

Brooke called me back a short while after I reached HotRescues. By then, I'd gone inside to retrieve Zoey from Nina and was taking her for a walk along Rinaldi Street.

"Antonio will bring Detective Greshlam to HotRescues at around three this afternoon," Brooke said as I held my smartphone against my ear to catch every word. "I'll be there, of course. Be ready to lay everything out for them, okay?"

"Absolutely."

"By the way—Gavin, the new trainer? He's amazing. Not that Cheyenne needs much instruction, you understand, but Gavin's still managed to teach him quite a bit. He's not just a pet now. He's becoming a trained security dog."

Interesting. I wasn't sure when they'd gotten together, but Brooke's praise of Gavin added yet another reason to keep him on at HotRescues.

The dance I'd been prepared to make as I drove finally found its way into my steps as I led Zoey back toward our shelter. Fortunately, she had been productive quickly, and I'd cleaned it even faster. She was energetic as always and thought our happy jogging was a game. She jumped in circles on her leash and barked enthusiastically as I laughed and ran.

Never mind that I'd have been happier if the contact from the Robbery Homicide Division with whom I'd meet that afternoon was Detective Stefan Garciana, who'd been the thorn in my side the last time I had to figure out the solution to a murder. He'd been the one to suggest looking at the least likely possibilities first, to try to eliminate them . . . maybe.

Not always. Like this time.

Detective Greshlam had been the one to interview me right after Bethany's death. She had stayed involved with this case. She was the right one to talk to. Plus, she'd be tempered—possibly—by Antonio, if she wanted to stay on her colleague's good side. Or not.

"What's going on?" Nina asked while Zoey, panting, hurried to the water bowl in the welcome room.

I was panting, too, and went into the adjoining kitchen for a chilled bottle of water. When I got back, I told Nina, "No guarantees, but I think I've found evidence that clears Mamie."

"Great!" My second-in-command leaped from behind the leopard-print counter and gave me a hug.

Zoey and I took a nice, slow walk around the shelter, including the center building where I checked on the cats and toy dogs. We again had empty spots that would soon be filled by more of the animals rescued from Mamie's.

We'd have even more empty spots in a couple of weeks when the work on the property next door was completed.

Which reminded me of the work I needed to do on my end to publicize Dante's fund-raiser, only about a week away.

For now, I led Zoey back toward my office, where I hoped I could concentrate on what I needed to do until the cops arrived that afternoon.

We sat in the conference room in the middle of the second floor of the HotRescues admin building. I'd told Nina to hold all calls—and that we weren't to be disturbed. By anyone.

I was sure she understood that to include her.

I watched as Detective Greshlam's eyes moved from one photo on the room's walls to the next. They each showed some of our successes—pets and their new owners, all smiling.

I sat on a blue upholstered wooden chair, the one at the head of the oval table. The detective sat at my right, and I wondered if her chunky girth was comfortable in the narrow seat. Brooke and Antonio sat across from her. We were a study in contrasts, with both detectives, Antonio included, dressed in suits, and Brooke and me in our own standard uniforms around here—hers a black security T-shirt over jeans, and me in jeans, and a blue HotRescues knit shirt.

"Detective Bautrel tells me you have some evidence to present to us in the Urber murder." Detective Greshlam's glare yelled that I should have butted out, but she didn't say so in front of her fellow officer.

Antonio didn't hesitate to stick up for me—which suggested he really wanted to impress Brooke. Or maybe he was the one who was impressed—with the theory I'd had Brooke describe to him. "I didn't get all the details, but what I heard puts a new spin on the case. Start where you want, Lauren, and tell us everything."

I didn't intend to get into a lot of detail, like naming everyone I'd considered as potential suspects and why I'd eliminated some. Nor did I want to mention how I'd settled on Cricket as the murderer . . . until that last conversation with Darya. As a result, I didn't actually tell them everything, only what mattered.

I explained first about what I'd determined last. "The day before Bethany was murdered, she held that meeting about hoarding. One thing she said that I had thought odd then, but hadn't glommed on to its importance, was something about how all shelter administrators who were part of Pet Shelters Together had to make sure their funds were used to help animals, nothing else. When I talked to Darya about Bethany's speech that day, and how I'd learned afterward that Mamie was far from the only administrator Bethany tried to coerce into joining PST by what amounted to blackmail, Darya got upset. I can't prove it, but maybe you can—that Bethany's comment was aimed at Darya, or Darya at least took it that way. Bethany may have learned that Darya was stealing donated funds from her own shelter and pressured her, on threat of disclosure to the world, to join the shelter network."

"That's not very convincing, Lauren." Detective Greshlam's tone sounded much too condescending. I curled my lips but said nothing. "Not without evidence."

Antonio responded. "Want me to go for the warrant to start checking it out, Joy?" I hadn't heard the detective's first name before, although her card had said her first initial was J.

"I'll handle it." The detective's tone remained professional, but she turned a seething look on Antonio. He took it in stride.

"Then there was the PST pin," I continued. "I heard one was found with Bethany's body. Since Mamie hadn't joined the network and gotten one, that should have kept her from being your top suspect." Joy's face remained impassive. If that was a reason they hadn't arrested Mamie yet, she wasn't going to admit it. "Were you aware that Darya had lost hers?"

"She'd gotten a replacement." The detective shrugged her shoulders as if this line of information was irrelevant and she was bored. But Antonio was grinning. "She showed it to us. Anyone could have taken her missing pin."

"And I'm sure all the other administrators showed you theirs, too, didn't they?" I asked.

"Maybe."

"I'd imagine you figured that the one dropped near Bethany was left on purpose by the killer, maybe to make you think that whoever did it was a PST member—which made you believe it *wasn't*. But maybe a member actually did lose it during the murder. Did you ever determine where it might have come from?"

Another noncommittal shrug.

"You might check with Darya. She got even more upset when I mentioned it in the same conversation."

The detective's eyes widened. I aimed a glance at Brooke, who was smiling as broadly as Antonio.

"One final thing. Darya worked in the Better Than Any Pet Rescues office now and then after joining PST. With some supervision, sure. But she could easily have learned where Bethany kept her gun."

"So could a lot of other people."

"Like Mamie," I agreed, "since she'd threatened Bethany once before, and had been threatened right back. But Darya and Bethany had been arguing. Quite a few people heard them. Those disagreements could have become threats. It's just one more thing you may want to look into about Darya."

"That's it?" Detective Greshlam didn't sound impressed.

"Taken all together, I've suggested a lot of motive and means for Darya's guilt," I said. Flimsy? Maybe, but I wasn't a detective. Put all together, with some official legwork . . . "You'll have to confirm them, of course. Opportunity, too, if she was there and dropped one of her two Pet Shelters Together pins in Bethany's blood. All that is up to you, of course. But I think Darya's a suspect worth looking into."

We were finished, so I took them both through the shelter area. Antonio hadn't visited here a lot, but he enjoyed the place.

I wasn't sure whether Detective Joy Greshlam had any kind of heart, but I suspected she did, since it seemed to break just a little, at least, as she gushed over some of our residents.

I wondered whether she'd be back someday to adopt one.

Antonio hung back with Brooke when his fellow detective eventually left. "What do you think?" I asked as we headed toward the parking lot. Greshlam and he had driven separately.

"You definitely gave some angles they might not have known," Brooke said.

"No guarantees," Antonio said, "but I like the way your mind worked on this, Lauren. If you're right, I'll call you so you can observe the arrest."

Chapter 30

Sunday was when I'd planned to visit the Tarbets again.

By then, only a couple of days had passed since I'd handed my theory and rationale over to the cops. Nothing had happened. At least I didn't think so. Even if the media hadn't gotten word about the focus on any different suspects in Bethany's murder, Brooke would have heard something from Antonio.

But she had assured me yesterday, and now today, that he hadn't let her in on anything the LAPD might be doing.

"That doesn't mean they're not actively pursuing what you gave them," she assured me early on Sunday morning when Zoey and I arrived at HotRescues. "But they can't tell regular citizens, even me, without potentially spoiling their case."

So, I just went about my regular business, making sure our residents were well cared for. Planning for our big fund-raiser, which would take place a week from today. Encouraging visitors to fill out our paperwork and, if they met our standards, adopt a dog or cat. Meeting with people who'd already been approved and had come to pick up their newest family members. And doing home visits.

That day, I called first, as I usually did. First, I went to the Northridge home where someone had just adopted a cat this week. I hadn't met the lady but had relied on her paperwork, plus recommendations from Nina, Mona, and Angie. All had liked her, and she took the cat home the day after the initial visit.

After I met her at her home, I couldn't help but agree with their opinions. I felt certain that the year-old Siamese mix she'd adopted would have a good forever home.

I next stopped at the people who'd referred her to HotRescues. The Tarbets were wonderful about doing that, and I wanted to thank them. I also wanted to invite them to our fund-raiser next weekend.

Davie was home, along with Margie. The teenager was the one to answer the door. "Hi, Lauren! Come in."

"I can't stay long," I said. "Your mother home?" She was, and she joined us in their living room with Nemo, Moe, and Beardsley. I chatted with them for a while, and thanked them for their latest referral, one of many recently. "It feels wonderful to save animals, doesn't it, Davie?"

He looked a little confused—and a little sheepish. But all he said was, "Mom's the one to thank. She's the one who gives out the most referrals."

"But you try to help, too, don't you? Anyway, come to our fund-raiser a week from today. I'll get the entrance donation waived for you, and you might enjoy seeing the Small Animal Rescue Team give a demonstration. Plus, there are some things I'd love to show you at HotRescues, including our newest facilities."

When I left, I felt sure they'd be there. A good thing. I intended to make it an event that Davie in particular wouldn't forget.

The week dragged on. Not that I wasn't busy.

I talked to Mamie a couple of times. She sounded depressed, and I attempted to cheer her without giving her particulars.

Until someone else was arrested for Bethany's murder, she remained a suspect. I knew the cops were smart, and I'd given them a wonderful lead. But you never knew . . .

Besides, I could be wrong. Just in case, I studied my suspect files daily, hoping to see something I had missed. Nothing leaped out at me, though. And my accuracy and intuition were usually as spot-on as a Las Vegas odds-maker's.

Yet I started to worry. I could have trotted down the wrong path in my eagerness to chase an answer I liked. Maybe I'd been right when I'd believed it was Cricket. Maybe Mamie was guilty after all.

Had I missed something? Was it someone I hadn't even considered seriously? Heck, I wasn't really a detective. I'd just been darned lucky—and smart—when I'd solved the last murder I'd been involved with . . . the one where I'd been the primary suspect.

Maybe I should just back off and avoid all this frustration. But that would cause frustration of another kind.

I at least got Mamie interested in coming to our fundraiser and SmART demonstration that weekend. And to see our animals—which by then would include more of those she had considered hers. Despite her expression of interest a while back, she hadn't returned to HotRescues in the interim.

Matt had let me know there were a bunch more animals from Mamie's hoarding available to be picked up. Otherwise, they'd be moved to one of the overcrowded city care centers—which would put their longevity in ultimate danger. I'd immediately notified the shelter managers and others who viewed the Southern California Rescuers Web site, including Kathy Georgio and Ilona Graye. I let Cricket know, too, and she promised that, after she spoke with her members, there would be no released animal left behind. Would she use Bethany's tactics? I didn't ask—not when pets' lives could be at stake.

I was at the Northeast Valley Animal Care Center on Thursday at the time Matt prescribed, along with Pete Engersol to help, and we accepted around a dozen dogs and cats. Kathy, Ilona, and some other shelter directors I knew from the Southern California Rescuers Web site, from as far away as Palm Springs and San Diego, were there, too. So were Cricket, Sylvia, Raelene, and even Darya. I acted entirely cordial with Darya, without hinting what I knew— or thought I did. Fortunately, she only had room for one or two animals, and I assumed she was there only because Cricket had insisted on it.

I wondered what would happen if Darya was arrested. When I'd visited her shelter, I had recalled that she wasn't the first director there. She wouldn't be the last, either. Right now, she had a staff and a husband, so presumably the animals at Happy Saved Animals would still be well cared for.

One way or another, I'd make sure of it.

Matt was there when we picked up the animals. I wanted to give him a big, grateful kiss, but we both decided to wait

till we were alone together. He promised me he'd be at the
HotRescues fund-raiser on Sunday. Plus, we made arrangements to have dinner together on Friday night.

I had to cancel out on that, though. Friday was the day
Brooke got the call from Antonio. The Robbery Homicide
Division had in fact been able to get hard evidence to prove
the allegations I'd made.

Darya Price was about to be arrested.

I was vindicated! I'd not only chosen the right suspect,
but I'd helped to point the cops in her direction.

I drove to Happy Saved Animals with Brooke. She'd met
me at HotRescues, and we'd left Zoey and Cheyenne there
in Nina's able care.

"You know this is a special favor to me." Brooke sat in
the passenger seat of my Venza, and her glowing smile lit
her entire face. "I mean, our getting notice and an unofficial invitation to watch, as long as we stay out of the way."

"Your Antonio seems like a great guy . . . for a cop."

She laughed. "What do you mean, *seems*?"

We reached the street where Happy Saved Animals was
located. I'd entered last time through a rear courtyard. Was
that the best place to hang out now? I wasn't sure, but the
entrance from the main street was a gate in a large fence that
obscured what was beyond it. I noticed a few police cars
parked in the vicinity and mentioned our dilemma to Brooke.

She made a quick call to Antonio. "Stay here," she said.
"This will be fine."

It was. We couldn't tell much of what was happening,
but in about half an hour the gate opened and Darya came
out, surrounded by cops. She appeared to be cuffed, with

her hands behind her. The police ushered her into the back of one of the marked cars, and it drove off.

"So justice has triumphed again," Brooke said.

"Amen," I responded, hoping—and believing—it was true.

Later I learned from Brooke, also unofficially, that the LAPD investigation had yielded that Happy Saved Animals did indeed have some donors who would soon be unhappy. Not all of their donations went to the shelter but instead were kept by Darya and, presumably, her husband.

Meantime, Lan had disappeared and was being sought as a person of interest in the ongoing investigation.

A PST pin had unsurprisingly been found at the shelter, in Darya's office. Detectives had questioned Cricket, and she'd told them what she had divulged to me: that Darya had received a second one after losing the first. Since the organization kept close watch on its pins, the logical conclusion was that the one found at the site of Bethany's murder was one of Darya's. And since there had been no indication that anyone else had taken the missing one, the assumption was that Darya had found it.

A lot of this was circumstantial evidence. So was the fact that Darya had argued with Bethany a lot, including the day before the murder.

What wasn't quite so circumstantial was the fact that Better Than Any Pet Rescues was equipped with security cameras, similar to those at HotRescues. That hadn't been made public. Mamie's car had been seen entering the parking lot, which was no surprise, since she was found there. Other vehicles had come and gone, too, including Darya's and her husband, Lan's—again no surprise, thanks to the meeting that night. But although Lan's had driven away with the rest of the crowd, Darya had stayed late, allegedly to help Bethany clean up. She had already been questioned over and over by the police, since she might have been the last one besides the murderer to see Bethany alive.

Or she might have been the murderer. The cops had been aware of that, which was one reason Mamie had remained free. What I'd told them hadn't made them turn the official investigation in an entirely different direction. Even so, my little bits of icing on their investigatory cake—the reason behind the arguments between Darya and Bethany, consisting of Bethany's threats to reveal the financial condition of Happy Saved Animals to the world, plus the added swirl of the missing pin—had provided enough evidence to finally lead to the arrest.

The media had learned about the arrest, too, and had vans and helicopters and reporters capturing the situation on film. It would be on the news that night.

Whatever the consequences ultimately were for Mamie's hoarding—and she should receive some credit against the animal cruelty charges for her decision to surrender her pets—she would not be arrested for Bethany's murder.

Except for finally doing the memorial Web site for Bethany that I'd promised the PST members, my involvement in the killing was finally over.

Chapter 31

Matt and I did get together that night after all. I really felt jazzed after witnessing Darya's arrest, and Brooke and I left the scene around seven o'clock.

A while later, Matt and I were seated outside at a family-style restaurant with Zoey and Rex lying happily at our feet. Matt was in casual civilian garb, including a navy T-shirt that hugged his substantial chest and biceps, which made me relish the evening as a hot date. Or maybe it was my need to celebrate in as many ways as possible that enhanced my awareness.

I still wore my usual HotRescues outfit. I hadn't had the time or inclination to don anything sexier, but judging from Matt's appreciative glances in my direction, he didn't care.

"We need a bottle of wine," I told him. "To celebrate. My treat."

He laughed. "No, mine. I need to toast the heroine of the day. And night." His dark eyebrows lifted suggestively, and it was my turn to laugh. And nod as I felt my cheeks redden.

We took our time over dinner and wine, but hurried back to my place when we were through.

Where we carried out my celebration more personally . . .

I remained in a festive mood the next day at HotRescues—and not entirely because of my night with Matt. Although that certainly helped.

So did the reports on radio, TV, and Internet about the arrest of Darya Price for the murder of Bethany Urber. Not to mention the pleased chatter from my shelter staff and volunteers.

I got a call from Miguel, who sounded really glad that his girlfriend's murderer had been caught. "I talked to both of her ex-husbands already, too. They told me to thank you."

Interesting, since I didn't gather they were high on the authorities' suspect list—or mine, either, for that matter. Nor did they particularly miss Bethany. Maybe they had just grown tired of being questioned.

Then there was Mamie. I didn't have to call her; she called me. Without animals in her life, she probably spent a lot of time watching television. "Lauren! It's so wonderful! That poor Darya, though. I know she and Bethany argued a lot because of Bethany's nastiness to her, too—but Bethany was nasty to everyone. We all hated her."

"Murder's a pretty extreme reaction, though. And even with Darya now in custody, I'd suggest you not go around talking about how much you hated Bethany. Darya hasn't been convicted yet."

"Oh. Right. I get it." She paused. "See you tomorrow. Right? That's when your fund-raiser will be?"

"Yes. See you then."

I had a surprise for her. One of the dogs we'd taken in at HotRescues this week had been her favorite, Herman. Even if she remained forbidden from keeping any animals, she could visit him here. We wouldn't push to find him a new home.

Matt called soon afterward—not just to congratulate me, or to thank me for last night, although he did both of those, too, which warmed my heart, and other parts of me, even more. "I'll be there later with the members of the Small Animal Rescue Team," he said. "They'll set up their equipment this afternoon and do some practice runs in anticipation of tomorrow, if that's okay."

"Absolutely."

"One more thing I need to let you know. Things are in chaos around Happy Saved Animals. Darya's husband isn't there, and the staff isn't proving capable of taking care of the animals. We'll probably need to take them all into Animal Services custody, but I'm not sure how many we'll be able to keep."

Meaning that the rest might be put down for lack of space.

"I'll find a place for any that need it," I assured him, even as my mind began somersaulting over all the issues. I'd just gotten help from a lot of other rescuers, but not all in the area or beyond. Plus, I hadn't pushed hard to enlist the help of fosterers, but I would now if that became necessary.

One thing that would help was that my own facility's added space would be available soon. I'd just have to make it happen faster, if necessary. Lives were in the balance.

"Great," Matt said. "Why am I not surprised? We can talk about it later."

Seven members of the Small Animal Rescue Team arrived around mid-afternoon. They were all employees of Los Angeles Animal Services, stationed at different animal care centers. I'd seen at least some of them before.

Matt was with them. He introduced me again to Renz Sharp—short for Lorenzo—the team leader whom I'd seen at the puppy mill rescue along with some of the others. Renz was of moderate height and wiry, with light brown hair and a broad and friendly smile. Like the other SmART members, Renz wore a darker brown T-shirt with a round logo that said Los Angeles Animal Services, Small Animal Rescue Team. Each had a short, appropriate nickname—a play on their real names—stamped in white on their shirts. Their work pants were deep green. Two were women, five were men, and all were friendly.

After introducing them to our staff and volunteers, and giving them a quick tour of the open part of our facility, I took them next door to show them the building that would be the center of their exercise. In addition to long metal tubes, each carried a large fabric bag that looked heavy, and undoubtedly contained part of their equipment.

I wasn't able to stay with them while they got ready, but they began adding safety equipment to their uniforms, including helmets, vests, and knee pads.

"It'll take them a while to get prepared," Matt said. "I'll come get you when they're ready to start testing their setup."

About forty-five minutes later, he came for me. I left Nina in the welcome area, poor thing, but someone had to be there in case any potential adopters arrived. She'd be back tomorrow to see the demonstration, so she was okay with it.

Everyone else came with me, Matt included.

The training session held by SmART was utterly amazing.

By the time I returned to our new building's second floor, they had already positioned things up on the balcony with a large metal tripod anchored by nylon rope to a heavy floor-to-ceiling pole they had set up inside. They had also run several thick strands of rope over the balcony rail to the ground below.

"We're going to do what we call a MARS exercise," Renz told me from beneath his red helmet. "That stands for Mock Animal Rescue Scenario. We need to be prepared for all kinds of rescues, including where animals have fallen down cliffs or other mountainous terrain. The best way to get to them is for some of us to traverse down lines like these to wherever they are, which may not be the bottom. Then we'd determine if we can take them all the way down from wherever they are and get them out from there, or if we have to haul our team members and the animals back up. We don't usually have the same issues off buildings, but this is a good training situation just in case."

I looked at the nylon lines strung downward, hitched together by metal gadgets I'd heard the team members refer to as carabiners. There were also pulleys and other gizmos. Thanks to taking my kids to amusement parks and fairs within the last few years, I recognized what this really was. Not that I'd encouraged Tracy and Kevin to participate in scary rides like that, but they'd insisted. I'd only watched, though.

"That looks like a zip-line," I said. "You just hook up to it and ride down on those pulleys, right?"

"Exactly. Ready to see this?"

I definitely was, and so were the other HotRescues people who'd joined me.

With some remaining at the top and others at the bottom to make sure the system remained stable, SmART team members slid down the lines one by one. Men and women were equally adept, and the exercises went perfectly.

We clapped and cheered as we watched. I felt glad it was them, and not me, sailing down those ropes. None of them looked scared. I'd have been terrified. I was okay with heights, as long as I was on something substantial, like a building.

"That's amazing!" I said to Matt.

"What's really amazing," he reminded me, "is that these folks are all volunteers, even though they work for Animal Services. They buy most of their equipment unless it's donated."

I'd talk to Dante, but I was sure that no matter what kind of money we brought in from our fund-raiser tomorrow, he'd send a healthy contribution their way.

Eventually, each team member had taken a turn zipping down the line. They'd do the same thing all over again tomorrow, the demonstration they had promised as part of the fund-raiser for animal rescues that would also publicize HotRescues.

The public was in for a great event, and so were we.

"We'll just leave everything set up for tomorrow, if that's all right," Renz said.

"Fine. We have security around all night, so no one should bother anything."

But it turned out I was wrong—and not for any reason I could ever have anticipated.

Later, after the SmART Team and most of my HotRescues crowd was gone, I joined Matt at a nearby Mexican restaurant for a quick dinner. Brooke had already arrived for the night with Cheyenne, and Zoey stayed with them for now.

Despite feeling some regret, I sent Matt home so I could return to HotRescues. He understood, since his earlier announcement about the possible demise of Happy Saved Animals was one reason I needed to go back and work on logistics.

At the shelter, I left my purse in my desk drawer and went outside with a notepad and pen in my hand, saying hi to the medium and large dogs on both sides of the shelter path as they greeted me. "You're going to get even more company soon," I told them, but they didn't give me their opinions—at least none I interpreted from their continued barking.

Brooke, the only human still around, was in the middle of her early walk-through under the shelter lights, with both Cheyenne and Zoey accompanying her. I told her about my dilemma.

"That sucks," she said, when I told her Matt's assessment of how endangered the pets from Darya's shelter now were.

"It sure does."

"Need me to do anything?" she asked.

"Nothing any different from your usual great security job," I said. "Come on, Zoey." We went through the gate into the new property so I could look around and stew over the problem. A lot of dogs behind us still kept up their noise. I knew my statement hadn't made them any more nervous than usual, but figured they were continuing to grump to Brooke.

I could have asked my staff members to help figure out how to handle this, but it was up to me to ensure that things get done right. Micromanagement? Who cared? This time, I needed to reassess the amount of space we'd have for more endangered pets once the new part of the shelter opened, and to figure out how we could open it faster—like right away.

The building, though close to being done, wouldn't be usable for a few more weeks. Most of the outside enclosures had already been started, but they still needed a lot of work.

No matter what Darya had done to Bethany, the animals in her shelter could not be permitted to suffer for it. Here or somewhere else, they'd be taken in and cared for.

I made notes as Zoey and I walked around. Not all the lights on the adjoining property were hooked up yet, but enough that I could see.

The configuration of the new enclosures would nearly double our capacity. Maybe we could shoehorn in most of the endangered pets, for a while, at least, if we came close to finishing our new areas. The outdoor fencing was up, but the long, shedlike indoor areas where the animals—mostly dogs—could go to get out of sun or rain, or just veg out, had only just been started. If necessary, we could bring in dogs of all sizes, and even cats, and somehow provide temporary covers for them. Maybe Dante would have suggestions of items HotPets could provide.

Zoey suddenly stopped walking and just stood on the path beside me, growling. Even baring her teeth. That wasn't like her.

"What's wrong, girl?" I asked.

She lunged forward, toward the nearest door to the building, though it was closed. Had some wild creature gotten inside? I hoped not, but at least if it had, it would be isolated. I could call Matt and he'd be able to get me some help. First, I wanted to see what it was.

Oddly, I remembered another situation where I'd gone

into our back shed building and found that a very human
enemy had set up a trap for me and one of our rescue dogs . . .

But that was months ago, and that situation had been
resolved.

Just in case, though, I didn't want Zoey to get into an ugly
situation where she could get attacked by a coyote or even a
raccoon, or sprayed by a skunk, if it did turn out to be a local
wild creature.

"Sit," I told her. "Stay."

She looked at me reproachfully, but no dog was smarter
or more obedient than a Border collie, the most obvious
part of her background. She sat and stayed as I opened the
building's door.

I reached for the light to flick it on. Too late, I noticed
movement off to my side.

In a moment, when light flooded the downstairs area, I
saw what had caused it.

A wild animal? Maybe—but one in human form. It was
Darya's husband—Lan Price.

He was brandishing a knife, and before I could react, he
had grabbed me.

Chapter 32

"Hi, Lan."

I tried to stay calm despite the way he held on to my arm. That knife was much too close. He was breathing heavily. His white T-shirt and jeans both had holes in them, and there was a feral quality in his eyes that reminded me of a cornered rabid dog—which I'd seen in my former life as a veterinary tech.

"What are you doing here?" I continued.

"What I should have done before," he hissed. "Getting rid of you." The fact that he was thin didn't mean he wasn't strong. I realized that as I made a not-very-subtle attempt to pull away. He just held on tighter.

Zoey knew I was in trouble. As obedient as she is, she had started barking outside the door. That meant Brooke would come to see what was going on.

She could be walking into trouble, too, if I didn't figure out how to warn her. Call her? Sure. But any attempt to get my BlackBerry out of my pocket might cause Lan to stab me immediately.

The room we stood in was an entry, where supplies and equipment would be kept for the cats and toy dogs for which the adjoining rooms had been designed. This whole structure was intended to take the place of the center building on our existing campus. Upstairs would be offices. By now, all the floors had been completed, and so had drywall on the walls, but only the second-floor improvements had been finished and painted.

But, foolish micromanager that I am, I'd insisted on having things as neat and clean as possible at the end of each day, so there weren't any handy tools or boards or other weapons lying around that I could use.

"Why don't we talk about this?" I said calmly. "Are you aware of our wonderful security system? We'd had some problems around here before, so I had our security company install hidden cameras. I'm not sure how you got in—"

"Not hard. Through the back door after some people in Animal Services uniforms went out."

The SmART team. They wouldn't have known that no one was to enter at the rear except for our staff and volunteers.

"Then your picture is undoubtedly on our system." That actually could be true. "We've just had some cameras installed in here, too. See that?" I pointed up at a flaw I'd just noticed in the drywall. In any other circumstances, I'd have read the riot act to Halbert, the chief contractor. Right now, I wanted to hug him. "Why don't we walk out of here? You can come into my office, and we'll talk."

And Brooke would see him and call the cops. All would be well. I hoped.

"No way. You know what? You've ruined my life already,

mine and Darya's. I did it. I killed Bethany Urber." He had glanced up to where I'd told him the camera was. "Not Darya. I was the one who did it all—stealing from our own shelter. I got into some trouble and needed money. Darya had me help with the accounting, so it was easy for me to do. Bethany was wrong when she accused Darya. My Darya's such a sweet, straight-laced woman . . . She's innocent of everything." That was all but shouted in the direction of the nonexistent camera.

"Then to help her, let's go talk to the police," I said calmly. "If you want to save her from a trial and prison and even worse, you have to step up now, Lan."

"I have to kill you first!" he shouted. His grip on my arm had relaxed a little, but now he tightened it again, brandishing the knife in front of my face. I shuddered. I felt my body start to tremble. What was I going to do?

"Killing me won't accomplish anything." Fear quivered in my voice, and I cleared my throat in an attempt to minimize it. "It'll just make things worse for you in the long run."

"I'm not going to the cops. I'm going to kill you, because of all the trouble you caused for Darya. Then I'll kill myself. She'll go free, and I won't be around to suffer."

"It doesn't work like that," I tried to say. But his arm raised and the knife he brandished started crashing toward me.

I yanked my arm free and moved just in time. I wanted to run out of there, but he was between me and the door. Zoey still barked outside. Was Brooke on her way?

I couldn't dawdle to find out. I needed to do something . . . fast.

I saw the steps to the second floor and got an idea. I've never trained in any self-defense classes, but I've watched TV and movies. I kicked Lan right in the genitals as he tried to grab me again. He groaned and cupped himself, and the moment of distraction was enough. I ran for the stairway.

I pulled my BlackBerry from my pocket. As I leaped up the steps, I pushed the button programmed to call Brooke. "Help!" I shouted. "Call 911!"

I heard her say something like, "What the hell's going on?"

"Lan Price is here. He's crazy." I hung up. I'd said all I'd needed to.

I reached the top of the steps. We'd planned on using this floor as a conference room and offices like our current center building, so there was no door to slam shut at the top. I could, however, go into one of the offices . . . and then another idea came to me. More foolish than the last one? Absolutely. And only to be used as a last resort—to save my life.

As Lan began running up the stairs behind me, I hurried into the office I'd been in earlier today. It had the largest balcony, so it had been the one where the SmART folks had set up their equipment to practice and get ready for tomorrow's demonstration.

There were no locks on the door, and Lan Price, crazy, furious, and carrying a knife, was right behind me.

The pole SmART had set up was in the middle of the office floor, wedged from floor to ceiling. The ropes were still attached to it. It didn't seem usable as a weapon, but that wasn't my intention.

The sliding glass doors were open, with the ropes extending out onto the sturdy tripod gadget and below. I hurried onto the balcony. There was a lock on the sliding door, but only from the inside. It would have done me no good to close it.

I leaned momentarily over the balcony and stared at the dimly lit ground below.

Then I looked again at the three ropes attached to the

tripod and extending downward. A pulley device with long straps on it hung near the metal contraption from one of the ropes.

Lan burst into the office. "I've got you now, you bitch!" he screamed.

I had only one option. I'd watched my kids do this sort of thing for fun, hadn't I? And I'd seen the SmART team do it before in the interest of preparing to save animals.

Now, I needed to save myself.

I wasn't wearing any of the protective gear required for the amusing or serious use of this equipment. I didn't know if I could hold on. I didn't especially like heights.

I didn't have any choice.

I wrapped the rope attached to the pulley around me, tugged for an instant to make sure it wasn't all falling over—and then, holding on to the top of the line nearest the pulley, I climbed over the concrete railing and let myself fall.

Chapter 33

Holding on to the line attaching my gear to the pulley, I sailed downward through the air, the breeze in the near darkness pelting my cheek.

What had I been thinking? Lan had a knife.

There were three nylon ropes tied parallel for safety reasons, but Lan would see which one held me. Would he have time to slice through it?

The descent had looked instantaneous as I'd watched the SmART exercise. Now, as I neared the midway point, I felt as if I was traversing the sky in slow motion. My legs dangled. I bit my tongue to avoid shrieking in terror.

With Zoey and the other dogs barking, no one would hear me anyway.

Something was suddenly different. The line holding the pulley—and me—seemed to go slack. I did scream then . . . just as my feet hit the ground. Nowhere near as skilled as the SmART members, I started to fall over—only to feel two hands grab me.

"Lauren, are you okay?" Brooke steadied me, her voice nearly inaudible over the cacophony of dogs nearby, and sirens in the distance.

"Absolutely." I gave my security director a big, trembling hug. Only for a second, though.

"Then what the hell were you doing? That guy Lan— what did he . . . ?" Her voice tapered off as the other end of the rope slapped down near us. She looked toward the balcony, as did I.

Lan stared over the side, backlighted from the faint illumination that emerged from the room behind him, his face set in a rictus of anger.

"That's Lan?" Brooke demanded. "Did he disconnect the line while you were on it?"

"He cut it with the knife he threatened to use on me. He's Darya's husband. Now, security expert, we need to try to keep him inside the building till the cops get here and arrest him."

"No problem."

I thought there were a lot of problems, but I determined to follow her lead. She was the expert, after all.

"The guy could be suicidal," I called to her as she ran toward the gate between the two properties. "But even so, he's armed and dangerous. Let's not do anything foolish."

"We won't." She opened the gate just long enough for Cheyenne to slip through onto the unpaved surface. She shut it in Zoey's face, though my dog pounded at it to get through.

"Cheyenne could get hurt," I yelled. "He's not an attack dog."

"You haven't seen him since Gavin gave him lessons."

No, I hadn't. Nor had I believed a golden retriever mix would excel in security work. The breed is too sweet. But Brooke had told me that Cheyenne had really gotten into it.

I hoped now that she was right.

There were only two doors in the building, at the front and back. Multiple windows looked out onto the grounds, though. Lan could break one and dash out. I doubted that Brooke was armed. That wasn't in her job description.

Nor mine.

If Lan did emerge, we'd have to let him go—although the sirens did sound as if the cops were closing in. Lan would probably not get far.

With Cheyenne at her side, Brooke paced the uneven ground at the side of the building, dashing between the front and the rear, where the only security lights were located—and they were dim. I decided to do the same thing on the other side, hoping I'd be able to see well enough to figure out what to do.

"Don't try to stop him if he does come out," I yelled to remind Brooke. "That knife of his is wicked."

"I figured," she returned. "I saw your rope."

I did again, too, as I reached the other side of the building. I couldn't see it well in the darkness, but it was mostly white, with blue stripes swirled around it. It lay on the ground in an uneven snake of lines and coils, still attached a short distance away, at ground level, to another of those tripods the SmART folks had erected, and anchored to stakes screwed into the ground. The other two ropes still hung above.

I saw Lan then—no longer upstairs. He was on the bottom floor, right inside the farthest window. With a crash, he broke it open. I wasn't sure what he'd used to smash it, but I didn't want to find out. Like Brooke, I wasn't armed. Unlike Brooke, I'd seen his knife.

I also had an idea. This side of the building was around the corner from the one I'd zipped down. I grabbed the end of the severed rope as I saw Lan beating away some of the sharp glass shards protruding around the window frame.

He saw me then, too, as he climbed out. He brandished his knife again. "I'll get you now," he shouted. If he'd had a mustache, I'd have expected him to curl it in his fingers like one of those old-fashioned caricature villains— Snidely Whiplash, maybe, on the aging reruns of *Dudley Do-Right* cartoons that had sometimes been on TV when my kids were little.

But caricature or not, he was dangerous with that knife.

I saw Brooke come running. Cheyenne was in front of her. The dog could get stabbed before we humans could protect him.

That couldn't happen. I took my end of the rope and ran not toward Lan, but away. The tripod held, and in moments I had used the length of the severed rope to shove Lan back toward the building and the open window. The contact and movement startled him—long enough to let Cheyenne get near. Exactly what I didn't want.

But the dog didn't attack. Neither did he approach while wagging his tail and attempting to make friends, as goldens were apt to do.

Instead, he stood there growling. Teeth bared, as if he was a vicious pit bull awaiting the chance to jump at Lan's neck.

So Gavin really had trained him to growl on command.

"Get him away, or I'll stab him," Lan yelled.

At the same time, half a dozen police officers ran into the yard through the gate, guns drawn.

"Drop your weapon," one called. "On the ground. Face-down."

I'd gathered that Lan didn't care whether he survived

or not. Would he decide to end this now by failing to cooperate—or worse, attacking until they had no choice but to shoot him?

He looked around, from the uniformed cops aiming guns at him, to Cheyenne, to me. The knife was in his hand, stabbing at the air, toward the dog . . .

Then he knelt, putting the weapon onto the dirt. He petted Cheyenne once. "I didn't really want to hurt you, guy," he said, so softly that I could barely hear him.

Lan lay facedown on the ground as the cops dashed toward him.

There was barely time for Cheyenne to give Lan's empty hand a lick. And then the angry, vicious, murderous human— who obviously loved dogs—was in custody.

Chapter 34

More than an hour later, Brooke, Matt, and I sat in the discussion area in my office. I felt exhausted.

I also felt happy—as happy as I could be after having nearly become another murder victim. But at least the situation was finally over. I could relax . . . eventually. Soon.

I didn't want to wake Mamie to tell her, but her ongoing problems would not include being a murder suspect.

Lan had been arrested. Had he been instrumental in Bethany's murder, as he'd claimed, or had he only said so to try to save Darya—before he attempted to take his own life?

After killing me.

I supposed all that would come out eventually.

Earlier, Detective Greshlam magically appeared not long after Lan was taken into custody. I assumed she'd been informed that something had occurred relating to a case she was investigating, and she'd hurried here.

As soon as I'd finished giving her my statement, I'd gone back into the main part of HotRescues. By then, poor Zoey was frantic, and I gave her a lot of hugs before checking on our residents.

I called Matt, too. Though his voice was groggy, he'd awakened immediately. This wasn't an event that needed Animal Services help, but I craved his moral support.

Besides, I felt certain he'd hear about the situation on the news, and wanted to let him know myself. When I'd peeked out the window from our welcome area, I wasn't surprised to see that media vans had already started pulling up on Rinaldi Street in front of HotRescues. Whatever their system for keeping track of police activities, they'd already done it that night.

Now, I sat on my office sofa, Matt beside me, his arm around my shoulders. Brooke sat on a chair facing us. Both Zoey and Cheyenne lay on the rug that protruded from under my desk.

"There wasn't much I could tell the cops," Brooke was saying. "I'd finished my rounds and had come back to the sleeping quarters, such as they are, in the middle building when you called, Lauren. You didn't give me many details."

"But you did as I asked and called 911." My smile couldn't have looked especially bright, as tired as I was, but I wanted her to know how much I appreciated her help.

Our protocol required that she notify EverySecurity, since the outfit that sent patrols to all of Dante's businesses was still our official security provider. One of their representatives was downstairs talking to the authorities.

"Our SmART team members will be surprised when they arrive tomorrow," Matt said, "to see that one of their ropes was cut that way."

"Today," I said, glancing at my watch. "Only a few hours from now. I gathered that they always take a belt-and-suspenders approach and have a lot more gear than they're likely to need, but I'd suggest that you call Renz and make sure they bring a replacement."

"Sure will." Matt's arm around me tightened, as if he was picturing how that rope got severed and when. The vision hadn't left my own imagination since I'd landed on the ground.

Alive and unhurt.

And angry. But Lan would pay for it. Even if no evidence appeared to prove his story about who'd killed Bethany, he'd at least be charged as an accessory—as well as for his attempted murder of me. That was what I'd been told by Detective Greshlam.

Both Darya and Lan would probably pay for Bethany's murder. It would be interesting to hear what Darya's role had been, if the cops ever sorted it all out. Had she been the killer, with Lan trying to protect her—or had he committed the murder as he'd claimed when he came after me? Either way, Darya knew the details, and her reactions around me indicated she had played a major role, even if it was just covering up the truth on behalf of her husband.

In any event, Cricket would be able to continue in Bethany's footsteps as the high-handed, demanding administrator of Better Than Any Pet Rescues and the Pet Shelters Together network.

PST would have to survive without HotRescues' membership.

And somehow I would make sure that all the animals now at Happy Saved Animals were saved again.

Brooke had started to droop. Sometimes, considering how well she was doing, it was easy to forget that she'd been hired by Dante only after he'd picked up her medical expenses and she had begun to get better.

"Go home and get some sleep," I told her. "I'll stay here for the rest of the night and make sure everything's okay."

"No, you won't," she said. "I've already made arrangements for the guy downstairs from EverySecurity to stay here on watch—and cooperate with the cops as long as they're around, too."

"Great. Then I'll head home. You, too, Matt."

The look we shared made me wonder whether he took that as an invitation to join me at my place.

Turned out he did. But, much to my regret, we were both too tired to do anything but sleep in each other's arms.

A few hours later, Matt ran back to his place to take care of Rex and to change clothes.

It was Sunday now, the day of the planned SmART demonstration and fund-raiser at HotRescues. Fortunately, the cops hadn't suggested that I postpone it—which I would have hated to do. A lot of planning had gone into it. Plus, it was important to a lot of people—including me.

I'd made certain last night that Detective Greshlam and the other police were aware of the event, and that we'd need to take control of that part of HotRescues again no later than eleven o'clock that morning.

No one had objected. But I knew always to expect things to go wrong, so I headed to the shelter as early as I could drag myself out of bed, figuring I might have to make some waves to get control back.

Turned out I didn't.

First thing when I woke, I called Tracy and Kevin. Like everyone else, they'd see the news. They had once viewed me on YouTube, which wouldn't be the case this time, but I nevertheless assured my kids that their mom was fine. "And I now know how to ride a zip-line," I told them.

Neither sounded thrilled, but they were sweet enough to thank me for letting them know I was okay.

Then I drove to HotRescues. The guy from Every-Security—Ed Bransom, whom I'd dealt with before we hired Brooke and who was, surprisingly, still a manager there—met me in the welcome area and told me all was in order. The cops had left an hour ago. Ed walked with me through the shelter and onto the new property. The nearly finished building looked completely innocent in the light of day. The ropes set up by SmART remained in place, including the sliced one now rolled up on the ground.

Even the yellow crime scene tape had been cut away, though some shreds remained tied around a few items on the new property, including the tripods set up by SmART. I didn't attempt to remove them. They gave the place an extra air of showmanship, which could be a benefit to the fund-raiser.

They also reminded me even more of my own close call.

I wondered if Detective Greshlam would attend. I'd invited her, and she had sounded enthused. But I guessed that she'd have a lot of work to do today, after the latest arrest in Bethany's murder.

By the time Ed, Zoey, and I returned to the welcome area, a lot of our regular crew had arrived—more than usually appeared on a Sunday. I'd expected the whole gang because of the fund-raiser, but I knew they'd come this early because of the news. All of them—Pete, Nina, Angie, Mona, and even Gavin, not to mention our group of volunteers—were full of questions.

Ed left, and the rest of us took a quick walk to check on the residents.

The SmART team was next to arrive, all in their uniforms. Renz told me that Matt had called and they knew they had to redo their equipment. He looked at me without his usual smile, his dark eyes keenly studying me. "You're okay, Lauren?" he asked.

"Absolutely, thanks to your setup."

He did smile then, as did the other team members. "Too bad we weren't here to see it and take pictures for our Facebook page and YouTube," he said.

I laughed and gave him a friendly shove. "Go to work," I told him.

I left Zoey in the office as the crowd wanting to attend the demonstration began to arrive. Cynically, I wondered whether we'd get a larger turnout than we otherwise would have, thanks to last night's news. But as long as we raised funds for animal rescue, including a hefty donation to SmART, it didn't matter.

Although if I'd been able to prevent what I'd gone through here last night, I still would have . . .

I was standing in a crowd near our leopard-spotted welcome table when Davie Tarbet arrived with his mom, Margie.

"Hi, Lauren," Davie said. He looked as youthful as he was in his "Animals Rule" T-shirt and jeans. Little did he know what I had in store for him today. "I saw HotRescues on the news this morning. What happened here?"

"If you saw the news, I expect you have a pretty good idea. It's usually pretty uneventful here, though—except for all the animals we take in and rehome." I looked into Davie's innocent blue eyes. "Like a lot of owner relinquishments that have been dropped off here in the middle of the night lately. Would you know anything about that?"

"Of course he wouldn't," Margie said. She spoke firmly,

but the pinkness in her round cheeks suggested she now knew what her son had been up to.

"Come with me," I said. They glanced at each other, as if debating whether I was about to flog them—or turn Davie over to Animal Services . . . or worse. Let them worry. Davie, at least, deserved it. But they did follow me.

First, I led them outside to the parking lot, and then to the alley behind HotRescues. Pete was out there unloading some food from the van. He looked at us.

"He the one?" he asked me.

"That's what I think," I responded.

"Well, look, young man." Pete approached and glared down with all the fury possible in a thin senior citizen who happened to love animals. "Those pets could have been stolen by someone else when they were left outside here. And even if they were okay, we have to follow the law, so if Animal Services had decided we couldn't keep any, we'd have had to turn them over . . . and their lives would have been in danger if they got into an overcrowded city shelter."

"But they were owner relinquishments," Davie protested. Then, more weakly, he added, "Weren't they?"

"You know the truth," I said, "no matter what the notes left with them said. I remembered that I told you the difference between our ability to take in strays and owner relinquishments during the time you and your mom started coming in while thinking about adopting another pet. You started asking a lot of questions about animal rescues. I suspect that the first animal you left here was before you had that bit of knowledge, since a stray mysteriously appeared one night, and the next time there was a note that it was a relinquishment. I talk about the difference a lot, so I didn't realize the connection with you at first."

I paused and looked him directly in his eyes—not easy,

since he kept them downcast, and his face was even more flushed than his mother's. But he said nothing.

"You'd mentioned hearing about the troubles we had here a while back, and we talked about security, so you knew to look for cameras and disguise yourself."

Still no verbal response from him. I was getting even more irritated, but I'd already decided how to handle this.

Besides, I understood the kid. Not that I'd tell him, but I'd been known to do things in the interest of saving animals that weren't always appropriate—like not looking too hard for a stray dog's identification where it was clear his owner had abused him.

"Was Shazam really the last dog's name? How did you learn it?"

His eyes still downcast, he mumbled, "He was wearing a string around his neck with a note on it. I wasn't sure it was real, but when I called him Shazam, he answered." Davie glanced up, aiming a pained look at my face. "I fed him but left him there for a week, hoping his owner would come back and get him, but no one ever did."

Poor kid. His heart was in the right place. But he still needed to learn reality. "Saving stray animals from the park where you're working is definitely commendable, Davie." I'd assumed that was where he found them all. "But you have to be careful if you really want them to survive. And that's why you're going to learn what to do. Officially. As a volunteer here at HotRescues. Okay, Margie? It's better than having Animal Services learn what really was going on."

She gasped. "You wouldn't tell them that . . . whatever you think, would you, Lauren?"

"We're having a volunteer orientation starting here next Saturday. Since it's summer and Davie isn't in school, this would be a perfect time for him to learn all about HotRescues and how our volunteers help out with our residents. It takes two sessions, and then we can set him up with times convenient for him to volunteer here when he's not working at the park's day camp—although you'll need to be here with him, Margie, since he's a minor. You can come at times convenient to both of you. I figure he's at least sixteen, has access to a car and a license, and knows the way, or we wouldn't have had those 'relinquishments,' so it should work out well for all of us. Okay?"

They again looked at one another. I wasn't certain of what they communicated, but it must have been something good.

"It sounds great to me!" Davie turned back to me and rushed forward, giving me a hug. "I don't see a lot of stray animals in the park, but the ones that are . . . well, I worry about them."

It wasn't exactly an admission, but it was close enough. "We all do," I said. "That's one reason we need to follow the rules. Even if they don't have a collar or chip, they might have worried owners who won't know where to look for them if they're not in the official system. That's why it's usually best to take them to Animal Services . . . and then we'll take them in if they're not found or rehomed from there. If not us, I've got a lot of friends and acquaintances who are rescuers that I can get in touch with." Even members of Pet Shelters Together.

We went back inside. It was nearly time. I walked them onto the back property, where the crowd had gathered. I stayed on the ground this time, although I figured I could have given the SmART members competition if I'd decided to do my own zip run down their lines again . . . not.

My zipping days were over.

Matt was already there. He stood with Dante and his

girlfriend, Kendra Ballantyne, a lawyer and pet-sitter who had been involved in some dangerous situations of her own. She had brought her dog, Lexie, a tricolor Cavalier King Charles spaniel. The three of them hurried over.

"Glad to see you're okay, Lauren," Kendra said. Lexie sat down and panted a tongue-hanging smile.

"Same here." Dante took my hand and squeezed it before letting go. "But next time you want to encourage a crowd to show up at one of our fund-raisers, how about finding a safer way?"

We all laughed, and Matt again put an arm around me.

Carlie arrived with a camera crew. I went to greet them near the gate to the new property and gave her my version of what had happened here the night before.

"Are you okay?" she asked, studying me. I assured her I was. "Can I interview you on camera?" My baleful look was my answer. "Okay, another time. Right now, I've got the SmART demo to film."

I used that as my excuse to return to Dante. "So what's our estimated take?" I asked him. Each person here was to donate at least a few dollars to get in, and judging by the crowd around us, we'd gotten a bundle.

"A lot," he said. "And I intend to triple it—in addition to what's needed to finish up this new area." He waved toward the building and the areas around us where new enclosures would be set up for rescued pets. "Some will go to SmART for more equipment, including a replacement rope. As we already discussed, you can help me figure out what other good causes the rest will go for. Mostly, I just wanted to make certain that the community sees HotRescues and all the good you do here."

"Like zipping down buildings in the interest of saving animals," I said with a smile.

"Like that," he agreed.

But it wasn't me who zipped just then. Renz was the first SmART team member to come down the line to rescue MARTE, their stuffed animal.

"That's amazing," said a high voice behind me. I turned. Mamie stood there, her red curls looking freshly washed and her black shirtwaist dress immaculate. I hadn't seen her arrive.

"It sure is," Dante said. "Welcome, Mamie."

I introduced her to Kendra, Matt, and the other HotRescues folks who stood around us.

"I walked through the shelter to get back here, Lauren," she said. "It really is wonderful. I even saw Herman in one of the enclosures. I reached in and petted him but wanted to hug him. I miss him so much. I . . . I'm really sorry for what I did. I know I said I'd come here more, but I've been so sad . . . Can I start volunteering here now?"

I knew she wanted to reclaim Herman, too, but I'd get Mona's psychological take on it first, and Matt's official one, too.

I glanced toward Dante. This was something we'd discussed. He knew how concerned I was about her living alone—especially in the place where she'd started hoarding before. She seemed to have improved, but without counseling, who knew if it was permanent?

Besides, I might have saved her from a murder rap, but I still felt responsible for her. I'd hated to acknowledge it to myself, but after all that had gone on around here, I'd let myself recognize it. A little. Not that I'd ever admit it to anyone else. But sometime after Mamie drew me into the situation, I'd started feeling a touch guilty for being part of the event that was the last straw in her difficult and lonely life, the thing that had plunged her into hoarding along with her marital woes. Not that she should have been chosen to run HotRescues. But now, I didn't want to just turn my back on her again, no matter what.

"If you're willing to move to an apartment complex for seniors near here," I said, "I think volunteering often at HotRescues will work out well." I'd checked out the assisted living complex. It was one where pets were restricted to one per person, and the residents were supervised. Plus, social workers were on call.

Dante and his employees would help Mamie sell her property, if she wanted, and the funds would go toward her living expenses. Dante would pick up the rest.

"Leave my home?" she squeaked.

"If you're not living there," Matt said, "but at the place Lauren has in mind, there's more of a possibility that we can get the okay for you to take Herman back—someday."

My former mentor threw herself into Matt's arms. Good thing she was small, since she nearly knocked him off balance. "Oh, that's so wonderful!" she exclaimed. "When can I move?"

"We'll get you a place right away," Dante said. Even if there wasn't space, I knew that he'd find a way to do it. His degree of wealth convinced anyone of anything . . . fast.

"We're having a class for volunteers here starting on Saturday." If Mamie was to volunteer here, she'd need to participate in a class. Our insurance required it.

"Of course." She hesitated. "Maybe someday I can even teach some of your classes."

"You've certainly got the pet rescue background for it," I agreed. As long as she didn't suggest taking in more animals than could be safely handled and fed. And of course I'd be sure she didn't. I would monitor everything she did.

Another SmART team member traversed the line from

top to bottom, and we all watched. I reveled in the way the crowd oohed and aahed. I even saw, at the other side, that Detective Greshlam had in fact made it back for the demonstration—even though I doubted it was as unusual an event for a member of the police department. Maybe she had something to tell me about the saga of Lan's arrest or Darya's incarceration for Bethany's murder. I'd ask her later.

For now, I drew closer to Matt, put my arm around him, and watched as one of the teams that reported to him continued to awe the visitors to HotRescues, and me, too—even as my mind veered off toward the additional animals we were about to take in.

We'd soon have room. I'd make certain it all worked out.

I smiled and looked on at the happy scene surrounding me.